ALSO BY AUDREY J. COLE

EMERALD CITY THRILLERS

THE RECIPIENT

INSPIRED BY MURDER

THE SUMMER NANNY: A Novella

VIABLE HOSTAGE

FATAL DECEPTION

BOOKS 1-5 BOX SET

STANDALONES

THE PILOT'S DAUGHTER

THE FINAL HUNT

THE ONE – Pre-Order Now

ONLY ONE LIE

AUDREY J. COLE

RAINIER
PUBLISHING

ISBN: 978-1-7373607-5-9

Only One Lie

Cover by Rainier Book Design
RainierBookDesign.com
Cover photos by:
Inara Prusakova @Shutterstock
@marcosrivas unsplash.com

To all the women pilots who served in World War II

1

Hattie sat up in bed at the sound of a door slamming. The hot water bottle between her feet was now cold. Although she was used to the heat being turned down since the start of oil rationing, the house felt even colder than usual. She reached for her robe before stepping out into the hall of the Queen Anne mansion. The house was completely dark.

The sound had come from Max's room at the other end of the hall. She'd been lying awake since Max's father, Vincent Ellis, stumbled into the house nearly an hour ago. He'd drunkenly hummed a tune as he climbed the stairs to the room he shared with his wife, not even bothering to hide his indiscretion.

Soon, his rough snores from the floor below made Hattie stifle a laugh. She thought of his older brother's call from the bank earlier that day, looking for Vincent. *Maybe he got into an accident.* Evidently, a board meeting about financing the war effort was not one a Pacific Bank heir should miss.

In the nearly four years that she'd been working as the

Ellis family's nanny, the advantages of being next in line to the Pacific Bank fortune never ceased to amaze her. While the country was burying itself in wartime debt, the Ellis family stood to get even richer.

A floorboard creaked under her bare feet as she continued down the hall toward Max's room. The sweet child was destined for greatness. So long as the family's money didn't ruin him—like it was doing to his father. Hattie thought of the hotel room in Chicago that she had shared with her mother and two younger siblings growing up, where she'd learned to make potato pancakes for dinner at the age of nine while her mother worked downstairs running the hotel.

How different my life would be if I'd been born an Ellis. Hattie pictured being served breakfast in bed on a silver tray by the family's butler in the late hours of the morning. The sleeves of her satin negligee would dip into the apple butter atop her waffle, but it didn't matter. The staff would launder it.

Max's door was closed when she reached his room. She pushed it open, wondering what would cause him to shut it in the middle of the night. At three, he was afraid of the dark and always insisted on keeping his door cracked. She hoped his parents hadn't heard the noise. His father, passed out cold, would be cross from the middle-of-the-night disturbance. A chilly draft hit her when she stepped into his room.

"Max?"

His curtains fluttered from the breeze blowing through the open third-story window. Hattie crossed the room and pulled the window closed. She turned away from the lights of Seattle that twinkled downtown.

"*Max?*"

He knew never to open it. A shiver traveled up the back of Hattie's neck. She felt for the light switch and flicked it on. The boy's bed was empty. She looked around the room with frantic eyes.

A gasp escaped her throat. "Max!" Max knew better than to disturb his parents in the night. He always came to Hattie.

An image of the boy's crumpled little body on the pavement below seared in her mind. She ran back toward the window, but then spotted a simple piece of paper atop the little boy's pillow. She moved to the bed. The note was pinned to the pillowcase. It ripped at the corner when she pulled it away.

The words blurred on the page without her spectacles. Hattie extended her trembling arm to read the short, typed message.

BRING $75,000 CASH TO THE PLAYGROUND AT KINNEAR PARK TOMORROW NIGHT AT MIDNIGHT. NO POLICE IF YOU WANT YOUR BOY RETURNED AND UNHARMED.

For a moment, she stood frozen in disbelief. Max was gone. Stolen from his bed while she and his parents slept in nearby rooms.

She crossed the room. The note fell from her hand as she fumbled to unlatch the window. She thrust it open, smacking it against the top of the windowpane. She stuck her head out of the third-story window.

The light from Max's room illuminated the side of the home enough that Hattie could tell there was no ladder or other obvious way someone could have carried Max down. She looked down at the abandoned street.

"Max!" Her cry echoed into the night without an answer.

She turned from the window and stared at Max's empty bed. His one-eyed teddy bear lay in the middle of his down-turned bedding. He hadn't slept a night without it since he was a baby.

Her mind burned with the image of the Lindbergh baby, his decomposed remains when the body was discovered. Tears filled her eyes thinking of the sweet child in the hands of some monster.

Her eyes moved to the note on the floor. She knew she should run downstairs and wake Max's parents. But she couldn't move. She thought of the noise that had awoken her. *Could the intruder still be in the house?* Maybe there was still time to stop him.

Hattie heard swift footsteps coming down the hall before Max's mother burst into the room. Her dressing gown was untied, exposing her ivory silk pajamas.

"What on *earth* is going on?" Priscilla's look of annoyance at being woken in the night was replaced with terror as she looked from Hattie's stricken face to her child's empty bed. Her gaze fell to the note on the floor before her wide eyes returned to Hattie's.

"Priscilla, what the devil is happening?"

Vincent appeared behind her, his dark hair a mess of waves on top of his head.

"He's gone," Hattie croaked, as Max's mother lifted the ransom letter.

Priscilla's knees gave out and she collapsed onto the floorboards. Hattie reached for her, feeling a sudden bout of sympathy as she watched the color drain from her face.

Vincent bent over and snatched the note from his wife's hand. He pressed his palm to his forehead as he scanned the paper.

Vincent narrowed his eyes at Hattie. "How could you lose our *child*?"

Priscilla brought a limp hand to her mouth as a whimper escaped her lips. Vincent stepped over her and pushed past Hattie. After sticking his head out the window, he screamed his son's name, drowning out his wife's sobs at the nanny's feet.

2

Vera pulled the yoke back as far as it would go and eased in full left rudder. The nose of the Aeronca Chief lifted uncomfortably high, and the plane shook before it rolled over on its back to the left. Dari's shoulders pressed against hers as the plane spun out of control, their only view the water of Lake Washington twirling beneath them. Vera forced her eyes to focus on a small dial among the controls. She tried to ignore the feeling of her lunch rising to the back of her throat as she pushed the yoke forward and waited for their airspeed to increase.

She moved her gaze to the altimeter. "Five thousand feet," she called out, louder than necessary with the engine in idle.

They'd been at over seven thousand feet before the maneuver, and they were losing altitude fast. Vera counted several more rotations as they spiraled dangerously closer to the water.

"Four thousand feet," Vera announced, preparing to put in full right rudder to stop the spin.

"One more rotation." Dari's Filipino accent filled the fuselage.

"I already did five!"

"I counted four. One more."

Against all instinct, Vera waited for the plane to rotate another 360 degrees before she stepped down hard on the right rudder, placing her hands on the dash and lifting out of her seat to put her full weight on the pedal.

"Three thousand feet."

Vera held her breath as the spinning stopped. They were pointed straight down toward the lake. She could make out two people staring up at them from a small sailboat as she gently drew the yoke toward her chest.

The G-forces pulled them down into their seats as the force of gravity tripled their body weight. Vera knew that pulling any harder might break off the wings.

Vera exhaled when they ascended scarcely above the tall evergreens that lined much of the lake.

"Not bad for a country girl," Dari admitted, as Vera leveled off.

Despite the adrenaline pumping through her, a smile reached the sides of Vera's mouth. She'd nailed every maneuver so far for her commercial license flight check. And she was especially relieved the spin recovery was over.

Dari looked up after making a mark on her clipboard.

"How does that not make you nauseous after spinning in circles?" Vera asked.

Dari grinned, her teeth white against her red lipstick. "What can I say? I was born for this."

Vera noticed the small white roll that poked through Dari's shiny dark curls and wondered how it managed to stay put during the spin. She turned her eyes to the small, faded photo of Amelia Earhart standing in front of her Lockheed Electra before her final flight that she'd stuck into the side of the dash before they took off. She was glad to see that, like Dari's cigarette, the photo remained in place.

Dari pointed out her side window. "Now, let's start your approach for the crosswind landing."

A flutter of nerves replaced Vera's sense of achievement as she started her descent over the north side of the lake toward the runway at the Kent Airport. Although she had over one hundred hours of flying time, she'd only completed two successful crosswind landings. And the wind today blew over ten knots harder than either of those times.

Vera scanned the surrounding skies for other aircraft before gradually pushing the yoke forward. Exactly a month ago, a Wildcat and an Avenger torpedo-bomber collided in this exact spot during a training exercise. Both pilots bailed out and were rescued, along with one radioman from the bomber. But the second radioman couldn't bail out in time and was killed.

Vera glanced in Dari's direction. From her somber expression, Vera wondered if she was thinking about the same thing. All four men involved in the crash were stationed at Sand Point Naval Air Station. Vera's husband, Hugh, knew them well. Vera and Dari had been tying up a plane at the Kent Airport when they heard the thunderous explosion in the air. They looked off in the distance to see the bomber's detached wing fall from the sky. A few men parachuted out as flames and black smoke erupted from both aircraft before they spiraled down into the lake.

Vera had cried out in terror, afraid it could have been Hugh. Dari had looked on in shock and later told Vera that, for a moment, she'd been afraid it was another air raid like she'd witnessed at Pearl Harbor nine months earlier. Dari had driven Vera home and kept her company until they saw Hugh's Ford Coupe pull up in front of their home. Vera ran outside and threw her arms around him as soon as he climbed out of the car. There were tears in Hugh's eyes when he came inside and told her and Dari that a good friend of his, a radioman, had gone down with the bomber.

Vera kept a firm grip on the yoke as the wind blew their light aircraft off course and forced herself to concentrate on the crosswind landing. After checking their surrounding airspace for other aircraft, she set her sights on the runway as she fought the wind to approach from the northwest.

"Watch your airspeed. Don't get too slow."

At Dari's warning, Vera checked her airspeed indicator. She eased the throttle forward an inch, knowing if she let the approach speed go too slow, they would stall. *Speed is life,* Dari had said one of the first times they flew together. *If there's no wind going over the wings, you're no longer flying.*

Another gust nearly blew them off their lineup to the centerline and it took all of Vera's concentration to maintain the proper approach path. It was a reminder of why her parents were so adamantly against Vera being a pilot. *Too dangerous for a woman.* They hadn't spoken since last Christmas.

It was only a few weeks after the Pearl Harbor attacks, and, after exchanging gifts, Vera confided that she hoped to serve their country as a pilot if women were given a chance. Her mother's words as she and Hugh sat around her parents' fireplace still stung.

A cockpit is no place for a lady. If you really wanted to serve your country, you wouldn't have dropped out of nursing school.

"You can do this," Dari said, as if reading her mind.

As they approached the runway, Vera eyed the orange windsock blowing perpendicular to the airstrip. Knowing this was going to be much more difficult than recovering from a spin, Vera banked the airplane into the wind and used the rudders to keep the nose pointed at the runway. The gusty winds made it difficult, and she had to keep making corrections with both her feet and her hands.

She managed to get the plane over the numbers at the end of the runway when another gust blew the airplane sideways and Vera struggled to maintain control. Despite all her concentration, her mother's voice popped into her head.

You're throwing your life away when you could be doing something useful.

The drone of an engine right above them startled Vera from her crippling thoughts. She felt the left wing dip toward the ground as a blur of bright yellow buzzed overhead. Vera yanked the yoke to the right and immediately knew she'd overcorrected. Their plane banked away from the runway as Dari took over the controls and righted the plane just before the wing would have dug into the ground.

Vera's heart pounded in her chest as she watched the Piper J-3, ahead of her now, climb into the blue sky. She had a good idea who was in the cockpit.

As Dari climbed away from the runway, Vera tore her eyes from Amelia Earhart's photo and stared at Mount Rainier's snow-covered summit in the distance. She couldn't bear to look her hero in the eyes.

"You want to try again?"

Vera shook her head. "No, thanks."

She was too shaken. Not only by their near-miss, but that she'd failed. Her parents had been right.

3

Priscilla paced back and forth on the imported hardwood floor of her two-story foyer. They'd given their butler the day off, not wanting to risk the news of Max's kidnapping getting out before his safe return. She'd also canceled her speaking engagement that afternoon for a hospital fundraiser, feigning a cold.

She ran her finger over the wooden mast of the toy sailboat she had taken from Max's room that morning. She'd been carrying it around with her all afternoon. The house was painfully quiet without him, and she could hardly bring herself to imagine what he was going through. Max was terrified of strangers, especially men.

Just a few days earlier, a young father had made a friendly comment to Max at the park while he'd been floating his toy sailboat on a large puddle. Max had scooped up his boat and run to Priscilla, burying his face in her trench coat. *How terrified Max must be now.*

As his mother, it was her job to ensure no harm came to him. Guilt stabbed her chest like a sharp blade. *I'm so sorry, my little sailor.*

As long as Vincent could get the money, they would have him back soon, she reminded herself. She could only hope no harm came to him before then.

Her family and friends had warned her about what her life would be like after becoming Vincent's wife. What it would cost to marry into the Ellis family. But she hadn't listened. While she'd known there had been some truth to their warnings, she never imagined things would end up like this.

She stared out at the darkening sky beyond the window. *Where the hell was Vincent?* The bank had been closed for nearly two hours. If he couldn't come through this once, she felt she might strangle him.

Vincent had an executive office at the Pacific Bank headquarters, but he was hardly ever there. He kept too busy enjoying the lifestyle of being an heir to the Pacific Bank fortune, leaving the corporate responsibility to his older brother, Rex. She hoped his going in today—and staying late—wouldn't raise too much suspicion.

The bank closed at five, and the vault's time lock started at six. He *had* to get the money. There was no other way.

His headlights shone through the window as he pulled into their drive. She waited at the front door when he came in and eyed the briefcase in his hand.

"Did you get it?"

Vincent walked past her to the bar cabinet and poured three fingers of Scotch. He knocked back half of the drink in one gulp. "Yes."

She crossed her arms. "And no one saw you?"

"Of course not!" He turned away and sauntered into the library, keeping his drink and briefcase in hand.

Priscilla glanced upstairs, thinking of her son's empty

bed. She locked eyes with Hattie, who looked on from the upstairs balcony. The judgement in the nanny's eyes was unmistakable.

Priscilla moved into the sitting room, out of Hattie's view. She'd never wanted a nanny. When she became pregnant with Max, she'd dreamed of raising her son herself. But that was not the way things were done in the Ellis family.

Her eyes gravitated to the large, family portrait mounted above the marble fireplace mantle. Vincent's mother, Ruth, dominated the focal point of the painting, managing to make her cane look like the scepter of a ruling monarch. She was flanked by her oldest son, Rex, on one side and Vincent, Priscilla, and a one-year-old Max on the other. Ruth's painted eyes stared back at her. There was no smile.

The artist had managed to remove the despair from Priscilla's expression, making her look almost happy. She turned away. Stepping in front of the fireplace, Priscilla imagined the conversations of future dinner party guests as they admired the painting decades from now: *Poor Vincent. Such a tragedy that his wife went insane…just like her father.*

But after tonight, the Ellis family's plan to get rid of her would fall apart. It was the only silver lining in this horrific scenario. There was no way they would institutionalize her against her will, not now. If Max's kidnapping got leaked to the press, it would be front-page news. They couldn't separate Max from his mother after all he'd been through. *How would that look to their precious reputation?*

The grandfather clock chimed seven o'clock. *Five hours to midnight.* She would do everything in her power to protect Max from anything like this happening again. But for now, there was nothing to do but wait.

4

Vera turned up the volume on the kitchen radio playing "Blues in the Night," hoping to drown out the memory of her failed crosswind landing that had been replaying in her mind since the bus ride home from the airport. After Vera declined to try again, Dari had brought the Chief down for a landing. Vera could only imagine what her parents would say if they'd witnessed her epic failure. For once, she was relieved they weren't speaking to her.

Ever since the recent announcement that test pilot and air racer Nancy Harkness Love had been put in charge of recruiting experienced women pilots to ferry aircraft from factories to military bases around the country, Vera had envisioned herself behind the controls of a B-17 bomber. So far, Love's handpicked recruits were some of the most highly qualified women pilots in the country. But how could she measure up to these top-notch female pilots if she couldn't even pass her commercial flight check? Maybe her mother was right—she was wasting her time. And she'd be better off helping the war effort in some other way.

Thank God she had Hugh. He always knew exactly what to say to lift her spirits. She smiled, remembering the first time she saw him. Since her parents had refused to pay for flying lessons, she'd volunteered at an all-male flying club in the hope of getting free lessons. While most of the men made her feel invisible, Hugh's green eyes caught hers from across the room, and he'd left his group of rowdy friends to talk to her.

"Are you a pilot?" he'd asked.

"No. I mean, not yet. I want to learn."

"I could take you up."

"Now?"

He flashed her a boyish grin. "Sure. Why not?"

Minutes later, she was strapped into the front seat of a Piper J-3, with Hugh seated directly behind her, and he gave her the first flying lesson she ever had. He'd struck Vera as a man who could do anything, and he made her feel like she could too.

She placed her homemade coconut cream pie in the icebox and heard Hugh's Ford putter to a stop in front of their home. Catching her reflection in the kitchen window, she tried to smooth her copper hair. She'd set her hair in pin curls last night, hoping to wake up looking like Rita Hayworth. But the morning rain had turned them into a frizzy mess.

The front door opened just as Vera peered inside the oven. The meatloaf was almost done. She spun around at the sound of Hugh's whistle from the kitchen doorway.

"Hi, kitten." He set his hat on the counter and moved toward her, holding a bouquet of yellow peonies in his arm.

Her heart quickened at the sight of him.

"Happy anniversary." He pressed his mouth to hers, squishing the peonies between their chests.

His tongue caressed hers. She took a step back, knowing if she didn't, she'd forget all about her meatloaf. And she wanted tonight to be perfect.

"Happy anniversary," she said, hoping he wouldn't ask about her commercial license. She'd tell him about her failed flight check before the night was over, but she didn't want to ruin their dinner.

He tucked a strand of her hair behind her ear. "Maybe dinner can wait."

She knew the look in his eyes. He was ready to carry her upstairs and make mad love to her. "Actually, it can't. If I don't take the meatloaf out in a few minutes, it'll burn."

Hugh shot her a playful grin. "All right. I guess I can wait a few minutes." He moved to the icebox and pulled out a beer. "You want one?"

"No, thanks. I thought we could open that bottle of Cabernet we've been saving with dinner."

She watched him lean against the counter and admired his thick brown hair and square jawline. He was even more handsome than the day she'd married him one year ago. "How was work?" She turned and stabbed a simmering potato with a fork.

He popped off the bottle cap. "Good. I spent the day at Sand Point and trained in the Wildcat. I was supposed to fly Vincent Ellis to the San Juans this afternoon, but he called and canceled this morning."

"Well, I'm glad you didn't have to go."

"And there's something I need to tell you."

Reminded of her flight check, her heart sank. *I have something to tell you, too.* "What's that?"

"I got a telegram today."

Vera spun around. The playful look had disappeared from his face, but there was a light in his eyes.

Vera waited for him to go on. Just then, the potatoes boiled over, and she reached back without looking to flick off the gas.

"I've been recalled to active duty."

Vera took a deep breath and leaned back against the oven. When Hugh was reactivated last month into the Navy Reserve, they both knew he could be recalled to active duty at some point. *"Already? But they're still training you in the Wildcat."*

He nodded. "They need more pilots. There's a B-17 departing Boeing for Hickam Field on Friday, and I'm ordered to be on it."

"Friday! That's two days!" She turned the radio dial off, the foxtrot melody suddenly driving her mad.

"I can't sit at home anymore, Vera. Not while men are giving their lives for our freedoms. I have to join the fight."

"You're not sitting at home. What about your job for the Ellis family?"

The owners of Pacific Bank were one of the richest and most powerful families in the Pacific Northwest. Hugh had been over the moon when they hired him that summer to pilot their Lockheed Model-10 Electra.

He ran his hand through his hair. "I haven't told them yet. I'll talk to Rex tomorrow. They'll have to replace me. And I can't expect to get it back after the war, which makes me sick after how hard I worked to land that job. God knows if I'll ever find another job that pays even close to $10,000 a year. But right now, Vera, there are more important things."

"Where is Hickam Field?"

Hugh set down his beer and put his hands on her shoulders. "Pearl Harbor."

She wasn't sure whether to push him away or hold him tight.

"I know it's a shock, but I have to go."

Vera blinked back tears. "It's just...so soon."

"It'll be okay, kitten. I'll be home before you know it."

But they both knew he couldn't promise that. He couldn't promise coming back at all. Smoke rose from the oven, interrupting Vera's thoughts.

"Oh, no!" Vera grabbed a hot pad holder. "My meatloaf!"

She opened the oven door and coughed from the waft of smoke that escaped as she lifted the blackened meatloaf onto the stovetop. She fanned the air. "What a waste of ration coupons...."

Hugh peered over her shoulder at the charred meat. "I have to say, I don't know that I'm going to miss your cooking."

She swatted him with her hot pad holder, unable to contain a laugh.

He wrapped his arms around her from behind. "Why don't we go out to Vito's? It's Rex Ellis's favorite restaurant; they say the drinks are the best in town. And you can tell me how your flight check went today."

5

Less than ten minutes to midnight, Priscilla pressed her fist against the Cadillac's horn. She'd been waiting behind the wheel in the driveway since eleven-thirty. She jumped when the driver's side door flew open, surprised to see it wasn't her husband.

"Where's Vincent?"

Hattie folded her arms across the robe pulled tight over her pajamas. "You know," she said, "this isn't going to keep them from sending you to the loony bin."

Heat rushed to Priscilla's face despite the cool breeze. "How dare you speak to me like that?"

Hattie leaned into the car. "I can speak to you any way I choose. You're not the one who signs my checks."

"If you'd been doing your job, this never would've happened." Priscilla's voice came out as a hiss.

Vincent appeared behind their nanny.

"Move over."

Hattie stepped aside, and Priscilla assumed his cold command was directed toward Max's caretaker. But when he put his hand on the wheel, she realized he was speaking to her. Her mink coat slid across the leather seat as she moved to the passenger side.

I should've known better. He would never address Hattie with such disdain.

Vincent set the briefcase full of money onto the seat and climbed behind the wheel.

"What took you so long?"

He turned the ignition. "I recorded some of the serial numbers from the bills."

"Why? It won't matter when we get Max back. We need to hurry. It's almost midnight."

Vincent scoffed and pulled out onto the street. "Damn it, Priscilla. You don't think I know that?"

He sped down the hill and ran through a stop sign. Headlights illuminated her passenger-side window. Priscilla gripped the door handle as Vincent stepped on the accelerator, while the driver of the oncoming car laid on the horn.

"Let's just get our son," he said. They drove in silence the rest of the way to Kinnear Park.

Vincent came to a stop on the street in front of the park. Priscilla scanned the dark street. They were the only car in sight. "What if they aren't here?"

"They'll be here."

Priscilla followed Vincent out of the car.

"What are you doing? Stay in the car."

"He's my son, too. I'm coming with you."

She could sense his eyes rolling even in the dark. Her heels dug into the wet grass as she struggled to keep up with Vincent's long gait. Vincent turned on his flashlight and they found the path that led to the playground.

Her stomach was in knots when they reached the play

area. The two park benches were empty. Vincent shined his flashlight across the vacant swings and slide.

"Where the hell are they?" Priscilla checked her wristwatch but couldn't see in the dark. "What time is it?"

Using his flashlight, Vincent checked his. "It's just a few minutes past midnight."

"Are we too late?"

"No, we would've seen them leave."

Priscilla sat on a wet bench. *They'll be here. They have to be.*

Vincent paced back and forth. Priscilla leaned forward, trying to ease the knot in her stomach. *Where the hell were they? Hold on, my little sailor. Just a little longer.*

She'd give her life to hold Max again in her arms. Since he was taken, she'd agonized over what he was going through. How frightened he must be. She hoped he would be too young to remember this as he got older.

"What time is it now?"

Vincent shined the beam on his wrist. "Twelve-twenty."

Something was terribly wrong. Priscilla stood from the bench. "Why aren't they here?"

Her question lingered in the air, neither of them wanting to face the answer.

"Do you want to call the police?"

"Of course not!" Vincent's tone was icy, even more than usual. But his face revealed his guilt.

Vincent had left the gate unlocked the previous night. Priscilla's bedside clock read two a.m. when he finally crept into bed. An hour later, she'd heard Hattie's screams.

"Get back in the car. I'll wait."

Priscilla glared at him through the dark. How dare he order her around at a time like this? She stormed away from him, but not in the direction of the car. She'd scour the park until she found Max. Maybe in the dark the kidnapper mistook the playground for another area.

She felt the gravel path under her pumps and followed its winding path along the grassy slope.

"Max!"

Her foot kicked something solid. She fell forward and used her palms to catch herself against the gravel before she went all the way down. Her heart felt like it would beat out of her chest. She knew what she had kicked.

"Vincent!" Her scream echoed through the park.

She put her hand on the wool trousers covering the limp legs of the man she had tripped over. She shook the pants leg, but there was no movement. She heard Vincent's footsteps flying up the path.

"Max!" she yelled out again.

Her cry was met with nothing but silence. The light from Vincent's flashlight illuminated the body next to her when he reached her side. Priscilla shrieked and jumped to her feet. She impulsively took her husband's arm and stared down at the man.

"Oh, no! Oh, dear God! This can't be happening!"

A bullet hole marked the middle of the blond man's forehead. Blood and brain matter speckled with gunpowder seeped into his hairline. Another bullet had pierced his chest just below his neck. A deep red stain flowed beneath the collar of his shirt. His blank eyes stared at her.

"Max!"

Vincent aimed his flashlight around the surrounding park as Priscilla continued to call out for their son. But there was no movement and no response.

"Max!"

"I know this man!" Vincent pointed to the bloodied corpse. "It's Howard Mills—the man Rex fired for stealing! The guy we called the police on!"

Only three weeks ago, this same man had appeared at their home like a raging maniac, banging on their front door and complaining that Rex had unfairly fired him.

"I remember—but Vincent!" She gripped the sleeves of his overcoat and spun him toward her. "Where's our *son*?"

6

Vera strode past the yellow Piper J-3 parked in front of one of the Kent Airport's hangars and felt a fresh spark of anger seeing the plane that sabotaged her flight check. Smelling coffee, she opened the door to the pilot's lounge attached to the hangar and heard Lily's high-pitched laughter when she stepped inside.

To Vera's dismay, there were several people already inside the small office space. Normally, Dari was the only instructor in the lounge at this early hour. She'd been hoping to catch Dari alone to tell her about Hugh's deployment. And her doubts about flying after yesterday.

Dari looked up from the sectional charts spread across the only desk in the room as Lily leaned toward Roger, the head of the flight school. She giggled with him, placing her red lacquered nails on the arm of his bomber jacket. When Lily noticed Vera, she turned serious and stepped away from Roger to come toward her.

Besides Dari, Lily was the only other female instructor employed at the flight school that operated out of Kent

Airport. Lily had been working as a hairdresser when she discovered her love for flying after winning free flying lessons in a contest at the Washington State Fair. Although she was a skilled pilot, she had a reputation for being reckless. But her latest stunt had crossed the line.

Lily locked eyes with Dari before turning to Vera. It was the first time Vera had ever seen the beautician-turned-pilot look sheepish. "I'm sorry about yesterday, doll. Really, I am. I was just having a little fun. I didn't mean to wreck your landing."

Vera folded her arms and watched Lily chew her wad of gum. As mad as she was at Lily, she was also mad at herself. She hated to admit it, but Vera could only blame herself for blowing the crosswind landing.

"Good morning, ladies." But Roger was focused only on Dari. "How 'bout a drink tonight?"

Dari let out a lighthearted laugh. "Just like last night, and tomorrow night, nope...."

Roger put a hand over his heart and winced as if she'd stabbed him. "You're killing me, Dari. What's a guy gotta do to get a date with you?"

"The only thing I want to date has at least one engine, two wings, and a top speed of one hundred and twenty knots."

"I thought all planes were female."

Dari grinned. "Not in my hands."

Roger's student whistled before he followed his instructor out the door.

"I'll take you up and redo your flight check," Lily said to Vera as soon as the men had gone.

Vera glanced at Dari, who looked mildly amused by Lily's offer.

Vera uncrossed her arms. "I'd rather fly with Houdini."

Dari stifled a laugh. Lily shrugged as Roger leaned his

25

head back through the doorway.

"Congrats again, Lil. The WAFS will be lucky to have you."

Vera gaped at her friend. "The *WAFS*! You've been accepted?"

Last month, when rumors were swirling of a female ferrying squadron being formed to free up more male pilots for deployment, Lily and Dari had both written to their congressman and the Army Air Forces expressing their interest in joining.

Lily nodded with glee. "I got a telegram from Nancy Harkness Love yesterday. I'm to report for training next Tuesday."

"That's in less than a week!"

Lily beamed proudly. "I know. Isn't it wonderful?"

"It is. Congratulations!" Vera enveloped Lily in a hug. "But this doesn't mean I'm not still mad," she said, after pulling away.

"Wait." Vera turned to Dari. She recognized the look of disappointment on her friend's face, even though she was trying her best to hide it. "Did you get a telegram too?"

Dari shook her head.

"It probably just got delayed somehow," Lily said.

Although both women held instructor ratings, Dari had over five hundred hours more flying time than Lily.

"It's fine." But Dari's tone said otherwise.

Vera knew how bad Dari wanted it. After her husband was killed in the attack on Pearl Harbor, Dari left her job as a private flight instructor on Oahu to join the Civilian Pilot Training Program in Seattle. She'd been waiting for an opportunity like this for the last ten months.

"Plus, you could always apply for the Women's Flying Training Detachment," Lily said.

Dari nodded. "Yes, maybe I will."

Vera cringed. She'd already planned on applying to the WFTD—at least until she almost got herself and Dari killed yesterday. The requirements to get accepted were lower than the WAFS, and the training more extensive.

But Dari held an instructor license and over fifteen hundred hours of flight time. Not to mention her experience flying in the National Air Races. She was one of the few women to claim the prestigious Bendix Trophy after winning the transcontinental race two years ago.

If Dari didn't get accepted with all her experience, how could Vera expect to?

The lounge door opened, and a petite dark-haired woman stepped inside. Vera recognized her as Dari's student. She was followed by a tall blond man Vera had never seen before.

"Hi, Opal." Dari forced a smile. "You ready to solo?"

A confident smile spread across the young woman's face. "As ready as I'll ever be."

Vera tried to meet Dari's gaze, wanting to console her, but her friend averted eye contact. Vera figured maybe it was better to let Dari keep busy than to dwell on it. And hopefully Lily was right—the telegram was still on its way.

Vera turned to Lily. "Have you told Joe you got in?"

Lily's expression soured. "I did. Right before he broke off our engagement."

Dari's eyes widened as she moved toward Lily. "Why on earth did he do that?"

"I told him I couldn't get married now until after the war is over, and he didn't want to wait. Said it was either him or the WAFS." Lily blinked the tears from her eyes as she fluffed the bottom of her blonde curls with her palm. "So that was that."

"I'm so sorry, Lily," Vera said. And she meant it. Even if Lily had ruined her flight check. Although, the way Lily made eyes at practically every man she met, Vera couldn't imagine her settling down any time soon.

"What a dope!" Opal said. "Sounds like you're better off without him, honey."

The man next to her looked around as if he were lost. "Excuse me, ladies. I'm looking for my flight school instructor. But I seem to be in the wrong place."

Opal chuckled. "Oh, you're in the right place, mister. And the right time."

Lily smiled and strode across the small office toward him with an outstretched hand, showing off her gleaming nails. "I'm Lily. I'll be your instructor."

"Oh. Hi. I'm Andrew." His cheeks flushed with color. "I guess I was expecting a little less of a looker."

Dari shook her head, watching Lily hold onto his hand a little too long.

"Well, Andrew," Lily drawled, "I guess it's your lucky day. Let's see what I can teach you."

He opened the door to the hangar and Lily winked at the women before stepping out of the office.

"Oh, brother," Opal said as soon as the door shut behind them. "That guy doesn't stand a chance."

Vera laughed. The only thing Lily liked more than planes was men.

"That Joe..." Dari said. "The dope's still thinking it's the twenties."

7

"What were you doing here so early?"

Dari had returned to the pilot lounge after watching Opal solo, and Vera was glad to have a moment alone with her friend.

"I realized you're not scheduled for any flights today," Dari added.

"I know." Vera had taken the bus not long after Hugh left for Sand Point. He'd offered to drive her, but she insisted on taking public transport. Gas rationing wasn't set to start in Washington until November, but, until then, she still wanted to do her part. Although, as the bus crossed over the Ballard Bridge, she realized Hugh wouldn't be using any gas after two more days.

"You should've seen Lily this morning. First time I've ever known her to be up before the sun. Watching her try to fit her entire wardrobe into her little suitcase was quite comical. Good thing she doesn't leave for another three days. It's going to take her that long to figure out she won't be needing all those heels from her pageant days." There was a smile on Dari's face even though they both knew she should be going too. "She's already daydreaming about all the eligible cadets she's going to meet. I told her she's not going to need ruffles and heels to impress them—they're going to be knocked off their feet when they see her climb out of a fighter."

Vera couldn't help but laugh, envisioning Lily's petite frame lifting the canopy of a P-38, shaking her platinum curls when she removed her helmet.

She sank into one of the worn-out leather chairs. "Hugh's being deployed in two days."

"Oh, Vera." Dari crossed the room and sat on the arm of her chair. "I'm sorry. Although, it's not entirely unexpected, right?"

"No, it's not. I think, in a way, he's glad to join the fight. And I understand. I just didn't expect him to go so soon. His reserve squadron hasn't been recalled yet, but they need more pilots. So, he's being flown out to Hickam Field the day after tomorrow. But he's worried about having to give up his job for the Ellis family."

Dari's expression darkened at the mention of where her husband, James, was killed. On the day of the attacks, Dari had been given the day off from her job as a civilian pilot instructor at Pearl Harbor. From her parents' home overlooking the harbor, she had watched the USS *Arizona* explode after being struck by the Japanese torpedo bombers, killing James and nearly twelve hundred other crewmen. One month later, Dari's maternal grandparents were killed in their home country after the invasion of the Philippines.

Dari put her arm around Vera's shoulders. "He's right, you know. We have to fight back."

On the side of Highway 99 that morning, Vera's bus

passed a billboard of a young woman being donned with a white nursing cap. *BECOME A NURSE. YOUR COUNTRY NEEDS YOU.* She'd felt a pang of guilt for dropping out to pursue her dreams of being a pilot, even though she'd hated every minute of nursing school.

Vera nodded. "I lied to him about my flight check yesterday, and now I feel horrible. He's always been so supportive, and I should've told him the truth. I just didn't want him to leave thinking I'm...incapable. Anyway, I'm thinking about reenrolling in nursing school."

A look of surprise washed over her friend's face.

"To help the war effort," Vera added.

"As soon as you get your commercial license and more flight time, you can apply for the Women's Flying Training Detachment. I sent my application in last night. This is what we've been waiting for, Vera."

"I could've killed us yesterday. I don't have what it takes to fly military planes."

Dari straightened. "You know why I recruited you into the Civilian Flying Training Program last year? When I met you, you'd given up your education to volunteer in a male-only flying club where you managed to get free flying lessons. You can't give up now."

Vera leaned forward, her head in her hands. "I don't know..."

"I thought you hated nursing school, anyway." Dari cocked her head to the side. "Didn't you tell me you were always passing out at the sight of blood?"

"Well...yes."

They both laughed. Vera remembered the moment she fell in love with flying—during one of the first lessons Hugh had given her. She'd never felt exhilaration like pushing in the throttle as she steered the plane with her feet down the runway. She was pulled against her seat as the wind caught beneath the wings, and she lifted the nose off the ground. She felt no fear. She felt unstoppable. The freest she'd ever been.

"If I'm going to keep flying, I'll have to get a job. I can't afford the flight hours with Hugh losing the Ellis job. There was a help wanted ad in the *Tribune* for waitresses at Blanc's café. I'm going to stop by and apply on my way home."

The drone of a plane taking off filled the small space.

"Hold on." Dari's face lit up and she pointed to Vera.

"What?" Vera could see the wheels turning in Dari's mind.

"If you get your commercial license, maybe you could take Hugh's place while he's gone. Then you could add up more flight hours to apply for the WFTD—and get paid. Well."

Vera looked up at her friend. "As the Ellis's private pilot?" She laughed. "There's no way they'd go for that. Hugh was lucky to get the job, even as an ex-navy pilot."

"I have a confession to make," Dari said.

"Oh, dear...."

"I told Lily to buzz you during your crosswind landing."

Vera stood from the chair. "You *what*?"

Dari cringed. "I'm sorry. I thought you could handle it. I just wanted to prepare you for anything. I didn't mean to make you fail your flight check."

Vera crossed her arms. She would've been angry if it weren't for the guilt written all over Dari's face. She sank back into the uncomfortable chair.

"Well, I obviously *couldn't* handle it. Maybe it's better I accept that now than waste more time trying to be something I'm not."

"You didn't fail because of your lack of skill. It was your

nerves." Dari stood and opened the door to the hangar. "Let's go. I have an hour before my next student arrives." She pointed at the red and white Aeronca Chief they'd flown yesterday. "I promise I won't pull any tricks this time."

Vera shook her head. "I can't."

"The only way to conquer your fears is to face them." Dari strode toward the plane. "Come on! This is your chance. Go after what you want, or someone else will."

Vera bit her lip and watched Dari start to pull the Chief out of the hangar. Despite not being accepted yet into the WAFS, Dari was unwavering in her determination to serve the war effort. Vera had wanted to fly ever since she watched a barnstormer land in a field beside her parents' Chehalis farmhouse when she was eight. When she read Amelia Earhart's article in *Cosmopolitan* a few years later, Vera realized she didn't just want to fly, she *had* to.

Damn it. She's right. Vera stood and followed Dari.

Dari had hold of the Chief's propeller with both hands and was pulling the airplane out of the hangar. A grin spread across her face when she saw Vera come out of the lounge.

"Wait up!" Vera called. "I'll help you." She gripped the back of one of the wing struts and pushed the plane forward.

Vera watched as her friend swung the nose of the plane toward the runway. Dari had seen the destruction at Pearl Harbor. The loss of human life. If flying was something Vera could offer the war effort, then she was going to give it everything she had.

8

Priscilla descended the maple staircase of her home, clutching Max's one-eyed teddy against her chest. His room was filled with people she didn't know—FBI agents and other investigators. Another stranger climbed the stairs holding a camera. He didn't look any older than twenty. While she was grateful for their presence, she was also terrified at what they might uncover.

Her knees wobbled and she gripped the varnished banister for balance. Her tennis bracelet knocked against the railing. Dawn had broken in the hours since the police had been called to their home. The early-morning daylight seeped through the home's many windows.

She felt disconnected from her body, as if someone else was moving her legs down the staircase. She hadn't slept a wink in the twenty-four hours since Max was taken. Her mind ran wild with imagining the endless horrors Max might be experiencing. She doubted she would sleep again until her little sailor was returned home. *If—*

Her butler, Gregory, came out one of the double doors to

the library, interrupting her thoughts as she reached the main level. He carried a silver tray of coffee cups and a large pot of coffee.

"Coffee, madam?"

"No. Thank you, Gregory."

She watched him march toward the kitchen. *How could anyone stomach anything at a time like this?* She moved toward the male voices coming from inside the library. Vincent flashed her an irritated glance out of the corner of his eye when she entered the room. *As if I don't have just as much right to hear what the investigation has yielded.*

Pronounced dark circles shadowed his eyes. A lock of over-pomaded hair hung loose over his right eyebrow. The agony in his face mirrored her own. If she didn't know him so well, she might have felt sympathy.

Her mother-in-law sat on the far side of him. Despite the early hour, her white hair was pulled into an elegant bun at the nape of her neck, which was adorned by the same three-strand pearls from that dreadful portrait. She appeared dressed for a social luncheon rather than a middle-of-the-night emergency. But Priscilla could see the worry lines on her mother-in-law's forehead that replaced her usual cold expression. This was not a part of Ruth's plan.

Ruth looked Priscilla up and down over her upturned nose before turning her attention back to the FBI agents. Rex stood beside them. Priscilla felt blood rush to her face. Did no one think to invite her to this briefing?

Priscilla sat beside Vincent on the davenport and caught a glimpse of her stockings, ripped from the park gravel, before she looked up at the two agents. The younger one had a half-smoked cigarette in his mouth, while his partner, an older stout man, held a small notebook in his hand. The older man assessed her with sharp discerning eyes. Priscilla shifted uncomfortably in her seat before he continued to address the Ellis family as if she wasn't there.

"So…it's a match."

The one with the cigarette pulled it away from his lips and blew a cloud of smoke toward the window.

Priscilla straightened. "What is?"

The agent locked eyes with Vincent before addressing her. "We found a footprint on the side of the house. It's a match to Howard Mills, the man you found dead in Kinnear Park."

She pulled the teddy closer to her heart. "Haven't you found any more? I mean, there had to be someone with him…?"

The older agent frowned. "I'm afraid we found only one set of footprints outside. It doesn't help that you waited so long to call us. Yesterday's rain might've washed away any footprints from an accomplice. We're still dusting for fingerprints inside your home—and on the ransom note. And we'll need to have you both fingerprinted, along with your nanny, to eliminate your prints from what we find."

"But there must be some proof of a second kidnapper!" She looked between the two agents while Vincent sat silent at her side.

The taller agent took a long drag from his smoke. Priscilla fought the urge to rip it out of his mouth.

"There might've been," he said after he exhaled, "if you hadn't been so concerned with keeping this out of the papers."

"But the note said—"

The agent held up his palm toward Priscilla. "Right now, it looks like he came in alone." He looked at Vincent. "Rex told us that you were the one who got Mills his job at the bank. What was your relationship with him?"

"We were friends." Vincent waved his hand dismissively. "Well, acquaintances really. We shared some similar interests."

"You mean drinking," Rex said.

Mouth agape, Priscilla turned to her husband. *Friends?* She had no idea Vincent had known him outside of the bank. *Why hadn't he said anything sooner?*

Vincent kept his gaze fixed on the FBI agent. "Mills was ambitious. He came from a family in the fishing business. He wanted more. So, I helped him get a job. He showed up at our house after Rex fired him and begged for his job back. When I refused, he spouted off and left. He was angry, for sure—but I would never have imagined he'd do *this*."

The older agent looked Vincent in the eyes, waiting for more. "Is there anyone you can think of who might've helped Mills kidnap Max for the money?"

Priscilla shot a wary glance at her mother-in-law.

Vincent hung his head. "We do have a fairly new pilot—"

"Oh, shut up, Vincent," Ruth interjected. "Clearly, it's some fanatic Priscilla met at those protests. One of those lowlifes probably followed her home."

Priscilla jumped to her feet. "Of course, you blame me! All I've done is try to support noble causes, while your son is fine to gallivant all over town with that tra—"

Her mother-in-law slammed her cane against the floorboards. "Enough!" In spite of her frail frame, the sharpness in her tone commanded the room.

The investigators exchanged a look while Priscilla sat back down.

The older one turned to Rex. "Other than firing Howard for stealing, have you had any trouble at the bank?"

Rex shook his head.

The agent's eyes moved to Priscilla. "Or with your domestic staff?"

"Our private pilot hasn't worked for us very long," Vincent interjected. "Maybe you should talk to him."

Rex scoffed. "That's absurd and you know it, Vincent."

"What's his name?" the older agent asked.

Rex turned to the investigators. "Hugh Chandler. He's a decorated navy pilot. I hired him six months ago, and he came very highly recommended. The idea of him being involved in this is preposterous."

Priscilla looked between the two agents. "So, who killed Howard? Where's my son?"

The older agent flipped his notepad closed. "After we finish searching your property, we're going to look into Mills's associates and see if we can find a connection to an accomplice. And we'll need to interview each of you individually."

Vincent scoffed. "*Why?* We aren't suspects."

Priscilla studied her husband's face as the younger agent leaned over and pressed the butt of his cigarette into her gold ashtray.

"Mills's murder did save you seventy-five grand."

Priscilla gawked at the investigator. "But we don't have our son! We would've gladly paid the money to get him back!"

"I don't like what you're insinuating," Rex said. "Seventy-five thousand might seem like a large sum to you two," Rex continued, "but I can assure you it's an insignificant amount compared to our family's fortune."

"And no amount of money would be worth losing Max!" Priscilla shifted her gaze from the FBI agents to her husband, who sat in silence, cradling his head with his hands.

Could Vincent have killed Howard before they went to the park? *But then where was Max?*

Priscilla watched Vincent slowly raise his head, trying to read his face.

"Surely, one could hire a hitman for much less than seventy-five grand, especially in these war-torn times." The younger agent stared down at Vincent. "Maybe you intended to get your son back, but things didn't quite go to plan."

The weight of the agent's words hit Priscilla like a ton of bricks. She gripped the arm of the davenport as her surroundings swirled in and out of focus.

"That's horseshit! I won't have you accusing me under my own roof! Interviewing us separately is a waste of time! Isn't that what you're doing now?" Vincent shouted. *"You need to find my son!"*

The sofa shook from Vincent's outburst. Priscilla turned to him. Despite her suspicions, she couldn't deny that Vincent looked as distraught as she felt.

"It's protocol," the older FBI agent said. "I assure you, we're just being thorough. It shouldn't take long—if you're honest with us. Then, we can move on with the investigation."

"And what are the chances that you'll find him?" Priscilla felt Vincent's hand tugging at her elbow. She pulled her arm out of his reach.

The agents exchanged a somber look as Priscilla stood from the davenport.

"How can you not have any *leads*? It's the twentieth century! There must be evidence of who did this. Surely, you've investigated this kind of thing before?"

"We have, but child abduction cases aren't that common in the recent years. The last one we had was a six-year-old girl kidnapped from her home in Tacoma last summer."

Priscilla stared at the agent. "And did you find her?"

The younger man glanced at his partner. "Um. Well, yes. But...."

Priscilla sat down, remembering the case from the papers...the little girl was abducted from her family's mansion in the Stadium District. She drew in a sharp breath.

Vincent exhaled an exasperated sigh. "She was found dead in the woods two days after she was taken."

9

Vera woke to darkness. She stared at her bedroom ceiling, surprised that she'd finally succumbed to sleep after lying restless for hours. When they had gotten home from their beautiful dinner, she'd scraped the charred meatloaf into the garbage, and Hugh helped her do the dishes in silence. She'd held back her tears as she leaned against his chest. After inhaling the scent of his aftershave, she led him upstairs where they tore each other's clothes off before devouring each other. They'd made love more passionately than usual, knowing their next two days with each other could be all they had.

She closed her eyes, wondering how long it would be before this dreadful war was over. And if Hugh would still be alive. With Japan's warships scattered across the Pacific, Vera knew the risks.

She'd passed her commercial flight check that morning with Dari. Although nervous, she'd pulled off a seamless crosswind landing. And Dari had been right, getting back behind the controls had restored her confidence as a pilot.

But she still had no idea where she was going to find a job so she could afford to get more flight hours. Since her only skill was flying, she knew it might not be easy. Her parents' last letter was etched in her mind. *Where is your sense of responsibility? You could have had a career. And you threw it away.* To them, a female pilot was no better than a circus performer.

Vera turned on her side, surprised to see Hugh was gone from their bed. She hadn't heard him get up. She sat up and flicked on her bedside lamp. The blankets were pulled back on his side of the bed.

"Hugh?"

Her eyes rested on the olive-green flight bag on top of his dresser. She stared at the brown letters, *U.S.N.*, stamped on the front of the bag. Below it, *H. CHANDLER* was stenciled in black. He would be packing it tomorrow. When his enlistment ended last year, the bag represented a thing of the past. Something they'd show to their grandchildren when they told stories of the years Hugh was a navy pilot before he worked for the most prominent family in the Pacific Northwest.

Hugh's sudden recall to the Pacific all but confirmed the rumors that another counterattack against the Japanese was imminent. She slid out of bed and ran her hand over the leather handle of his flight bag that might, along with Hugh, never return.

"Hugh?" she called out when she stepped into the hall.

"In here."

His voice came from the spare room beside theirs that they hoped would one day be a nursery. When Vera reached the doorway, she spotted Hugh's silhouette in front of the window. She padded across the empty room and wrapped her arms around him.

She followed his gaze and looked down the hill beyond their quiet street. The beam from the West Point Lighthouse flashed in the distance.

"Are you okay?"

"I can't stop thinking about that poor little Ellis kid," he said. "The last time I saw him. How happy he looked."

She'd been shocked when Hugh told her of the boy's kidnapping when he got home from Sand Point that evening. Vera knew Hugh had encountered the boy several times in the last six months he'd been working for the Ellises and had taken a liking to the child. He'd been visibly shaken when he'd shared the news.

"And it's more than that." He put his arm around her shoulders. "I'm sorry I won't be able to provide for you the way I planned on. I don't want you to give up your dream of flying because of me."

She looked up at Hugh. "Do the Ellises have a pilot in mind to replace you?"

"No. I couldn't even speak to Rex directly. He was too busy trying to help the FBI find Max. So, I had to give my resignation to his secretary. I feel horrible leaving them without a pilot in the midst of this kidnapping."

"Hugh." She cleared her throat. "What if I replaced you while you're away?"

"What do you mean?"

Vera straightened in his arms. "As the Ellis's pilot. Now that I have my commercial license, I could take your place. It would also give me more flying time so I could apply for the WFTD. Then, hopefully, you could have your job back when you return."

He was quiet for a moment, and Vera prepared for him to shoot down her proposal.

"I'm not sure the Ellises will go for it."

Vera exhaled. She should've known better than to think that they would.

"But it's a great idea. With my leaving so suddenly, it just might work."

She tilted her head back to look him in the eyes. "Really?"

"I'll speak with Rex tomorrow." He kissed the top of her head. "The Electra is a lot different from flying an Aeronca Chief. But with the right training, I know you could handle it."

Vera rested her head against his chest. "Thank you."

"I have my final day of training tomorrow in the Wildcat, so I won't have time to show you how to fly the Ellis's Electra. But they brought in a Lockheed test pilot to teach me how to fly it, so I'll ask if they could do the same for you."

She took his hand and pulled him away from the window. "Good. Now let's try to get some sleep."

10

Priscilla stared at the newspaper covering her husband's face as Gregory poured coffee into her antique china cup. *How could he concentrate on anything other than Max?* She wasn't sure whether to envy or pity him.

There was a small photo of Max in the bottom corner of the front page. His kidnapping made the front-page headlines for only one day. Now, news of the war, and Japan fighting to retake Guadalcanal, filled most of the space.

In the last decade, child kidnappings grew rampant across the country, putting fear in parents and caretakers — especially among wealthy families like the Ellises. But since the December attack on Pearl Harbor and America joining the war, the country's concerns centered on the possibility of another home-front attack and their loved ones being shipped out to fight with no promise of return. Child kidnappings almost seemed a forgotten worry. Until now.

She turned to the sound of Gregory's steps leaving the dining room, unsure if she'd thanked him or not for serving her. Vincent folded the paper before plopping it on his empty plate. His eyes were bloodshot from the half a decanter of Scotch he'd polished off last night before passing out fully dressed in their study. By the deep wrinkles in his dress shirt, she knew he hadn't bothered to change this morning.

She had lain awake in her bed for several hours before tossing back the comforter and crawling inside Max's twin bed. She snuggled his teddy and breathed in the fading scent of his lavender shampoo until dawn finally broke.

The days since Max was taken felt like years. She couldn't stop herself from fixating on abduction cases that ended badly, like the Lindberghs and the girl from Tacoma last summer. Horrific scenarios constantly replayed in her mind like a motion picture.

Investigators continued to comb their property until yesterday evening and assured them they were exhausting all their resources for the investigation into Max's kidnapping. *But then why couldn't they find him?*

The only fingerprints on the ransom note were Hattie's, Priscilla's, and Vincent's, leaving the FBI to believe Mills had worn gloves. Other than his footprints outside, there was no trace of Mills—or an accomplice—at their home.

The doorbell chimed when she reached across her untouched plate for her coffee cup. She jumped, spilling the hot liquid onto her fingers as her cup clamored against the saucer.

"I'll get it." Vincent wiped the sides of his mouth with his napkin and rose from the table.

Vincent beat Gregory to the door. Priscilla was at his heels. The two FBI agents who were leading the investigation stood on her porch. Their somber expressions sent a ripple of fear through her chest.

"Come in." Vincent opened the door wide.

"Have you found him?" Priscilla burst out as they stepped beneath the chandelier.

"I'm afraid not," the younger one said. "May we sit down?"

Vincent led them into the library, where the two agents sat in matching Italian armchairs across from him and Priscilla on the davenport.

The older man spoke first. "As you know, Max has been missing for over forty-eight hours. We interviewed your private pilot, who has an alibi for the night Max was taken. Like Rex said, he's a decorated navy pilot who, as you're already aware, is being deployed this morning."

Priscilla looked at Vincent. Although she didn't know him well, their new pilot was always kind to her. She'd had no idea he was being deployed. But she was always the last to know anything in this family.

"Also," the agent continued, "we've interviewed every associate of Mills we could find. He was unmarried and kept long hours at the bank, so there weren't many. Everyone we've spoken to appeared genuinely shocked by his involvement. A good fisherman, not a mean bone in his body. His cousin, Bill, seems to have been his closest friend. He left on a week-long fishing trip out of Lake Union three days ago, so we can't interview him until he gets back.

"And there's still no proof that anyone was working with him. Mills had no criminal past, other than his alleged stealing from the bank. We've given the investigation our best effort."

Priscilla clutched Vincent's shirtsleeve. "You can't be giving up!" The Lindbergh investigation went on for over two months.

"We are at war," the agent continued. "With the Japanese

expansion in the Pacific, the threat of another attack is imminent. Especially here on the West Coast. We're having to assign agents to espionage prevention at Boeing, the Bremerton Navy Yard, and other government projects. We will continue to investigate Max's case, but we don't have the manpower to continue at the same capacity as we started."

Priscilla's jaw fell open. "But you can't stop until you've found him!"

The younger agent withdrew a pack of cigarettes from his pocket. "We aren't going to stop." He withdrew one from the package and tapped the end against the top of his thigh. "And we will continue to employ the public to help. The reward you've offered will hopefully bring in some useful information."

Priscilla wanted to scream. She squeezed Vincent's bicep, willing him to do something as the two agents stood from their chairs.

"Wait." Vincent held out his hands. "We have money. I can pay for your added resources. Whatever you need."

"We don't have the personnel." The agent lit his cigarette. "And we don't take bribes."

"Please!" Vincent stood to his feet.

The older agent turned before he reached the double doors. "Look, I understand you're distressed. But your family's money has made you quite a target. The people who took your son thought this through. And carefully. Although, killing Mills before they received your seventy-five thousand doesn't make sense. Unless whoever did this is planning to send you another ransom note for more money. In which case, you need to call us immediately. But, until then, there's not much more that can be done."

Priscilla brought her hands to her face after the two men

let themselves out. She crossed the room and grabbed Vincent's arm with both hands. "We have to do something!"

Vincent shook her hands away. "Like what, damn it?" He pointed to the chairs where the men had been sitting. "Those guys are FBI! Why can't you ever listen to anyone?"

"How can you sit here and just agree with them, Vincent? Your family must know someone…aren't there private investigators?"

"I already hired one."

"*What?* Why didn't you tell me?" What else was he keeping from her?

"It's not your concern."

She stared at him in disbelief. "Not my concern? He's my *son!*"

"You heard what my mother said. Who knows how many enemies you created against our family by attending those protests! As if your father's suicide wasn't enough of an embarrassment."

Her throat tightened. When she thought she couldn't hate him anymore, Vincent stooped to a new low. "My father was a better man than you'll ever be."

"This is all your fault!" Vincent stormed across the room and used both hands to push the grandfather clock on its side. It crashed against the floor, landing a few feet from her heeled slippers. Priscilla yelped as the floorboards shook from its weight.

Gregory appeared in the doorway. "Are you all right, madam?"

Vincent marched toward him. "Get my overcoat!"

"Yes, sir." Gregory eyed Priscilla with caution before turning away.

A minute later, she heard the front door slam. She took careful steps over the shards of glass and peered out the front window. Vincent's red Auburn convertible revved down the street. She clenched her fists together as Gregory returned to the room holding a broom and dustpan.

She knew exactly where Vincent was going. *How could he see her at a time like this?*

11

A gloomy fog hovered over the runway at Boeing Field that Friday morning. Vera looked on as Hugh and a half dozen other servicemen prepared to board the four-engine bomber. A camera flashed as the men huddled together for a photo for *The Seattle Tribune* in front of the plane. Their olive flight suits matched the aircraft's paint job, with their bright yellow life vests providing a vivid contrast. As Hugh posed for the picture, Vera couldn't shake the gnawing sensation that she was seeing him for the last time.

"Bye-bye, Daddy!"

In the small crowd beside her, a little girl in blonde pigtails stepped out in front of her mother, waving proudly. Vera swallowed and wondered if they would get the chance to have children.

Yesterday had passed in a blur. Hugh had spent most of the day at Sand Point completing his final day of training in the Wildcat he'd be piloting in the Pacific. When he got home, they'd savored every moment they had together, making love late into the night—not knowing when the time might come again.

Vera watched Hugh move toward the nose of the plane in his flight suit and was filled with longing. The little girl's mother pulled her back as the plane's engines roared to life. One by one, its four sets of propellers slowly started to spin, each sending a cloud of smoke spurting into the air from the exhaust stacks. Vera put a hand on her hat to keep it from blowing away.

Fortunately, Hugh had spoken to Rex briefly on the phone last night and he agreed to have a test pilot take her, along with Rex and his mother, to Portland in the Lockheed Electra tomorrow morning. They would then make the decision to hire her based on how the flight went.

"You'll meet Rex, Ruth, and the test pilot tomorrow at nine a.m. at the Everett Airport," Hugh had reminded her in the car on their way to Boeing Field.

"I got it."

On the side of the highway, a soggy poster pasted to a telephone pole caught her eye. *MISSING: MAX ELLIS*. She recognized the beautiful boy from the papers. Two FBI agents had come to their home last night to question Hugh about his alibi the night Max's kidnapper was killed. While Vera felt initially defensive that they'd come to interview her husband, she later felt saddened, knowing they must be grasping at straws by not having any better leads. Her gaze settled on the boy's smiling face beneath dark curls, holding a teddy bear in his arms as they sped past.

"And this doesn't mean you'll have the job for sure. But if the flights go well with the test pilot, which they will, hopefully they will hire you."

Vera squeezed his hand. "I understand. I'm going to give it my absolute best."

Before Max's kidnapping, Vera had seen photos of the Ellis family members in the society pages. From her photos, Ruth Ellis intimidated her more than the other Ellises. Maybe because the Ellis matriarch was never smiling. Vera remembered reading about her in the papers several years ago after Ruth's husband died. When he left her the Pacific Bank fortune, along with the bank, she became one of the richest women in America.

It's just a job, she told herself as butterflies started to form in her stomach.

She'd been so preoccupied by Hugh's sudden deployment that she hadn't given much thought to the pressure of flying for such an elite family. Until now.

"I might've left out the detail that you're a woman."

Vera turned to him and saw that he wasn't kidding. "*What?* Why did you do that? You don't think they'll guess as soon as they see me?"

"I wasn't sure if Rex would agree if I told him their new pilot was my wife. Plus, as soon as they meet you and see firsthand what a great pilot you are, they'll love you. I figured this was our best chance of you getting the job."

"You should've told them. You're not the one who has to show up, knowing they'll be expecting a man."

He pulled her hand onto his lap. She was tempted to pull away, but she knew she'd regret spending their final minutes in a petty feud. Instead, she entwined her fingers with his.

"You don't have to do this you know," he said.

"Do you not think I can handle it?"

"Of course, I do. It's not that."

He turned off the highway for Boeing Field, and her heart sank knowing how little time they had left together.

"Then what is it?"

"There's something you should know about the Ellises…" His voice trailed off as he pulled into the airport.

She eyed him curiously. "What?"

"It's nothing." He kissed her forehead before opening his car door. "I was just going to say they're not like us—their money and power make them act differently. But I don't want them to overshadow our last few minutes together. Forget I said anything."

"Promise you'll write to me," she said, as they walked hand in hand toward the tarmac.

"Of course. I'll write as soon as I can. Oh, and don't forget about my tomatoes in the garden. They should be ready in a few more days."

She nodded. "I'll check them."

"If there's going to be a frost before they're ripe, you can pick them early and let them ripen in the garage. Otherwise, an early cold snap could ruin them."

She smiled at his concern over the tomatoes. He'd been laboring over their small victory garden for months, but those tomatoes were his prized vegetable.

"Don't worry. I'll be sure to take care of them." She had never kept so much as a houseplant alive but figured she could handle picking tomatoes off the vine.

"I love you, Vera!" Hugh's shout over the bomber's whirring engines snapped her back to the present.

Hugh winked at her before he started to pull himself up into the hatch.

"Hugh!" Vera held onto her hat and ran a few steps toward the plane. "I love you, too!"

But he'd already disappeared inside the plane.

Vera stepped back in line with the other families of the servicemen, aware of the open-mouthed stare from the girl in pigtails at her outburst. She watched the plane take off through tear-filled eyes. *Did he hear me?*

She wondered if she'd been too hard on him for not telling the Ellises she was a woman. Hugh had only wanted to help her get the job.

She stayed on the taxiway until the bomber disappeared into the clouds. She thought of the dangerous battles he might face in the Pacific and prayed she'd have the chance to tell him again.

12

Priscilla shuffled the poached egg around her plate as Gregory entered the dining room with the morning paper. He set it in front of Vincent's empty chair.

Priscilla tapped her fork sharply against her plate. "I'll take that."

Gregory handed it to her. She felt a ripple of relief as he left the room, making no comment regarding her husband's absence.

She scanned the front page, but there was no mention of Max's disappearance, nor the reward the family offered for information leading to his whereabouts. She sank against her chair.

BUY WAR BONDS was written in bold letters beneath the front-page headline: NATIONAL GAS RATIONING NEAR. It was as if Max's kidnapping was completely forgotten.

Tears blurred her vision as she skimmed the rest of the articles: a US aircraft carrier torpedoed in the Pacific Ocean near the Solomon Islands, killing nearly 200 of its crew; a woman charged with running up a bill at a Seattle hotel after impersonating an army nurse on leave from California; and a plane crash in eastern Washington during a navy training exercise.

She was about to turn the page when she recognized their private pilot's photo at the bottom corner.

NAVY WILDCAT PILOT DEPLOYED TO THE PACIFIC

How is it that our pilot made the front page but not our missing child? Hearing Vincent's car pull into the drive, she set down the paper. A moment later, the front door opened and slammed. She heard Gregory greet him.

"I'm heading to bed," Vincent huffed.

Vincent moved through the hall and came into her view. His eyes glazed over hers as he sauntered past the dining room doorway. In that brief moment, she spotted the lipstick on his shirt collar and his undone tie. His hair was disheveled.

She wondered how she could have ever thought she was in love with him. Even worse, how she once believed he loved her.

His appearance reminded her of the first time Vincent came home smelling of another woman's perfume—right after Max was born.

"What kind of marriage do you think this is?" he'd shouted when she confronted him, waking Max in his bassinet. "It's a social one," Vincent continued over his son's cries. "You didn't think I married you for your looks, did you?"

Tears sprung to her eyes.

"Don't give me tears." He took a step toward her, his lover's perfume permeating from his neck, and slapped her upside the face. "You know how many women would kill to be my wife? I provide for you better than any man could, including your nutcase of a father. And all I need is for you to be grateful."

The telephone rang in the hallway, jarring her from the memory. Vincent answered before Gregory could get to it. Priscilla started to get up, realizing it could be Max's kidnapper.

"Oh. Hi, Mother," she heard Vincent say.

Priscilla sank back onto her seat.

"Are you sure that's still a good idea?" he asked after a few moments. "No, I'm not against it. I just think we should wait. I'm worried how will it look, only a few days after Max was kidnapped."

Priscilla gaped at the open doorway to the hall. Vincent had to know that she could hear him. He could be bluffing her, but she was aware of who was on the other end of the line. If the Ellis family committed her to Rainier Psychiatric Hospital, who would believe Priscilla's side of the story, even if she had the chance to go to the papers? She was the one with the crazy father, as Vincent loved to remind everyone.

"The *airport?*" Vincent said after a moment. "I thought that was tomorrow." He let out a sigh. "Fine, I'll see you soon."

"Gregory, bring my breakfast upstairs," Vincent called, after hanging up the receiver.

Without so much as a word to her, she heard him pound up the steps. She took a deep breath, wanting to throw her coffee cup through the window. She could withstand living with him for the rest of her life if she had to. What she couldn't bear was going on without her son. Unwilling to let Vincent get the better of her, she forced her attention back to the *Tribune*.

She turned the page, which yielded a mugshot of a wild-eyed young man with unruly hair sticking out in every direction.

FORMER MENTAL PATIENT FATALLY STABS FATHER IN THE BACK

Priscilla's eyes fell to the article below the headline, which stated the man was twenty-five-year-old Jack Pierce, who had been paroled from Rainier Psychiatric Hospital last May after undergoing a psycho-surgical treatment known as lobotomy. Often a last-resort treatment for the mentally ill, the procedure sought to break down the emotional control center in the brain and replace its authority with a normal control center of reason.

There was a smaller headline in the middle of the article. *Mind Was Blank.* Betty Pierce, widow of the dead man, recalled that following the operation her son's mind was blank, and he required training—like an infant—to perform minor tasks. She added that while he developed seizures and incontinence, Jack's memory had begun to improve over the last several months.

"We consider Jack's operation to be a scientific triumph and sincerely hope that this tragedy does not weaken the public's confidence in brain surgery."

Priscilla's hands trembled as she flipped through the rest of the paper. Is that what Vincent had planned for her?

On the very last page, she found a smiling photo of Max. The $10,000 reward for information was printed in small text below his picture. *Did no one care?*

There were posters of Max with the reward offer all over town. *So, why hadn't they found him?*

She heard Vincent tread down the staircase before opening the front door and slamming it behind him. Gregory appeared in the dining room to take her plate as Vincent's convertible sped away from their house.

She turned to their butler. "Do you know where they're taking the plane today?"

"To Portland, I believe, ma'am."

Pacific Bank didn't have any branches there. "To do what?"

He hesitated, and she could tell he knew the answer.

"To meet with an investigator," he finally said. "Mr. Ellis said he specializes in child abductions."

"Without me?" She pushed back her chair and stood. How could she not be included in that? He was her *son*.

"Pull my car around, please."

Her plate dipped in Gregory's normally steady hand, causing her fork to slide to the floor. "Are you sure that's a good idea, Mad—"

"I'm sure." Priscilla marched past him to retrieve her coat. "Bring it around."

13

Vera tucked an auburn curl behind her ear that had blown in her face. She dried her damp palms on her trousers, feeling Amelia Earhart's photo in her pocket as she strode across the tarmac of the Everett Airport toward the Ellis's Lockheed Electra. It was nearly twice the size of the planes she'd flown before, and its polished aluminum exterior shone brightly in the morning sun.

She'd had no idea what to wear that morning and wished she'd thought to ask Hugh before he left. Hugh had always worn a suit. While she felt underdressed, she'd hoped to be taken more seriously in pants than a skirt, and finally decided on pleated navy slacks and a white blouse.

Last night, she'd stayed late at Dari and Lily's Renton apartment, not wanting to go home to her empty house. It was also Lily's last night in Seattle before she left this afternoon for her WAFS training in Delaware. Opal was there too, and the four of them shared a bottle of a wine. As they sat out on the tiny apartment balcony until nearly midnight, Vera learned that like her own father, Opal's dad was a cop, and she'd grown up on a farm in Olympia.

Selfishly, Vera was grateful Dari wasn't leaving for the WAFS, too. She felt guilty for feeling that way, but with Hugh gone, she was glad that Dari would still be close by.

Vera smiled inwardly, thinking of Dari's response last night when she shared her concerns about flying for the Ellises today.

"You're going to knock their socks off! As soon as they recover from you being a woman, that is," she'd joked. "Besides, without Lily around to sabotage you, what could go wrong?"

She paused before climbing onto the stepladder at the back of the plane, feeling a wave of nervous excitement at being at the helm of the same plane Amelia Earhart flew on her fateful trip around the world.

She wondered if she should offer her condolences for Max's kidnapping.

It was so horrible, it seemed wrong not to express her sympathy to the boy's family. But this was a job interview, and she also didn't know the Ellises.

She inhaled before climbing aboard. She had one shot to convince the Ellises she was capable of taking Hugh's place. Ducking her head as she entered the back of the plane, she saw that three of the ten passenger seats were already occupied.

Vera recognized Ruth Ellis's white hair. She was sitting across from a broad-shouldered man holding a briefcase whom Vera had never seen before. He looked rough compared to the Ellises. She wondered if he was a bodyguard. In front of them, a man with slicked black hair turned around when Vera stepped inside.

His brow furrowed when he saw her, and Vera knew him immediately from the society section of the *Tribune*.

"I'm sorry, miss. But you can't come aboard here," Rex said. "This is a private plane."

Ruth and the burly man across from her turned to face Vera, along with the man seated in the cockpit, who Vera assumed was the Lockheed test pilot.

She forced a smile, hoping to appear confident to the four pairs of eyes staring back at her. "I'm Vera. The pilot Hugh recommended."

Ruth raised her eyebrows. Rex's eyes travelled up and down, assessing her, as he put out his cigarette on the ash tray on the arm of his seat. "Hugh did recommend a pilot. But he failed to mention *this*." Rex waved his hand in her direction.

"He probably didn't think it relevant." She cleared her throat. "I'm also his wife."

"His *wife*?" Rex scoffed. "And you have your commercial pilot's license?"

"I do."

Rex shot a glance at his mother before returning his pointed gaze to Vera. "How long have you been flying?"

"Nearly two years."

"Are there no male pilots left? Don't tell me they've *all* gone to war!"

While she'd been prepared to be underestimated as a woman, she hadn't expected this kind of backlash. She bit the inside of her cheek, steeling herself for getting kicked off the plane.

Vera wanted to stand up straight, hoping the move would exude confidence. But slumped over, her head was already touching the ceiling. "I can assure you, I'm perfectly capable." She strived to keep her tone even. Sounding anything close to emotional would only reinforce his doubts about her competence.

Rex opened his mouth in rebuttal, but his mother spoke first. "People said the same thing about me after your father died. And I've been successfully running the bank for nearly a decade. Let's see what the girl can do."

Vera watched Ruth turn forward in her seat. She wasn't expecting to find an ally in the Ellis family matriarch.

"Fine." Rex motioned toward the front of the plane. "But you're not hired until you prove you can do it."

"Excuse me."

Vera felt a hand on her lower back and turned to see Vincent Ellis wink as he brushed past her.

"About time we hired a stewardess," he said, after he plopped into a seat.

Vera saw Ruth shoot him an icy stare.

"Oh, shut up, Vincent," Vera heard Ruth say as she moved toward the cockpit.

"Hi, I'm Tony." The test pilot offered a friendly smile and extended his hand as Vera climbed into the seat beside him.

"Vera," she said, shaking his hand.

"My wife's a pilot, too," he said. "Just got her private license last month through the War Training Program."

"That's great." Vera scanned the overwhelming number of controls in front of her. This was going to be much more complicated than the two-seater lightweight aircraft she was used to flying.

"So, first time flying the Electra?" Tony asked, following her gaze.

She nodded. "Yes. I've only flown smaller planes. Mostly a Piper J-3 and an Aeronca Chief."

"Don't worry. It's not as complicated as it looks."

"Do you mind?" Vera pulled Amelia's photo from her pocket and tucked it into the corner of the windshield. "I never fly without her."

Tony chuckled. "Not at all. I'm sure she feels right at home."

After going over the controls, Tony guided her through starting the engines. He picked up a headset.

"Here, this is yours."

"Oh." She took it from him, admiring the mint green ear cups. "I've never used one before."

"You'll get used to it quick. These engines are a lot louder than what you're used to."

They were nearly through the pre-flight checklist when a black Cadillac parked a few feet in front of the aircraft.

Tony straightened. "Don't they know this is a flightline?"

"What's the hold up?" Rex called from the back.

Tony turned around and pulled his headphones away from his left ear. "There's a black Cadillac blocking our way."

Vera watched a beautiful woman get out of the car. She pulled her mink coat around her neck as the propellers blew her dark brown curls about.

"Shit! It's Priscilla," Vincent shouted from the back.

"Who invited her?" Ruth asked.

"No one," Vincent mumbled, before he climbed out of his seat and moved toward the back of the plane.

Vera heard him open the rear door seconds before he marched past the wing toward his wife. Vera and Tony looked on as Vincent threw his hands in the air and shouted something incomprehensible over the plane's engines. Priscilla narrowed her eyes and motioned toward the plane before shouting back at him.

Vincent pointed to the parking lot beyond the flightline. Priscilla shook her head before tossing her car keys at Vincent. His eyes shot daggers at her as she stormed past him, bumping his shoulder with her own.

Vera watched her as Priscilla strode past the cockpit. From her photos in the society pages, Vera had always thought the socialite looked like Vivien Leigh. But she could see now that Priscilla Ellis was even more beautiful than the British actress.

Priscilla disappeared from her view as Vincent started the Cadillac and pulled the luxury town car around the side of the plane. Seconds later, Vera turned to see the woman board the Electra with purpose.

"Good morning, Priscilla." Ruth's voice was calm as her daughter-in-law took a seat in the back.

Priscilla didn't respond, just looked out the window. Tony and Vera exchanged a glance as Vincent jogged across the tarmac and reboarded the plane. After closing the rear door, he climbed back into his seat without a word to his wife.

Vera hadn't expected to see the wealthy couple at each other's throats. In the society pages, Vincent and Priscilla appeared to be a picture-perfect couple. Vera had imagined them madly in love. With all their money, she'd assumed they had everything. Until their little boy was kidnapped.

"Sorry for the delay." Rex put his hand on Tony's shoulder. "Apparently there was a bit of a misunderstanding. We're ready now."

The tension between them must be due to Max's kidnapping, Vera concluded. Surely that would put a strain on even the happiest of marriages.

Tony replaced his headphones and announced their departure to the radio room.

"Roger that," a male voice crackled through their headsets.

Tony turned to Vera. "Here we go."

14

Priscilla looked out the window at Puget Sound as the plane climbed south toward Portland. She found herself looking for Max in every yard, street, sidewalk until they flew into a patch of clouds.

She faced forward, shaking off the revulsion that ripped through her at the sight of Vincent's head in the row in front of her. She shifted her gaze to the large man seated across the aisle from Ruth. His well-muscled arm hung over the side of his seat, and he held a small briefcase on his lap. She'd never seen him before and assumed he must be the private investigator Vincent had hired behind her back, probably with Rex's help.

She felt a fresh irritation at not being invited to their meeting today with this special investigator in Portland. She was Max's *mother*. She eyed the backs of Vincent, Rex, and her mother-in-law. None of them loved Max like she did.

They cared for him, sure. But they treated him more like a possession than a child to be loved. Someone to be managed. To be owned. She could only pray this meeting with the investigator would bring them closer to finding him.

Turning back to her window, she gnawed on a manicured nail and stared down at the emerald landscape as they broke out of the clouds. She thought back to four nights earlier, when she and Vincent sped down the narrow streets of Queen Anne to Kinnear Park. They'd been so close to getting him back. *But where was he now?*

That night, she'd been certain Max would be returned to them. She'd pictured him standing by his captor, wearing the same navy pinstriped pajamas he'd worn the previous night. His brown eyes would be tired, his curls unbrushed, and he would be scared. But alive. And he'd come running into her arms, screaming *Mommy!* as soon as he saw her.

How had it all gone so wrong?

She blinked back tears, refusing to entertain that they might never be reunited. That she may never see his little freckled face again. He was out there somewhere, and she was determined to find out where.

Beneath them, a sailboat passed between the remaining towers of the ill-fated Tacoma Narrows Bridge. It had been nearly two years since its infamous collapse, but the war had delayed its dismantling and replacement. She nearly smiled, remembering the last time she'd taken Max sailing on their sixty-foot yacht. It was hard to think it was less than a month ago.

Unlike his father, who only wanted to sit back and enjoy the ride, Max loved being behind the wheel of the boat. Just like her. Vincent always insisted on taking a hired sailor with them, which drove Priscilla mad. *Why bother having a yacht if you didn't learn to sail?*

"Can I turn it, Mr. Smith?" Max had asked Vincent's hired man as Priscilla trimmed a sail.

Vincent complained about the wind as he reclined at the stern, finishing his fourth whiskey, as they prepared to turn into the Fremont Cut.

"Are you sure, little lad?" Mr. Smith had replied. "It's going to be a hard turn."

Max beamed at him. "I'm sure!"

"All right. Put both hands on the wheel and turn us left."

Priscilla looked on in delight at the fire in Max's eyes as he turned the wooden wheel, and the boat dipped to the side.

"A little more."

Max did as Mr. Smith instructed, laughing when he was sprayed with salt water from the speed of the turn.

"Now, hold it steady." Mr. Smith reached out his hand when the wheel began to slip from Max's grip. Together they held the turn, and Max smiled through gritted teeth as the boat turned into the narrow waterway from Elliott Bay.

"Look, Mommy!" he'd cried. "I'm turning us!"

"You've got a sailor on your hands," Mr. Smith told Priscilla.

"I can't wait to sail my own boat when I'm grown up," Max announced as he helped tie up the boat to the dock on Lake Union.

Vincent snorted as he swayed off the boat onto the dock. "You can hire a captain when you're older, son. You're going to be a banker."

Seeing the light in Max's eyes dampen, she'd been inwardly furious at Vincent. *How dare he crush Max's dreams like that?* "No child wants to go grow up to be a banker, Vincent." Plus, Vincent himself wasn't even a banker. She refrained from reminding him that his only profession was getting drunk and chasing women.

"You can grow up to be whatever you want," she'd told

Max that night while she stroked his hair until he fell asleep.

Where are you, my little sailor?

Priscilla tore her eyes from the window at the memory and moved her gaze to the front of the plane. The curtain was drawn behind the cockpit. She needed to speak to Hugh. He was insightful, and more importantly, he knew people that weren't under the Ellis's control. She remembered he was due to be deployed. *Was he already gone?*

She tried to recall what the FBI had said about Hugh's deployment. She wondered how fast something like that happened and realized how little she knew about how wars worked, even though they were in the middle of one.

Her thoughts drifted back to Max for the rest of the flight. There were countless times since Max was born that she worried he would grow up to be like his father. Now, she was terrified he might never grow up at all.

15

Tony's voice came through Vera's headset as he taxied off the runway at the Portland airport on Swan Island. "I'll have you land when we get back to Everett."

Vera felt a rush of nerves as he brought the aircraft to a stop in front of the terminal. Tony had touched down with a perfectly smooth landing. Vera could only hope hers would go as well.

Her mouth nearly dropped open at the sight of a Packard limousine pulling up beside the plane. A uniformed driver jumped out and waited outside the car. She'd only ever seen such a car in the pictures.

Rex pulled the curtain aside and put his hand on Tony's shoulder as the test pilot pulled off his headset. "We'll be back in a few hours."

"Roger that," Tony said.

Without as much as a glance in Vera's direction, Rex turned for the rear door.

Vera heard sniffles coming from one of the seats behind her and turned to see mascara-streaked tears streaming down Priscilla's face.

Rex and the large man with a briefcase were already crossing the tarmac toward the limo. Ruth slapped Vincent's hand away as he tried to assist her down the narrow aisleway.

"Good God, Priscilla!" Vincent exclaimed as he moved past his wife's seat. "Get ahold of yourself!"

Ruth started out the plane's rear door, ignoring her son's shouts.

Did he always speak to his wife this way? Vera couldn't imagine Hugh yelling at her like that. Ever.

She'd been too focused on mastering the Electra's control panel during their short flight to reflect on the marital dispute she'd witnessed before they took off. But now, Vera was shocked to hear the disdainful tone in which Vincent addressed his wife.

Vincent was no doubt distressed after his son's kidnapping. *But did he have no empathy for what his wife must also be going through?*

She watched Priscilla glare at her husband through tear-filled eyes. "Our son is *missing!* We don't even know if he's alive! So, don't tell me to get ahold of myself!"

Vincent leaned forward, and Vera thought he was finally going to console her. Instead, he brought his face an inch from Priscilla's and hissed loudly enough for Vera and Tony to hear.

"Priscilla, if you're going to put on a circus act, you should've stayed home. I'll tell the driver to wait while you gather your composure—but not for long. We don't need any more people thinking you're cutting out paper dolls."

Vera turned back around in her seat before Priscilla caught her staring. *How dare Vincent insinuate she was crazy for caring about her abducted son?* Vera seethed for the way

Priscilla's husband had treated her. *How else was the woman supposed to act?*

Out the side window of the cockpit, Vera eyed Vincent striding across the tarmac, greeting their driver with a winning smile as his wife cried alone in the back of their plane.

Tony shot an uncomfortable glance in Priscilla's direction before he unbuckled his seat belt and climbed out of the cockpit. "I'm going to find some lunch while we wait. You want to join me?"

Vera looked back at Priscilla, still weeping in the back of the plane, and shook her head. "No, thanks."

"Suit yourself," Tony said. He stood and straightened his tie. "I'll be back in about an hour and we can go over the controls and landing procedure again before we take off for Seattle."

Vera turned and watched Tony offer Priscilla a sheepish nod before disembarking the aircraft. Vera climbed out of her seat as Priscilla brought her hands to her face, her body shaking from her sobs. Vera pulled a handkerchief from her blouse pocket as she moved slowly down the aisle.

She rested a hand on Priscilla's shoulder when she reached her seat. Priscilla looked up and Vera extended the handkerchief, noting the socialite was even more striking up close.

"Thank you." Priscilla accepted the monogrammed cloth and dabbed her cheeks.

Vera sat down in the seat across from her. She pulled out the worn copy of *Speak No Evil* that protruded from her pants' pocket and set it on her lap. She'd already read the Mignon B. Eberhart novel once but brought it along not knowing how long she'd be waiting.

Priscilla stared at Hugh's initials on the handkerchief.

"Where is Hugh?"

Vera straightened, surprised to hear Priscilla say her husband's name.

"He was deployed to the Pacific yesterday morning."

Priscilla's expression darkened. "Oh. I didn't realize he'd already gone. I wish he could've stayed out of this awful war. I was hoping he might be able to help me. With Max. He was always so…kind."

Priscilla's concern for her husband caught Vera by surprise. She hadn't thought Hugh interacted with the Ellises on a personal level. Especially Vincent's strikingly beautiful wife. *And how would Hugh have helped her find her missing son?*

"I'm his wife."

Now it was Priscilla's turn to look surprised. She sniffed. "Oh." Her eyes assessed Vera more closely than she had before. "That's right. I remember him saying you were hoping to apply to the Women's Flying Training Detachment."

Vera stiffened. Priscilla knew much more about Hugh — and herself — than she would have expected. An uneasiness crept over her. *If they'd been on such friendly terms, why hadn't Hugh ever mentioned her?*

"So, you're taking over his job while he's at war?"

Vera nodded. "Well, as long as I can prove myself. They haven't exactly given me the job yet."

The limo's horn blared from outside, but Priscilla appeared not to hear it.

"I'm so sorry about your son."

Priscilla dabbed the corners of her eyes with Hugh's handkerchief. "I feel like I'm going to lose my mind if we don't find him."

Vera swallowed, unsure of what to say. Another loud

honk resounded from the waiting limo.

Priscilla's gaze moved to the book on Vera's lap. "You read detective novels?"

Vera expected Priscilla to join the others in the limo after the obnoxious honk, but she stayed put.

"Oh. Sometimes. I wasn't sure how long we'd be here today. My father is a detective, so I guess I've always had an interest in it." It was the only thing she'd ever been interested in doing other than flying, but her parents found that as equally unacceptable.

Priscilla's eyes darted to the limo waiting outside. "They're trying to keep me in the dark about the investigation. And I have to know why."

Her hand clamped around Vera's wrist as she stood from her seat. Vera inhaled her gardenia perfume as she leaned toward her.

"I need someone who can help me find answers. Someone who's on my side. *Please.* I can't trust my husband. And I must know what's happened to Max."

The horn honked again, longer this time.

Vera shook her head. "I'm sorry but I don't—"

Priscilla gripped her wrist tighter before letting go. "I can put in a word for you with Nancy Harkness Love. I know her personally."

Vera straightened at her mention of the head of the Women's Auxiliary Ferrying Squadron. That was quite an offer. She thought immediately of Dari.

"Actually, I'm not quite ready to apply yet. But I have a close friend who's a highly qualified pilot. She'd be excellent to serve in the WAFS."

Vera surprised herself by bringing up Dari. *I can't accept this favor.* She had no qualifications to help Priscilla find her son.

"What's her name?"

"Dari. Dari Ramos."

"Consider it done." Priscilla turned back when she reached the rear door. "Please help me. I have no one else to turn to."

Vera thought of Hugh, wondering what he would do if he was here. Priscilla seemed to know Hugh better than she should. And Vera needed to know why. *Had Priscilla planned to seek Hugh's help merely because he was kind? He was nothing like the men in the Ellis family. Or was it something more?*

Vera locked eyes with Priscilla, who was waiting intently for her response. Her mind burned with the image of the young child on the poster, and the striking resemblance to his mother.

"I'm not sure I can help. I'm not any kind of investigator, ma'am."

Priscilla's eyes bore into hers. "I only need you to try."

Before Vera could respond, Priscilla turned and stepped off the plane. Vera moved toward the door at the rear of the airplane's cabin and watched Priscilla scurry toward the parked limo in the rain.

As the luxury car pulled away, Vera pushed her worries about Hugh and Priscilla's relationship out of her mind, trying to convince herself there was nothing to worry about. Instead, she sat alone on the private airplane and thought of the problems money had brought upon Priscilla: a controlling husband backed by a powerful family, and her only child stolen from under her own roof.

How dreadfully awful it must be to be rich.

16

Vera lowered the Electra's landing gear as she started her approach to the airport on Ebey Island. She thought of Hugh, who would have landed here his first day on the job, too. Her landing had to be as good as his. If not better. After she announced their arrival to the Everett Airport radio room, the radio operator informed them of the fifteen-knot crosswind.

"So," Tony said, "you'll want to crab into the wind to keep the airplane tracking the centerline of the runway. You've done crosswind landings before, right?"

Vera glanced at the faded photograph that stuck out from the dash on her side of the controls, hoping it would calm her nerves. Amelia's smile exuded nothing but confidence.

"Yes, of course," Vera replied.

The wind gusted against them, but Vera put the memory of her failed crosswind landing out of her mind. She tried to imagine herself as Amelia, effortlessly landing the Electra no matter what the weather conditions. And certainly without any Ellises in the back judging her flying skills.

"This might be a little different than what you were taught. With a low-wing airplane you will have to crab into the wind to maintain runway centerline. As you flare, you'll want to straighten the nose with the rudder just before you touch down. Then you must immediately turn the yoke into the wind to keep the wing from rising. Also, with an aircraft of this size, the controls are going to be quite a bit heavier, and the airplane will be slower to react than with the lightweight aircraft you've been used to. So, you will have to be very aggressive with the controls in this wind," Tony instructed.

Vera nodded. *How am I supposed to remember all that?* She turned the plane into the wind to keep it heading for the center of the runway.

Speed is life. Vera glanced at the airspeed indicator as Dari's words sounded in her mind. She waited until the plane crossed over the end of the runway before she righted the nose. As soon as they touched down, she turned the yoke into the direction of the wind to keep the upwind wing from lifting.

"Nicely done," Tony said as she stepped on the brakes. "Slight bump there after we first touched down, but I couldn't have done it better myself under those conditions."

"Thank you," she replied, saying the words as much to Amelia as the Lockheed test pilot.

She was amazed at how well the complicated maneuver had gone, having never done it before. Her hands shook from the adrenaline in her system. She hoped Tony didn't notice.

After returning the plane to its original parking place, Vera turned off the engines and removed her headset.

"Not bad," Rex announced. "But next time—no bumps."

Tony tried to contain a smile at Rex's ignorance of the skill required to land in those conditions. Vera turned around to face him.

"We'll keep you on—for now. With everything going on, I don't have time to find another pilot. Your salary will start at five hundred a month."

"Hugh was making ten thousand a year," Vera said, after doing the math in her head.

"Don't expect us to be matching your husband's salary. None of the women employed by Pacific Bank even come close to making ten thousand a year. But I'd be willing to make it seven. If you're as good as Hugh said you are."

Vera worked to keep her jaw from dropping. While relieved she got the job, she wasn't expecting a pay cut for doing the same job as her husband. She opened her mouth to protest but quickly closed it. However unfair, she was in no position to argue.

"I'll have my secretary call you later today with the rest of this week's schedule." Rex turned and followed the others off the plane, except for Priscilla who remained in her seat. Vera hadn't heard her speak a word since they reboarded the plane in Portland. When the other passengers had left, Priscilla came up to the front.

"Pleased to make your acquaintance, Mrs. Chandler."

"Yours, too." Vera accepted her gloved handshake, feeling a folded paper between her fingers after Priscilla pulled her hand away.

Beside her, Tony held out a business card as Priscilla climbed out of the Electra.

"Well, you're an excellent pilot, Vera, and the Ellises are lucky to have you."

"Thanks for all your help." Vera slipped the piece of paper Priscilla had given her into her left hand before accepting his card.

"My number's on the bottom. Feel free to give me a call if you have any questions after today. I'm going to stretch my legs and get some coffee from the pilot lounge before we go back up to do your multi-engine training. Then, you can do a few more landings before they day's over."

"Sounds great," she said, as Tony climbed out of his seat. "I'll join you in a minute."

She waited for him to deplane before unfolding Priscilla's note. She recognized the bold Pacific Bank letterhead at the top. *Come tomorrow morning at ten* was scrawled in perfectly neat cursive above a Queen Anne address.

Vera had no idea how she could possibly help find Max Ellis. But after seeing the way the Ellises treated his mother, she didn't have the heart to refuse. She'd been shocked to see the way the Ellises treated Priscilla. In the papers, Priscilla was idolized. Glamourized. Respected. Everyone adored her. She was Seattle's golden girl, always in the news for using her status to bring awareness to good causes. Her family definitely didn't see it that way.

Plus, Priscilla's connection to Nancy Harkness Love felt too good to pass up. It could get Dari into the WAFS.

Vera stared at Amelia's photo on the dash as she slid the note into her pocket. *What on earth have I gotten myself into?*

17

Vera spotted Priscilla's shiny black Cadillac when she pulled Hugh's Ford through the open wrought iron gate of the white three-story mansion. When she stepped onto the cobblestone driveway, she took in the breathtaking view of downtown and Puget Sound glistening in the mid-morning sun at the bottom of the hill. She could only imagine the views from the home's second and third floors. She put a hand on her hat to keep it from blowing away as she climbed the marble steps toward the double front doors.

After ringing the doorbell, she smoothed the front of her fitted tweed suit jacket. The large door swung open, and a gray-haired man in a dark suit stared down at her with a grim expression.

"Can I help you, miss?"

"That's all right, Gregory." Priscilla's voice echoed through the grand entryway before Vera could open her mouth. "She's here to see me. I'll let her in."

Gregory studied Vera for a moment longer before he stepped aside and Priscilla appeared in his place. She opened the door wide.

"Please come in."

Priscilla was dressed just as impeccably as yesterday, her short sleeve angora sweater reminding Vera of Jean Arthur in *The Talk of the Town,* the last picture she and Hugh had seen together. But her eyes were tired and her smile looked forced.

"Thank you." Vera tried not to gawk at the enormous crystal chandelier that hung from the ceiling as she entered the large foyer.

Priscilla turned toward her butler before he disappeared down an adjacent hallway. "Gregory, won't you bring some tea into the sitting room, please."

He nodded. "Yes, madam."

Vera noticed the strained pleasantry in Priscilla's voice when she spoke to her butler, and that it disappeared as soon as they were alone.

"Thanks so much for coming." Priscilla placed her hand on Vera's back and led her toward a large room with a fireplace at the front of the house.

Vera glanced at Priscilla's sling-back open-toed pumps, then at her own wooden-sole oxfords. She'd worn some of her best clothes, but still felt frumpy beside Priscilla.

"Of course." Vera was suddenly reminded that despite the opulence around her, she had no idea how to help the bank heiress find her son.

Movement from the top of the stairwell caught Vera's eye as she moved alongside Priscilla. Vera looked up, expecting to see Vincent, but was taken aback by the woman staring down at her. She looked around ten years older than Priscilla. Her plain clothes were a sharp contrast to Priscilla's, and her dirty blonde hair was pulled into a low, tight bun. But it wasn't her attire that had startled Vera. It was the fierce judgment in her prying eyes.

Priscilla turned her head to follow Vera's gaze. "That's Hattie. Don't mind her."

Hattie's eyes continued to follow them until Priscilla shut the double doors after they had entered the formal sitting room.

"Is she your housekeeper?"

Priscilla shook her head and moved toward the fireplace. "She's Max's nanny." She pulled a silver cigarette case off the mantle. "She lives here," she added, extending the opened case toward Vera. "Cigarette?"

After Vera shook her head, Priscilla placed a cigarette in her jade holder and motioned toward the sofa. Vera recalled from the papers that Max's nanny had been the one to find him missing from his bed in the middle of the night. She took a seat on the sofa as Priscilla snapped the case shut and lifted a crystal lighter off an end table.

She didn't miss the tremble of Priscilla's hands as she lit her cigarette before inhaling a sharp breath.

"Is your husband home?" Being a weekday, Vera presumed he must be at the bank.

Priscilla jumped when one of the doors swung open. Vera turned to see Priscilla's butler holding a silver tray with a small blue-and-white teapot and two matching cups and saucers. The women watched him set the tray down in silence on the glass coffee table.

"Thank you, Gregory." Priscilla waited until the door closed behind him to answer Vera's question. "No, Vincent isn't here."

There was a harshness to her tone as she spoke her husband's name. She stood, folded her arms, and moved toward the front window.

"Yesterday, in Portland, we met with a federal

investigator who specializes in child abductions. Apparently, he's solved the most kidnapping cases in the country. He was frank with us and said the odds of finding Max alive are not good, especially with the unusual circumstances of finding his kidnapper murdered days ago."

"I'm not sure how I can help you." Vera remembered the photos from the *Tribune* of the federal agents combing the Ellis property for fingerprints and clues the day after the boy's kidnapper was found murdered in Kinnear Park. "Isn't the FBI investigating?"

Priscilla shook her head after taking a long drag from her cigarette. "Technically, Max's case is still open. But they told us they've done everything they could and had to put their resources toward preventing another Japanese attack. Vincent hired a private investigator, which I'm sure his brother is behind. The guy who was on the plane yesterday...looked like a wrestler."

Vera let out a little laugh, despite the gravity of the subject.

"But Vincent won't share any details with me. And even if he did, I'm not sure I can trust him."

Vera watched Priscilla step away from the window, wondering what she wasn't saying. She witnessed her husband's appalling treatment of her, but did Priscilla actually think Vincent had something to do with their son's kidnapping?

Vera decided not to ask, knowing she likely wouldn't get a straight answer. At least not yet.

She wondered what Hugh would think of her getting wrapped up in the child's kidnapping. If the FBI couldn't find Max, how could she? The desperation in Priscilla's eyes made Vera wish she hadn't agreed to help. *I shouldn't be here.*

Priscilla read her thoughts. "Please." She snuffed out her cigarette on a gold-edged ash tray. "I have to find him. And I have no one else to turn to."

Vera inhaled a deep breath as the cigarette smoke finally dissipated from the air. "There must be someone you could hire to look into this who has experience with this sort of thing?"

"Not without Vincent knowing. The FBI learned that Max's kidnapper, Howard Mills, has a cousin he was close with. His name's Gilbert, and he could very well have been Howard's accomplice. The FBI agents have gotten word that this Gilbert is out working on a fishing boat, so they're not even bothering to look for him." Priscilla took a seat beside her. "But what if Gilbert never went on that fishing trip? What if he has Max?" She reached for Vera's hands. "I need you to go down to the Fishermen's Terminal and see if you can learn where this man is. Someone must have seen his boat leave and know whether he was on it. Maybe you can learn where he lives."

Uneasiness crept up Vera's spine. *Why does this family have so many secrets from each other?* "But why me?" If Priscilla was so desperate to find her son, why wouldn't she go down to the terminal herself?

"If I go down there, they'll know."

Before Vera could ask who Priscilla was referring to, she spoke again. "Why don't I show you Max's room before you go?"

"Okay...."

There was a glimmer of hope in Priscilla's expression before she turned for the doors. "Follow me."

As Priscilla led Vera up the hardwood stairwell, there was no sign of the nanny. Vera was surprised when they ascended the second flight of stairs to find that Max's room was on the third floor. She felt an unexpected well of emotion when they stepped through the doorway to the child's empty room.

His twin bed was neatly made, and a worn-out, one-eyed teddy bear lay beside his pillow. As Vera stood next to Max's mother, there was an unspoken realization that the boy might never sleep another night in his bed.

"The window was open when Hattie discovered Max was gone." Priscilla's voice sounded strangely void of emotion. Robotic. Numb. "Vincent and I woke to her screaming Max's name in the night."

Vera moved toward the window, forcing herself to focus on the facts. She looked out at the magnificent view of the Port of Seattle before lowering her gaze to the cobblestone driveway three stories below.

"Was there a ladder found?"

"No. The FBI believe the kidnapper took it with him after getting Max down. The downstairs doors were locked. The front gate was open, but that's because Vincent forgot to close it after coming home drunk in the middle of the night."

Vera turned around. She knew they hadn't called the police until twenty-four hours later, after they'd found Max's kidnapper's body. "And you haven't received any more ransom notes?"

Biting her lip, Priscilla shook her head.

Hattie appeared in the doorway behind her employer with crossed arms. Her eyes narrowed at Vera. "Who are you? Another reporter?"

Vera was shocked by her brash questioning. That a member of Priscilla's staff would speak to her guest with such rudeness. Although, she supposed, she was Priscilla's staff too.

Priscilla spoke before Vera could respond. But not with the reprimand Vera expected.

"No, Hattie. This is our new pilot, Vera. She and a friend of hers are interested in flying for the Women's Auxiliary Ferrying Squadron. I told her I could put in a word for them with Nancy Harkness Love."

Vera glanced at Priscilla, wondering why she felt the need to over-explain herself to her employee, before she turned to Max's nanny.

"We were just discussing the night Max was abducted," Vera added. "How did you discover him missing? That must have been a horrible shock for you."

"I heard a door slamming shut. That was all." Hattie's expression remained flat.

Vera looked out the window again. There seemed no way Max's kidnapper could have carried the child down a ladder or rope in the middle of the night without Max waking and screaming.

She turned to ask Hattie to recollect the night of Max's kidnapping, but the nanny was gone. Vera looked instead at Priscilla, who started at the sound of the front door slamming.

"Priscilla!"

Vera recognized Vincent's shout from two floors down. There was a flash of fear in Priscilla's dark eyes before she turned toward his voice.

"Whose cheap car is blocking my spot in the drive?"

Priscilla clamped her hand around Vera's upper arm. "Let me do the talking," she said in a lowered voice.

Vera peered out Max's bedroom window one last time before Priscilla guided her out of the room. She thought of the infamous photo of the ladder leaning against the Lindbergh home beside their baby's second-story window.

But there was no ladder or even rope left behind outside Max's room.

As the two women stepped into the hall, Vera could hear Vincent stomping up the wooden staircase. She thought of what Priscilla had said about Vincent leaving the gate open the night Max was taken. With her hand still around her arm, Priscilla led Vera toward the stairwell. As Vincent neared the top, Vera glanced back one last time at the door to Max's room.

"What the hell is she doing here?"

18

Vincent's bloodshot eyes locked with Vera's when he reached the top of the stairs. Vera froze. The top few buttons of his shirt were undone. His eyes glazed over hers and moved back to Priscilla.

"I asked you, what's she doing here?"

"How good of you to finally come home."

His eyes narrowed at his wife's icy tone. "Answer me, Priscilla."

Vera looked back and forth between the couple who, just like yesterday, made no effort to hide their contempt for each other.

"I invited her for tea. I'm going to put a word in for a friend of hers for the Women's Auxiliary Ferrying Squadron." She lifted her chin. "Vera wants to fly for them too, eventually."

He scoffed. "By showing her our son's room?"

Vera stole a glance at Priscilla. "I was actually just leaving."

"Good." He kept his gaze focused on the women as they

started down the steps. "Then she can move that hideous automobile out of my driveway."

The women descended the staircase in an uncomfortable silence as Vincent looked on from the third floor. When they had nearly reached the bottom, Vera heard Vincent start down the stairs behind them. She wondered about Priscilla and Vincent's relationship.

From the way Vincent spoke to her, she could see why his wife would despise him. *But was she also afraid of him?*

It made Vera all the more grateful to have Hugh in her life. A lump formed in her throat at the thought of him, and the dangers he'd be facing in the Pacific.

A door slammed on the second floor. Priscilla glanced up the staircase before she turned to Vera. "Vincent knew Howard, the man who kidnapped Max. He helped him get his job at the bank." Her voice was so quiet Vera could barely hear her.

Vera looked into Priscilla's dark brown eyes and wondered if she *was* crazy.

"You think Vincent had something to do with this?"

"I don't know what to think anymore. I haven't slept in days. I was hoping Hugh might have overheard something, on one of his flights. But I can't ask him now, so I need you to find out."

Vera felt a pull of jealousy hearing Priscilla say Hugh's name again.

"You're lucky. Hugh loves you," Priscilla said. "He was so proud of you being a pilot."

But Priscilla's words did little to quell her growing suspicion. *When were Hugh and Priscilla having these heart-to-heart conversations?*

Gregory appeared in the entryway, and Priscilla whirled around to face him. *Her jumpiness bordered on paranoia.*

"Gregory, please get Vera's coat."

He nodded and pivoted down the adjacent hallway.

When he disappeared from their view, Vera turned to Priscilla. "I'm not sure I can help you." She didn't want to say it, but she was starting to see why the FBI had all but given up. "But I'll go to the Fishermen's Terminal and ask about this Gilbert Mills."

Priscilla gripped her manicured fingers around Vera's arm again. "*Thank you.*"

"If I learn something, how will I tell you?"

"*Priscilla!* I need to speak to you!"

Both women turned toward the sound of Vincent's voice from the upper level. Priscilla released Vera's arm from her hold.

"I'll phone you later." There was relief in Priscilla's tone before she started up the stairs, leaving Vera alone in her grand foyer.

Vera was still waiting for Gregory to reappear when she heard a woman's whispers coming from behind the stairwell. Vera crept closer to the source of the hushed voice. She stepped softly, careful not to let her heels clack against the floorboards.

"They were in Max's room," she heard the woman say when she got a few steps closer. "She was asking about the night he was taken."

Vera peered around the corner and saw Hattie with her back to her holding a telephone in her hands.

"I'm not sure," Hattie continued. "But I can find out."

Hattie spun around, and Vera lunged backward, pressing her back against the stairwell.

"I have to go," she heard Hattie say, before she slammed the handset onto the cradle.

The nanny's footsteps headed straight for her, and Vera

searched for somewhere to hide. Hattie was already suspicious of her. Vera couldn't have her knowing that she was eavesdropping on her phone call.

Hattie rounded the corner behind the stairs. Seeing nothing in the hallway to hide behind, Vera ducked into the small dark alcove beneath the stairs. She held her breath as she watched Hattie's low-heeled, lace-up shoes move down the hallway beside her. When she heard the nanny climb the stairs above her, Vera exhaled a sigh of relief.

She stepped out from under the stairs and glanced toward the empty entryway before tiptoeing to the phone. After lifting the handset, she dialed the operator.

Gregory waltzed down the adjacent hallway with her coat slung over his arm. Vera waited for him to move past the stairs before she spoke into the phone.

"Operator, can you reconnect me to the same number I just dialed? We seem to have gotten disconnected."

"I can't hear you ma'am. I need you to speak up."

"Madam?" Gregory called out from the entryway.

"Please reconnect me to my last call."

"One moment."

"Madam?" Gregory's footsteps moved around the stairs.

There was ringing on the other end of the line. Vera heard Gregory walking toward her. *Come on. Pick up.* She would have to hang up if someone didn't answer in the next few seconds.

The ringing stopped. "Rex Ellis, Pacific Bank."

Vera replaced the handset onto the cradle as Gregory came around the corner.

"Can I help you, madam?" He eyed her with suspicion before his gaze moved to the phone behind her.

Vera smiled. "Oh. No, thank you. I was just calling Ebey Island to check the weather reports for tomorrow."

Gregory stared at her in silence.

"That's the airport in Everett."

"I'm aware, madam."

She pulled her coat from his forearm. "Anyway, I'll just be on my way."

He assessed her, and for a moment, Vera thought he might confront her about using the telephone without asking. She leveled her eyes on him and didn't blink. *I work for the Ellises just like you.*

"I'll see her out, Gregory." Vincent appeared behind him.

"Very well." Gregory turned down the hall, leaving Vera to follow Vincent to the front door.

She noticed Vincent had changed into a fresh suit since he confronted her on the stairs. His hair was slicked back, and he'd transformed from looking like a hungover playboy to a suave professional. After he opened the door, Vera braced herself to be fired for being in his home.

"I need you to fly me to Orcas Island in the San Juans today. Be at the airport at two."

"Oh." She felt her shoulders relax. "Okay. I'll be there."

Vera turned around after the front door closed behind her, glad to be out of the mansion. She thought about the telephone call that she'd overheard. *Was Hattie paid to spy on Priscilla?*

Vera looked up at Max's bedroom window after she climbed behind the wheel of her Ford, startled to see Hattie staring down at her. She tore her eyes away and threw her car into reverse. Spotting a bright red Auburn convertible in her rearview mirror, she slammed on her brakes. Her Ford jerked to a stop inches from the expensive Speedster, and she exhaled against her seat.

Vera glanced at the upstairs window before she pulled out of the large driveway, glad to see Hattie was no longer watching her. No wonder Priscilla didn't trust anyone in her house. These people had more secrets than they did money.

19

Vera's stomach turned as she pulled her Ford into the Fishermen's Terminal parking lot, seeing it filled with squad cars and an ambulance. She got out and headed toward the water, where several dozen fishing boats were packed into the busy commercial moorage sites.

A cool breeze came over Salmon Bay and she cinched her plaid trench coat tighter as she walked toward a uniformed officer at the edge of a pier. At the end of it, Vera spotted a small group of police crouching down over something. Or some*one*.

The officer held his palm in the air as Vera approached. "You can't come through here, ma'am."

Vera strained to see what the police were examining on the dock. "Why? What happened?"

"Looks like murder." He pointed behind her to where a group of onlookers, mostly fisherman, were gathered on an adjacent pier. "I need you to stay back."

Vera turned and moved to where the small crowd was gathered, coming to a stop beside the only other woman in sight, who looked about Vera's age. She chewed a large piece of gum in the side of her mouth as she stared intently at the scene unfolding on the end of the pier. A teenage boy stood beside her, holding a camera.

The woman looked away from the crime scene just long enough to size Vera up. "You from *The Star*? I know all the faces at *The Tribune*."

Vera's hand flew to her mouth when she saw the short brown hair of the lifeless form that lay on the dock, peeking out between the fishermen who kneeled over him. *Max?*

Just then, a police officer stepped away from the body for a moment and Vera exhaled, seeing it was that of an adult man, not a child.

"Do they know who he is?" Vera asked the gum-chewing reporter.

She shrugged. "Some fisherman. Name's Mills."

Vera swiveled her head in the woman's direction as she flipped open a small notepad.

"*Gilbert* Mills."

Vera followed the reporter's casual gaze back to the pier, where Gilbert lay dead. One of the policemen was speaking to another and pointed at the water and then Mills's body.

The young cameraman leaned into the reporter. "How long do you think he was in the water?"

She smacked her gum. "From the looks of him, my guess is a few days at least."

Vera looked away from Gilbert's bloated, discolored face, which was obvious even from that far away—and much more grotesque than the carefully preserved cadavers she'd observed in nurses training. She fought the urge to vomit over the side of the pier.

Vera turned back to the woman beside her. "How do they know he was murdered?"

Her eyes were trained on two men in suits walking off the pier. "He's got a couple of bullet holes in his chest. But don't go stealing my scoop. You'll have to find out the rest for yourself."

With one hand on her hat, the reporter jogged toward the two men who moved past a group of fishermen hauling their catch up the dock. She waved her other hand in the air when she reached them.

"Excuse me, detectives!"

One of them stopped, looking only too happy to answer the pretty reporter's questions. The other detective strode toward a heavyset fisherman who stood taking in the scene around Gilbert's body from beside a large blue and white fishing boat.

A seagull screeched overhead as Vera moved closer to hear what the two men were saying.

"Are you Roy Fitz?" the detective asked.

The fisherman nodded.

"I'm Detective Gamble with the Seattle Homicide Bureau. I heard Mills was supposed to be out on a fishing trip. On your boat."

"Supposed to be. But he never showed. Me and the rest of my crew had to leave without him. We were planning to be out for a few more days but came back early due to the storm rolling in."

Vera glanced at the patchy blue sky, making a mental note to telephone the Orcas Island airport about the weather before she took off for the San Juans.

The detective crossed his arms. "When was the last time you saw him?"

Roy seemed to think for a moment. "Last Tuesday. His girlfriend came down here. The two of them got in a screaming match on one of the piers." He shook his head.

"Caused a huge scene."

The detective's eyes lit up. "Do you know who she is?"

"I do...."

The detective's brows furrowed. "Well?"

"Scarlet Fox."

"The actress?"

Roy nodded. "That's the one."

Vera felt as surprised as the detective looked. The ex-Hollywood star was now known for being an out-of-work partygoer who had returned to her hometown of Seattle after her acting career dried up. Although she'd been in the news last year after she was arrested for being drunk and disorderly and then assaulting a police officer, Vera had seen her in the papers only last month promoting a local campaign selling war bonds.

"And do you know what they were arguing about?"

Roy shrugged. "Money, I'd guess. According to Gil, she's hard up for dough these days. Somehow, though, she's got a nice houseboat on Lake Union."

Vera glanced at her wristwatch as the detective thanked him and handed Roy his business card. She'd have to leave soon to make it to the airport on time. She waited until the detective walked away before she approached Roy.

"Get back to work!" Roy yelled at a couple of men who stood staring at the commotion around Gilbert's body. "That net isn't going to repair itself!"

A strong fishy odor filled her nostrils when she reached the boat, where Roy was bent over rinsing his hands in the water. When he spotted Vera standing over him, the large man stood and wiped his hands on his dirty slacks. He looked her up and down before he spoke.

"You one of Scarlet's friends?"

"Um. Yes...." Vera was shocked at the man's assumption,

but she would run with it. "She wasn't at her houseboat, so I thought she might be here...with Gilbert."

He narrowed his eyes. "Well, you can tell her she doesn't have to come around here anymore. Although, the police will probably get to her before you do."

"Could you hear Scarlet and Gilbert's argument last week?"

He'd told the detective it was about money, but Vera wondered if it could have been about Max.

He shook his head. "I was too far away. Just sounded like a lover's quarrel."

They both looked toward the sound of Gilbert's covered body being rolled off the pier on a stretcher.

"There was a rope tied to his ankle when they pulled him out. I'm guessing his body was weighted down somehow...until the rope came free," Roy said. "I wonder if Gil was still alive when he went into the water."

Goosebumps formed on her arms as Vera imagined being shot and then shackled to an anchor, drowning and bleeding to death at the same time. After a moment, Roy turned to Vera.

"I told Gil that woman was trouble." He leaned toward her, his expression grim. "If I were you, love, I'd find better friends."

20

Priscilla walked slowly down the third-story hall to Max's room. She straightened when she reached his door. Was she hearing things? But then she heard it again. There was no mistaking the sob coming from inside Max's room. She pushed open the door.

Her heart sank, seeing Vincent sitting atop Max's bed. His body shook as he cried, holding Max's one-eyed teddy in his hands. Knowing how he must feel, she almost felt sympathy for him.

She could tell from the dark circles beneath his eyes that he'd been drinking more. She stepped inside the room, and he started, seeing her for the first time. He sniffed and wiped away his tears with the back of his hand.

Priscilla crossed the room cautiously, as if a wrong step might trigger Vincent to explode. To her surprise, he opened his arms to her as she neared him. She found herself sinking onto his lap, and they held each other for the first time in years.

As much as she'd grown to despise him, there was a

familiar comfort in his embrace. If nothing else, they were bonded by their love for their son. Even though that bond was now one of grief.

"I can't understand what would make Howard do this," Vincent finally said. "I keep thinking about it. I mean, I know he was upset after getting fired. And, sure, he may've been stealing from the bank. But we were *friends*. I told him that if he *ever* needed money, he could come to me."

Priscilla stiffened, thinking of the man who'd taken Max away from this very room.

"And who the hell killed him?"

Priscilla shrank as Vincent raised his voice, even though for once it wasn't directed at her. She leaned back to look him in the eyes. "Did you tell *her* that Max was taken? Before we went to the park?"

The broken expression on his face turned to a scowl. "Tell who?"

She couldn't bring herself to say the name of Vincent's lover out loud. "You know who."

Vincent stood, knocking Priscilla off his lap. He threw Max's teddy onto his bed as she scrambled to her feet.

"What the hell have you been doing? *Spying on me?*"

"Maybe she told someone about Max's abduction." Priscilla could practically feel Vincent's blood boil at what she was suggesting. "Maybe she wanted the seventy-five thousand for herself. Or maybe—"

Vincent jabbed a finger toward her face. "You better watch yourself, Priscilla." His tone was ice cold. "You have no right to throw out wild accusations."

The truth in his words jabbed at her heart. As Max's mother, it was her job to protect him. And she had failed.

"I'm just trying to find out what happened to Max. Same as you!"

Despite everything he'd done to her, she took a step toward her husband, hoping to calm him. But he marched past her, knocking her shoulder with his arm on his way out of the room.

"I'm leaving," he said. "I can't stay in this house anymore."

"Vincent!" She chased after him. "Please don't go!" She grabbed his arm, but he pulled it away, knocking her off balance.

She fell to the floorboards in the doorway of Max's room. Vincent was already bounding down the stairwell by the time she stepped into the hall. Her hands gripped the banister. Vincent's reluctance was likely the only thing keeping her mother-in-law from having her institutionalized, even after Max's abduction. But now, she'd crossed a line.

"Vincent, please! *I'm sorry!*"

Without looking up, he opened the front door and slammed it behind him. She'd known better than to ask where he was going. She looked out over the empty foyer of their grand mansion, overcome with being utterly alone. A cry escaped Priscilla's lips and her knees buckled beneath her. She pulled her knees to her chest and sobbed after collapsing to the wood floor.

She wasn't sure how long she had been crying when she felt a cool hand on her shoulder. She opened her eyes, surprised to see Hattie standing over her, looking almost kind.

"You're not well, Mrs. Ellis. Let me help you to bed."

Priscilla pushed herself off the floor and allowed Hattie to help her stand. She was going mad. Just like the Ellises wanted.

"That's a girl," Hattie soothed, leading Priscilla down the

stairs with a firm hold on her arm. "Come and lie down for a bit. If you don't feel better, I can call a doctor."

Priscilla remembered the article she'd read in yesterday's paper about the man who killed his father after receiving a lobotomy. An image of a white-coated psychiatrist driving a pick through her skull filled her mind. "No! No doctors."

Hattie gave her a worried look, and Priscilla softened her tone. "You're right. I just need to lie down."

They had almost reached her bedroom when the front door chimed. Priscilla turned toward the sound. She envisioned the two FBI agents standing on her front porch with news that Max had been found.

Before Hattie could stop her, Priscilla pulled her arm from the nanny's grip and flew down the stairs.

21

Vera sat alone in the cockpit of the Electra, refamiliarizing herself with the controls in preparation for her first flight without the test pilot. She tucked her faded photo of Amelia into the dash and tried to shake Gilbert Mills's bloated blue-green face from her mind.

She considered stopping to tell Priscilla, but she would have arrived late at the airport. She was already on Vincent's bad side. Now, there'd been not only one but two men murdered with connections to Max's kidnapping, and the boy was still missing. Maybe she'd been a fool to get involved.

On the other side of the chain-link fence that surrounded the airport, Vera saw Vincent's convertible come to an abrupt stop. She checked the time. It was ten minutes after two.

There was a bleached-blonde woman in the passenger seat and Vera watched her with curiosity as she climbed out of the Speedster. Keeping her eyes on the woman, Vera held in the talk button on the microphone.

"Electra 8619, taxiing to runway 16 for takeoff."

"Roger, Electra 8619. What's your destination?"

"Orcas Island."

"Are you aware of the storm coming in?"

Remembering the fisherman's storm warning, she reproached herself for not checking the weather again when she arrived. Since Vincent was late anyway, she would have had plenty of time. "When is it supposed to hit?"

"Not until nightfall. So, you should stay ahead of it. As long as you land before dark."

Vera did a quick calculation in her head. That would give her enough time to get back.

"Roger that."

She spotted Vincent sauntering across the flightline with his blonde companion hanging on his arm. She stiffened, wondering if Priscilla knew he was having an affair. The pair made no effort to hide their affection. *Had Hugh known?* It seemed so brazen for Vincent to bring his mistress aboard their private plane. Especially after Max has been taken. Did he have no regard at all for his wife—or shame?

The couple neared the plane, and despite the pleasant smile Vincent offered to the woman beside him, Vera recognized the same anguish in his eyes that she'd seen in Priscilla's.

She tried to turn her focus to her pre-flight checklist, but she couldn't stop her mind from reeling. If Gilbert killed Howard and took Max, then who killed Gilbert? And why would Gilbert off his cousin before they got the ransom money? Unless he was planning to ask for more.

Her thoughts were interrupted by a woman's laughter coming from the back of the plane. Vera turned to see the blonde climb inside, followed by Vincent. Vincent grabbed her waist and the woman giggled as she slowly took off her hat, and then rummaged through her oversized purse.

"Mr. Ellis," Vera said, "I've been informed there's a storm coming in tonight. It's not supposed to hit until dark, but it would be safer to wait until the weather clears. Especially if it's not...imperative that we fly."

Vincent frowned after turning his head toward the cockpit. "You let me worry about what's *imperative*. Your job is to fly the plane. Can you take us or not?"

"I can take you. But I thought you should know."

"Good." Vincent turned back to the grinning woman at his side.

Up close, Vera could tell she was pretty, but she didn't compare to Priscilla's stunning beauty and effortless glamour. Her lips were overdrawn with a bright red rouge, and her dark roots were visible where her hair parted.

Still, here she was on the Ellis plane, holding a bottle of champagne by the neck.

"Scarlet, you naughty, naughty girl! You must've read my mind."

This wasn't just any Scarlet, Vera knew now. She was Scarlet Fox.

With the curtain drawn behind the cockpit, Vera flew the Electra north over the Sound toward the San Juan Islands, alone with Amelia staring back at her and the drone of the twin engines. Plus, the occasional faint squeal from Scarlet in the rear.

Left alone with her thoughts, questions whirled in her mind. *Did Scarlet kill Gilbert...or have him killed? Did she know where Max was?*

Her mind reeled as she tried to piece together how Vincent could be having an affair with the girlfriend of one of Max's kidnappers. Who were now both dead. *Did that make Vincent a pawn or was he involved somehow?*

She thought of Priscilla's distrust of her husband, which was apparently a sound judgement when it came to their marriage. But was Priscilla right to suspect Vincent of something worse? She had thought Priscilla was paranoid, but now she wasn't so sure.

A few thousand feet below, the channels of Puget Sound opened to the larger waters of the Strait of Juan de Fuca. When Vincent told her to fly him to the San Juans, she'd assumed it must be for a business meeting. There was no way the company's gas rations allowed for joy rides with his mistress.

And what would she tell Priscilla? She'd promised to help her find her abducted son, but now she was flying her husband and his lover to a weekend getaway. As the San Juan Islands came into view, she thought of Hugh.

Had he flown Vincent and Scarlet to secret rendezvous? He must have. Why hadn't he told her? Especially when he knew she was going to take his place. A sudden downpour of rain showered the windshield, blurring the islands in the distance.

Vera assessed the darkening clouds above as she started their descent toward the horseshoe-shaped island. *How much had Hugh known about the Ellises?* Had he been willing to overlook their corruption for his sizable salary? If so, she hadn't known him as well as she'd thought. *Maybe not even at all.*

Before she could give it more thought, an updraft lifted the nose of the plane, requiring Vera's full attention to level out. A bright flash of light appeared outside her windshield as a deafening boom reverberated through the cabin.

The cockpit and cabin lights flickered. Scarlet screamed. Vera felt a hand on her shoulder and pulled off her headphones.

"What the devil was that?" Vincent yelled.

Wasn't it obvious? Vera took a steadying breath as she scanned the instrument panel and saw that her ammeter was reading zero, which meant the generators were no longer charging the batteries. "We were struck by lightning!"

22

Priscilla held her breath as she swung open her heavy front door, simultaneously hoping to see Max and bracing herself that her worst fears had come true. When she saw the two FBI agents' now familiar faces, the air deflated from her lungs. She recalled envisioning them on her front steps, afraid it had been a premonition of what would become the worst moment in her life. That they were back at all, after saying they were pulling back on Max's investigation, could only mean that something was terribly wrong. Beyond them, hail pelted from the overcast sky, bouncing when it landed atop her front lawn.

"Is it Max? Have you found him?"

Their cold expressions told her nothing. Except that they hadn't come with good news. She heard Hattie's footsteps approach from behind her.

The older man removed his hat. "I'm afraid we don't have any news about Max, madam. This is about Howard Mills's cousin, Gilbert. May we come in?"

Priscilla felt the floor begin to sway. The false hope was

almost too much to take.

"Of course," she heard Hattie say.

The nanny put her arm around Priscilla, leading her away from the door to make room for the investigators.

"Why don't you talk in the library?" Still guiding Priscilla, Hattie led the way to the room across the foyer.

"Is your husband home? It's important we speak with him, too."

Priscilla was vaguely aware of the younger agent's question as Hattie sat next to her on the davenport. But she couldn't focus on anything other than the fact that Max was still gone.

"Ma'am?"

Priscilla lifted her head to see the younger agent eagerly awaiting her response. "Um. No. He's out. He's having trouble being in the home with Max gone. I'm not sure when he'll be back."

The agents exchanged a glance, and the older man gave his partner a nod.

The tall man crossed his arms. "Howard Mills's cousin was found dead earlier this afternoon. His body was pulled out of the water at the Fishermen's Terminal. He'd been shot twice in the chest. The coroner has opened an investigation, but he appears to have been killed a few days ago."

Priscilla looked back and forth between the agents. "What...what does this mean? Do you know who killed him?" Maybe this was the breakthrough they needed. Whoever killed him must have Max.

"We don't know yet. We just learned that Gilbert was seeing the actress Scarlet Fox, whom you might know lives in Seattle again now?"

Priscilla drew in a sharp breath at the mention of

Vincent's lover.

"Does her name mean something to you?" The older agent eyed her intently.

Her head was spinning. *What could this mean?* The Ellis family worked so hard to keep Vincent's affairs out of papers. They'd be furious if she told the FBI about Vincent's infidelity.

Was Scarlet involved in Max's kidnapping? Suddenly, it all seemed to make sense.

"You should ask Vincent. She's his lover."

Out the corner of her eye, Hattie shot her a wide-eyed look of warning.

Both agents raised their eyebrows. "Well, that's an interesting development," the older one said. "Do you know where your husband is?"

Priscilla shook her head. "But I'm sure he's with her. He probably won't be home for days."

"Ok...I see," replied the older agent. "It's no secret that Miss Fox has had her share of financial troubles over the last few years. That could be enough incentive for her to be involved in something like this."

Priscilla laughed, clearly disgusted. "I don't *care* about that woman's money problems."

The agent nodded. "Call us as soon as your husband comes home, please. Or if you learn where he is. We're on our way to visit your brother-in-law. We can see ourselves out."

"Wait!" Priscilla jumped to her feet as the agents crossed the room.

The two men turned back.

"Aren't you going to search Scarlet's houseboat? I mean, what if she's keeping Max there?"

"We did, ma'am. And there was no sign of your son

having been there. Don't worry. We have our patrol units out looking for her."

Priscilla stood in the middle of the library, unable to move as the two agents left her home. Hattie moved past her, leaving the room without a word.

Her breathing quickened as rage formed in her chest. *Vincent, you fool.* He'd been had. And his infidelity might have cost them their son. She made a fist with both hands, her almond-shaped nails digging into her palms.

All this time, she'd been blaming herself for Max's abduction. But now, this was all his fault.

23

Thunder cracked from above after Vera brought the Electra to a stop at the small airport on Orcas Island. She'd never been more relieved to be on the ground. As she removed her headset, a flash of lightning lit up the darkening sky above the rain-streaked windshield. Her hand trembled slightly from pulling off an intact landing through the storm. She'd never flown in such tumultuous weather and poor visibility.

Vincent opened the plane's rear door, and Vera felt a gust of cold air enter the fuselage.

"Come back and pick us up tomorrow at four," he said.

"Wait!" Vera turned in her seat. "I can't fly back tonight. The lightning strike knocked out the generators. I had just enough battery power to run the fuel pumps and radio until we landed, but I can't take off again until I get the generators reset and the batteries recharged."

From the look on her employer's face, Vera could tell he wasn't accustomed to being told no.

"And besides, I can't fly in this storm."

Did he really have no idea what it had taken to land in these conditions? He had to have noticed the plane bouncing violently about on their descent. As she'd fought the wind to keep them on course, her visibility had all but disappeared. If her navigation hadn't been so exact, they would've ended up in the Sound.

"Of course, you can! This plane is equipped with the most modern instruments. Just ask Amelia Earhart."

Vera felt her brows knit together. She wasn't amused at his disregard for Amelia's standing as a pilot, nor her own safety.

"Plus, Rex needs the plane tomorrow morning. If he finds out I had you take us on a joy ride, he'll have my ass. So, I'm afraid you don't have a choice. I shouldn't have to remind you what's at stake here. You work for *me*. Don't make me fire you for insubordination."

Scarlet snickered behind Vincent. Vera glanced in her direction, seeing from her glassy eyes that she was already drunk on the champagne she'd uncorked mid-flight. Vincent turned for the door.

Vera climbed out of her seat. "With all due respect, Mr. Ellis, my getting fired won't matter to me if I'm dead. And if I crash on the way back to Seattle, your plane won't be waiting for Rex in the morning anyway. I'm afraid *you* don't have a choice."

Vincent stuck out his jaw. "How long will it take to get the generators reset?"

"If we can get an airplane mechanic out here tomorrow, probably less than an hour. But I need to find someone here who can charge up the batteries in the meantime."

Scarlet tugged on his arm. "Oh, come on, baby. I'm cold. Why don't you just let her stay in the guest house, and we can all fly back after the plane gets fixed and the storm

114

clears?"

He let out a dramatic sigh. "Fine. Let's go."

"Thank you." Vera turned and flipped off the master switch before following Vincent and Scarlet out of the plane.

The town car wound down a steep road lined with moss-covered trees before pulling into the circular drive of the expansive landscaped grounds of the Moore Mansion. Vera nearly gasped when the lights from the impressive white structure came into view out her rear side window. As they drove closer, she took in the three-story mansion, which was over twice the size of the Ellis's Queen Anne home. She'd never seen a private home this large. It seemed more like a luxury hotel.

"It's haunted, you know." The Dom Perignon hung off Scarlet's breath as she whispered into Vera's ear.

Vincent had reluctantly taken the front passenger seat after Scarlet insisted that she and Vera share the back. It was evident they'd been pawing at each other the entire flight, and Vera was surprised Scarlet didn't want to share the backseat with her lover.

Vera turned to her. For the first time since they'd landed, Scarlet looked completely sober.

Scarlet lowered her voice a touch more as Vincent instructed the driver where to park. "This is where his wife's father hanged himself. You know, the shipbuilder who went cuckoo." She circled her pointer finger by the side of her head for emphasis, then smiled. "His butler found him dangling from the balcony in his music theater."

Vera tore her eyes back to the grand estate as Scarlet

continued. "It's why she hates coming here."

The car came to a stop in front of the steps leading up to the covered wrap-around porch.

"I don't mind it, though. Sometimes, at night, I hear him wandering the halls. Once I even heard him play the pipe organ. Vincent was too drunk to remember, but he heard it too." Scarlet winked at Vera before getting out, grabbing Vincent's hand as the couple trod up the hail-covered steps into the house.

A shiver crept down her spine as Vera slid across the seat and followed them inside. Had Scarlet wanted to spook her? The actress clearly had a morbid sense of humor. Thunder rumbled beyond the house, and Vera wondered if she should've taken her chances flying through the storm rather than staying there with these two. After stepping onto the herringbone floor, she gaped at the grand chandelier hanging from the top of the foyer, and the ornate stained-glass windows above the front door.

A butler in a tailed tuxedo stood at attention beside the door. He nodded at her as she moved past. "Good evening, madam."

"Oh. Um. Good evening." She hadn't expected there to be staff at the island home. When Vincent told her where they were going, she'd pictured a small seaside cottage. Nothing like this.

On either side of the room, two sets of curved stairs led to the next level. She was at a momentary loss for words. It was hard to imagine this was how part of the world lived.

"What about your pilot?" she heard Scarlet say.

"Oh, blast!" Vincent stopped midway up the staircase and turned around.

Scarlet giggled.

"Marcus! Show this woman to our guest cottage, please."

"Of course, Mr. Ellis."

"But first, leave a couple bottles of champagne outside the door to my room." Vincent grabbed Scarlet's hand and continued pulling her up the staircase. He stopped when they reached the top of the stairs. "Oh, and Marcus. Make sure the indoor pool is ready to go for tomorrow. I plan to have a swim."

"Very well, Mr. Ellis." Marcus turned to Vera. "I'll be right back to show you to the guest dwelling."

The butler turned on his heels and disappeared down a hallway before Vera could even say thank you. Recognizing a painting on the wall, she took a step closer to admire the print. But as she examined the pastel of Edvard Munch's *The Scream,* she realized it was an original.

"Unbelievable," she muttered, taking in the colorful strokes of one of the most famous art pieces in the world.

A moment later, he returned with a bottle of champagne in each hand. Vera watched him bound up the stairs with surprisingly swift movements for his age.

"Ready?" he asked when he reached the base of the grand stairwell.

Vera nodded and followed after him. Marcus weaved in and out of seemingly endless hallways leading to the back of the home as Scarlet's squeals resounded from the upper level.

The butler grabbed an umbrella and held it over Vera's head as they walked down a cobblestone path to a tiny cottage perched on the rocky shores leading down to the bay. Vera looked back at the grand estate, wondering why a house so big would require a guesthouse. The home itself had to contain over thirty rooms.

"Here we are," the butler announced, after unlocking the cottage door. He flicked on the lights and held the door open for Vera to come inside.

The small cottage was less opulent than the main house, but to Vera, it held more charm. The four-poster bed faced the stone fireplace on the other side of the room. She could hear the waves lapping against the rocky shore below. The checkered curtains were drawn, but Vera could only imagine the breathtaking view of the bay during the day.

Marcus assessed her as she took in her surroundings. "If you find this unsatisfactory, ma'am, I can show you to the other two guest cottages on the property."

"Oh, no." She smiled at the butler who'd mistaken her awe for disappointment. "This is more than satisfactory."

It reminded her of the cabin she and Hugh rented for their honeymoon on Whidbey Island. She felt strange staying in a place like this without him. The cottage was cool and damp, and Vera rubbed her arms to warm herself.

"I'll get a fire going for you," he said, moving across the room. "And I'll bring over some dinner."

Her stomach panged at the thought of food, and she realized she hadn't eaten since breakfast. "Thank you."

As Marcus added kindling to the fireplace, she pushed aside the gingham curtains and peered back at the mansion. The lights were on in a room on the second floor, and she could make out Scarlet's silhouette as she pulled off her dress and flung it across the room.

Vera thought of Priscilla alone in her home with her prying nanny, her husband off gallivanting with his lover while she was left to worry about the fate of their only child.

Scarlet stepped away from the upstairs window, giving Vera a full view of her lace panties. It struck her how different Scarlet and Vincent were to those in her own life. She thought of Hugh, off to fight in the Pacific, and Dari and Lily, training to become the first women pilots to serve their country, while Vincent and Scarlet ignored any sense of responsibility. For anything. If this was what became of being famous and wealthy, Vera was grateful for the opportunity to find purpose in her *normal* life.

Her thoughts returned to Scarlet as she disappeared from the window frame. Maybe she could find a way to talk to the actress before they flew back. Without Vincent. See how she reacted to the news of Gilbert's death. Scarlet had seemed amused by the death of Priscilla's father, but maybe she would change her tune when she learned about Gilbert.

If Scarlet was mixed up with Howard and Gilbert, was Vincent also in on their plan to abduct Max? She thought about Priscilla's words earlier that day. *Vincent knew Howard.*

There would be much at stake in a divorce in the Ellis family. *Was Vincent hoping to drive his wife insane—or worse— by staging their son's abduction?*

She thought of Priscilla's father, remembering what Scarlet had said about the estate being haunted. She recalled hearing about the famous Seattle shipbuilder who killed himself three or four years ago after the stress of his hugely successful business ventures drove him insane. He'd traded the city for this island mansion, only to hang himself a few months later.

She scanned the rest of the huge home for lights, even looking for a sign that Max might be there. There would be plenty of room in the remote mansion to hide the young child. After what she'd seen of Vincent these last two days, she wouldn't entirely put it past him. Although it seemed more likely that Scarlet had been keeping Vincent occupied while her boyfriend and his cousin kidnapped Max.

"I'll be back shortly with your supper."

Vera jumped at the butler's voice. She'd already forgotten

she wasn't alone. She let go of the curtain, embarrassed to be caught peering at the house.

Marcus stood, shaking wood splinters off his hands. "Sorry, madam. I didn't mean to startle you."

She flashed him a sheepish smile. "It's not your fault—I shouldn't be so jumpy. I was just thinking about the weather. I need to fly back to Seattle tomorrow." She thanked him again before he left.

Vera waited until after she'd eaten the rosemary lamb roast Marcus brought back to her before she opened the curtains again. It was perhaps the best meal she'd ever had, and it made her wish she was a better cook. Vincent's bedroom light was turned off, and the mansion was dark aside from the porch lights.

She was about to turn away from the window when she saw a flicker of light from an upstairs room on the other side of the house from Vincent's bedroom. Goosebumps formed on her arms as the light went out. *Could that be where they are hiding Max?*

Or had the actress been telling the truth about the ghost of Priscilla's father walking the halls at night?

Vera closed the curtain and moved toward the cottage's front door. There was only one way to find out.

24

Rainwater dripped from Vera's hair onto the floor when she stepped inside the mansion, using the same door Marcus had led her through earlier. Despite running the entire way from the cottage to the house, she was drenched. Luckily, she'd found the back door unlocked.

The house was quiet as she wound along the dark hallways, trying to find her way to the front staircases. Despite not believing in ghosts, she found herself holding her breath, listening for the sound of Priscilla's dead father. She chided herself for letting Scarlet's words get to her. The actress was drunk on champagne and making up stories. *Besides, you're here to look for Max.*

Vera stepped through a doorway and realized she must have taken a wrong turn. Lightning flashed from beyond the stained-glass windows, casting colorful shadows on a two-story pipe organ that lined the walls on either side of a grand piano. She had never seen anything like it, let alone in someone's private home.

Lightning struck again and Vera lifted her head to see a

curved mezzanine above her, that looked to serve as a viewing area to the pipe organ. She glanced back at the piano, envisioning the silhouette of Priscilla's father hunched over the instrument. Thunder cracked from beyond the windows as Vera fled the grand music room. She rushed through a series of hallways until she came to the front entrance.

She gripped the mahogany railing and ascended the curved staircase. In the darkness, the mansion's charm was erased, replaced with an eerie atmosphere. Vera slowed, thinking Scarlet wasn't lying about it being haunted. She forced herself to continue up the steps, reproaching herself for her pounding heart.

When she got to the top of the staircase, she heard Vincent's snores coming from a room at one end of the hall. She steeled herself before she crept in the opposite direction, remembering her promise to Priscilla. She owed it to the woman to find out if her son was here.

Vera stopped halfway down the hall, hearing a noise coming from inside the doorway to her left. It was right about where she'd seen the flicker of light from the cottage. Surely, Marcus didn't sleep in an upstairs guestroom.

The door was slightly ajar, so she pushed it open. The room was quiet when she stepped through the doorway. The lights were off, but her eyes had adjusted enough to the dark that she could make out a four-poster bed, much like the one in the guest cottage.

"Max?" She kept her voice to a whisper as she tiptoed toward the bed.

She took a steadying breath, preparing herself to find the Ellises's sleeping child. And then what would she do? There had to be a telephone somewhere in this huge home.

"Max?" She spoke louder, straining to see if there was a

child beneath the blankets. She had almost reached the end of the bed when a cold hand clamped around her mouth from behind.

25

Vera screamed through the hand that muffled her cry.

"Don't!" A woman's voice spat sharply into her ear. "If you scream, so will I. And I'll tell Vincent you broke into the house and attacked me."

Vera recognized the fruity scent of Scarlet's cheap perfume.

"Can you keep quiet?"

Vera nodded, and Scarlet's hand fell away from her mouth. Vera spun around.

"What are you doing?" Scarlet asked.

I could ask you the same thing, Vera thought. "Looking for Max Ellis." She saw no point in lying.

Her eyes had adjusted enough to the dark that she could tell the bed was empty.

"Max!" Scarlet scoffed. "Why on earth would you think he'd be here? Go back to the cottage and I won't tell Vincent I saw you."

Vera's gaze fell to the array of several gleaming necklaces around Scarlet's neck. She took a step toward her, deciding to call her bluff. "Go ahead. I'd like to see you explain what you were doing on the other side of the house in the middle of the night." Vera lifted Scarlet's hand, which held another jeweled necklace. "Does Vincent know you were going on a treasure hunt?"

Scarlet fell silent, and Vera figured this was her chance to press her about Gilbert. "I was down at the Fishermen's Terminal today when a man's body was pulled from the water—Gilbert Mills. It appeared he'd been dead for a few days."

Scarlet stiffened. "You're lying!" she yelled.

Vera worried she might wake up Vincent at the other end of the hall.

"Gil's on a fishing trip."

"No." Vera shook her head. "I spoke with his boss, Roy. Gilbert never showed up."

Outside, a break in the clouds allowed the moonlight to filter in through the large window. She watched Scarlet's eyes widen.

"And he hadn't drowned," Vera added. "He was shot. Just like Howard."

"No!" Her voice wobbled.

"I have no reason to lie."

Scarlet's expression hardened. "I think you better mind your business and go back to the cottage."

"Fine, let's go wake up Vincent. And I'll tell him you were in cahoots with Howard's cousin. And after you explain that, you can tell him you were looting jewelry from the house."

"Stop!" Scarlet grabbed her wrist. "Please!"

Vera folded her arms. "Or you can be straight with me. Were you involved in Max's kidnapping? Do you know where he is?"

"What? *No!*"

"You're saying that dating the cousin of Max's kidnapper while you're screwing his father is purely a coincidence? I don't think so. Maybe you and Vincent were in on it together. Is Max here?"

Scarlet didn't respond.

"Max!" Vera called out.

Scarlet tried to put her hand over Vera's mouth, but Vera shook her off.

"Stop!" the actress hissed. "He's not here. I had nothing to do with it, I swear! Is Gilbert...is he really dead?"

"Yes."

"I don't believe you."

"It will be in the papers in the morning."

Scarlet sank onto the bed. Her shoulders shook as she sobbed into her hands. When she finally spoke, her voice came out a whisper. "I was shocked to learn Howard had been involved in Max's kidnapping. Scared actually. I've been trying to find Gil ever since. At first, I was worried he might have Vincent's kid. But I can't imagine Gil getting mixed up in that."

Vera sat on the bed beside her. "You were in love with him."

Scarlet nodded, sniffing back her tears. "We were high school sweethearts. Gil wanted the simple life. I wanted fame. Stardom. Money. We found each other again after I came back to Seattle." She sighed. "I didn't even want to come on this trip, but I couldn't let Vincent suspect anything."

"So, what are you doing with him? Distracting him while Howard and Gilbert kidnapped his son?"

"What? No! Do you know who I am?"

Vera nodded. "I've seen a couple of your films."

"Well, after I washed up in Hollywood, I blew all my money on trying to look like I still had it all. After my second arrest, I borrowed money from some bad people to pay for my lawyer. And rehab. Now they want it back."

"I see." Vera pondered how this sob story fit with the woman she'd seen flinging her dress off not even an hour ago.

"Gil and I were planning to blackmail Vincent about our affair. Gil was going to take photos of us when Vincent and I were together—at least that's what he told me." She turned to face Vera. "It was Howard's idea. He knew Vincent was a womanizer. But I had no idea Howard was plotting to kidnap Max. I can't believe Gil did either." She looked up at Vera. "Please don't tell Vincent."

"I won't...for now. But you need to tell the police what you know. It didn't take me long to learn you were seeing Gilbert. I'm sure they'll find out too."

Scarlet exhaled a deep sigh.

"It will be better for you if you tell them yourself," Vera added.

"Fine. I'll go to the police." Scarlet stood from the bed, wiping her tears from her cheeks. "But now I need to go back. I don't want Vincent to wake up and find me gone."

Vera followed Scarlet back to their room, where Vincent's snores continued to reverberate into the hall. Vera couldn't imagine how Scarlet could sleep next to him.

Scarlet turned to Vera when they reached Vincent's bedroom. "Promise me you won't say anything to Vincent."

"I won't, if you're telling me the truth."

After Scarlet softly shut the door behind her, Vera tiptoed back down the hall instead of going downstairs. She was inclined to believe Scarlet but decided to check the rest of the upstairs rooms anyway. Scarlet was an actress, after all.

After opening every door along the long hallway and quietly calling out for Max, Vera went downstairs, satisfied the boy wasn't there. And the light she'd seen from the cottage must have been Scarlet. When she passed by the music theater, Vera stopped cold, seeing the outline of legs dangling from the ceiling. Lightning struck, illuminating the room, and Vera realized the shadow she'd seen was a chandelier.

Nevertheless, she ran through the back of the house and all the way to her cottage, locking the door after she got inside.

26

Dusk had settled over the city when Vera touched down at Everett Airport. It had taken nearly all day for the weather to clear enough for the return flight from Orcas Island. She and Scarlet hadn't spoken another word since last night. While the ex-Hollywood actress was putting up a good front for Vincent, she was notably quieter than yesterday.

Vera felt a hand on her shoulder as she slipped off her headset.

"Thanks for getting us back safely."

Vera turned to see Vincent smiling at her, close enough for her to smell the Scotch on his breath.

"I spoke with Rex this morning. He'll need you to fly him to Boise on Tuesday morning at nine."

"Okay." Vera nodded, and Vincent turned for the rear door.

Scarlet waited for him at the back of the plane. Her tired eyes met Vera's before she followed him out.

Vera shut down the plane, leaving the photo of Amelia

Earhart stuck in the dash for her next flight. Gravel crunched beneath her shoes when she reached the parking lot.

"Vincent, stop!"

Vera had nearly reached her Ford when she heard Scarlet cry out. She was surprised to see Vincent's convertible still in the parking lot. In the fading light, Vera watched him press Scarlet against the side of the car, his hands traveling down her sides.

Scarlet tried unsuccessfully to push him away. "I just want to go home!"

Vincent turned toward the sound of Vera opening her car door and allowed Scarlet to shove him backward before she climbed into his front seat. Vera watched him shoot a disapproving look at his mistress before he climbed behind the wheel and peeled out of the gravel lot.

Vera started her car. Scarlet had nearly convinced her last night of her innocence. But what if she was only putting on an act? If her money troubles were true, who's to say she didn't kill Howard and Gilbert to keep all the money for herself...or have them killed? Maybe they'd argued, and the kidnapping hadn't gone to plan.

She pulled out of the parking lot and sped after Vincent's car. She spotted his taillights up ahead before he turned onto Highway 99. There were hardly any other cars on the side streets, and she ran a red light after briefly stopping at an intersection.

After following them onto the highway, she stepped harder on the gas so she wouldn't lose them. She stayed a safe distance behind as the Speedster wove in and out of its lane. After they crossed the Aurora Bridge into Seattle, she drove slowly behind them along Westlake Avenue that stretched beside several marinas along the shores of Lake

Union.

The convertible parked beside the lake, and Vera pulled over, turning off her headlights a couple of blocks behind them. A damp breeze came off the lake when she stepped onto the street. She pulled her coat around her waist as she crept forward toward the sound of Vincent's obnoxious laughter that was much too loud for the late hour.

Vincent swayed as he and Scarlet moved arm-in-arm beneath the marina lights. The couple turned onto a dock, and Vera trotted down the shore after them. She reached the end of the dock that led to a neat row of houseboats.

She stayed in the shadows and watched Vincent and Scarlet step into one of the small floating structures before she moved down the dock. Across the lake, steam blew from one of the buildings at the gasification plant. The houseboat's lights came on when Vera got closer and boisterous swing music began to play from inside. Vincent and Scarlet appeared in the window. She was shaking her head as he pressed his body against hers. He stripped off her coat before she staggered backward toward the window.

Vera ducked reflexively so she wouldn't be seen. She moved closer to the houseboat as Scarlet shouted something that Vera couldn't make out over the music. Vera reached the houseboat's front door when the music suddenly grew louder, and Scarlet's voice came from outside, only a few feet away from her.

Vera froze, realizing they'd stepped out onto the back deck of the houseboat.

"I said not tonight! I'm tired, Vincent. Let me back inside. I'm going to bed."

"Oh, come on," he slurred. "No one can see us."

Vera stared at the door to the houseboat, wondering if she

should just go home. She doubted Scarlet would keep Max here, even if she *was* involved. But there might be evidence of the boy's whereabouts inside.

Scarlet let out a shriek but was quickly silenced by what sounded like an open-palm slap.

As Scarlet's protests became muffled, Vera twisted the doorknob. She stepped inside and scanned the small space. The main level consisted of a small kitchen and living area with a narrow staircase against the wall. The deck door flew open, and Vera bolted up the stairs.

The door slammed shut when Vera reached the upper level. Scarlet's sobs were audible over the music.

"Vincent, please!"

"You will not deny me tonight, Scarlet. Not after I risked my ass to take you to Orcas! You whined and whined about going there, darling."

Scarlet pleaded with Vincent as Vera went into the first room she came to. From the neighboring houseboat's outdoor lights shining through the small window, Vera could see this was Scarlet's bedroom. Several publicity photographs of Scarlet and leading men from her films hung on the wall. Vera hurried toward the bedside table and ran her hand over its top. There was only an ashtray, perfume bottle, and a lamp, which she didn't dare turn on.

Unsure of what she was looking for, Vera moved to a dresser on the other side of the small room. She opened the top drawer and slid her hand along the inside, wishing she had a flashlight. The drawer seemed to be filled only with satin negligees. Vera closed the drawer and stepped into the hall.

"Come on!"

No sooner had Vincent spoken when Scarlet's footsteps sounded up the stairs. Vera rushed back into the room and dove under the bed.

"That's more like it."

There was a loud rap on the houseboat's front door. Vera peered out from under the bed and spotted Vincent's wingtip shoes at the top of the stairs.

"Who the hell is that?" Vincent's shoes pivoted toward the stairs. "So, that's why you wanted me to leave. You're expecting someone else!"

A fist pounded against the door three more times. "Seattle Police! Open up!"

"What the—"

"Vincent, wait! Don't open it!" Scarlet's heeled footsteps echoed down the stairs behind his.

Vera's heart hammered against the floor. What would the police do if they found her hiding under Scarlet's bed?

She slid out from under the bed and opened the window. It squeaked as she lifted it away from the windowpane. She grimaced, hoping the noise couldn't be heard downstairs. The music suddenly stopped, and Vera fell still. The pounding on the door ceased and she heard it creak open.

"What is this?" Vincent demanded.

"Scarlet Fox, you are under arrest for conspiring to kidnap Maxwell Ellis."

"*What!*" Vincent roared.

Scarlet screamed her innocence as another policeman shouted at Vincent to calm down. There was a thud as something—or someone—slammed against the wall. Vera swung one leg out the window and then the other, figuring there was no better time to get out.

She perched on the edge of the windowsill, looking at the dark water below as more commotion erupted from the lower level. She closed her eyes, inhaled a deep breath, and pushed herself off the ledge.

27

Vera scrambled for the surface after plunging deeper than she expected into the frigid lake. She sucked in a sharp, shallow breath after breaking the surface, using all her willpower not to cry out from the cold.

She forced herself to swim past the adjacent floating house instead of heading straight for the dock. She struggled against the drag of her clothes. The water was paralyzingly cold, taking her breath away as soon as it entered her lungs.

Vera grunted as she swam the last few feet to the dock. After pulling herself onto the floating structure, she lay on her back and stared at the half moon as she tried to slow her breathing. She knew she should get up before the police came out of Scarlet's houseboat, but she felt too numb to move. After a minute, she shakily pushed herself to her feet. A glance back told her they were all still inside.

She moved to her car as fast as her numb body allowed. She passed two empty squad cars on her way, hearing their radios squawk from inside. She opened her driver's door, grateful she'd left her purse on the front seat. If not, it would've been on the bottom of the lake.

Voices sounded from the dock as Vera stripped off her sopping trench coat.

"Let's go!"

"I didn't do it!"

"Save it for the station, lady."

Vera slid behind the wheel. After fumbling to get her keys into the ignition, she made a U-turn before turning on her headlights. Her teeth chattered as she turned on the car's heater. She sank against the leather seatback as warm air blew against her face. Now that the police had Scarlet, maybe they'd get to the bottom of whatever she was wrapped up in—and find Max.

Vera wound along the road that lined the shores of Lake Union. She was about to turn around the bend along the Fremont Cut when her Ford was rammed from behind. The screech of metal scraping against metal filled the car as her head smacked against the side window. Her headlights reflected on the canal's surface, and Vera realized she was no longer on the road—but headed straight for the water.

She jerked the steering wheel to the left and skidded back onto the street. Headlights blinded her vision as an oncoming car blared its horn. Vera swerved out of the oncoming lane a second before they would have collided.

Out of breath, she gripped the wheel and slowed, just as she was rear-ended again. Her head whipped backward from the impact. She checked her rearview mirror. All she could see were two blinding beams shining right behind her.

She stomped on the gas, swerving into the now empty oncoming lane as she sped along the canal. The headlights remained on her bumper as the road straightened. As she neared the Ballard Bridge, the tailing car finally backed off a little. Vera loosened her grip on the wheel. Maybe it was just a drunk driver.

When she turned onto the bridge, though, the car sped up, pulling beside her in the adjacent lane. Vera shot a glance at the sedan's passenger window, but it was too dark to make out the driver. Her eyes were drawn to lights flashing up ahead as the wooden barricade began to lower on the drawbridge.

As Vera slowed for the opening bridge, the car beside her slammed into her Ford, propelling her onto the sidewalk and toward the guardrail at the side of the road. Vera jerked the wheel to her left, but her car continued toward the edge. With her right bumper inches from the railing, she floored the gas pedal and broke free from the other car.

As Vera sped up the ramp, she stole a glance in the rearview mirror. The other car had skidded to a stop and was parked sideways across the centerline.

The barricade snapped in half as Vera plowed through it and she willed her Ford more speed as the incline of the rising bridge grew steeper. Holding her breath, Vera pressed her foot to the floor and squeezed her eyes shut as the coupe's front tires lifted off the edge of the half-open bridge.

28

Priscilla unclenched her fists as Vincent came through the front door. From the sound of him fumbling to get his key in the lock, she knew he was already drunk.

"You were with her, weren't you?"

She stood from the base of the stairs and stepped toward him. The fear she usually felt in his presence had been replaced by the rage building inside her since the FBI's visit yesterday. Uncharacteristically, Vincent hung his head. Without sympathy, she watched his chin quiver.

"Does she have him? Do you know where Max is?"

Vincent's eyes brimmed with tears. He shook his head. "I don't know." His voice came out a whisper.

Anger surged inside her chest. "You're such a fool." She had never dared to address him with such unleashed disdain.

Vincent turned his head to avoid her gaze.

"Your dicking around might have cost us our *son!*" she screamed. Before she knew it, she was pounding her fists against his chest. "*Where! Is! Max!*"

He raised his hand in the air, but Priscilla didn't stop.

"Vincent!" Her mother-in-law's voice cut through the room like a knife.

Vincent lowered his hand and gaped at his mother standing in the doorway to the library. Without consulting Priscilla, Ruth had installed herself in the library to wait for her son to come home. No doubt she had gotten wind of the FBI's discovery of his affair with Scarlet Fox. And from there—Scarlet's connection to Max's kidnapper.

Priscilla took a step back, out of his reach, her chest rising and falling with each rageful breath.

"Mother?" He looked sheepish, blood rushing to his face like a guilt-ridden child.

Priscilla eyed him with repulsion.

"Come in here," Ruth said, tapping her cane on the floor. "We need to talk."

Vincent gritted his teeth, his eyes shooting daggers at his wife as he brushed past her. After Vincent disappeared behind his mother, Priscilla turned for the stairs.

She lifted the hem of her negligee as she ascended the steps, aware of Hattie eavesdropping from the third-floor banister. She tried to calm her breathing as all of Vincent's offenses over the course of their marriage swirled in her mind. Offenses she'd once been prepared to overlook.

She locked eyes with Max's nanny when she reached the second floor, noting that Hattie didn't even bother to pretend she hadn't been listening.

"What the hell are you looking at? The show's over, Hattie. You can go back to your room, and when you get there, mind your own damn business!"

She'd shouted loudly enough for Ruth and Vincent to hear, and for a moment Hattie looked taken back at being called out by the woman she usually controlled. Then a look of smug satisfaction crept over her face.

"I don't even know why you're still here!" Priscilla waved her arms through the air. "It's not like there's a child here for you to care for anymore, is there? He's *gone!*"

Hattie turned her nose up, seemingly unruffled by Priscilla's outburst, before she slowly turned down the upstairs hall. Shaking with rage, Priscilla steadied herself on the staircase railing. She was aware that her behavior would only make it easier for the Ellises to institutionalize her. But she couldn't sit still and pretend her heart wasn't being wrenched out of her more and more each day that went by without her son.

If they didn't find him soon, she probably *would* go crazy. But what mother wouldn't? Even her ice queen of a mother-in-law must have some empathy for what she was going through.

"And get control of your wife—before I do."

Hearing Ruth's voice, she peered downstairs to see her mother-in-law standing in the half-open door to the library. *Had she no heart at all?* Priscilla shook off her mother-in-law's comment. *Get control of your son, more like.* If Vincent's affair caused any harm to come to her son, so help her—she'd kill him.

29

Vera's body lifted away from the seat as her car flew off the edge of the bridge opening. Time stood still as she watched her headlights disappear into the dark sky. She caught a glimpse of the water below before she began falling to the other side of the drawbridge below. She held her breath as the ramp on the other side came into view and she suddenly slammed onto the pavement.

She bounced against the seat before her head hit the steering wheel. Her vision blurred as she laid on the brakes, skidding to a stop at the bottom of the open drawbridge after her front fender mowed through the other barricade.

She looked out at the lights of a tall fishing boat approaching the bridge, its horn blaring. She glanced behind her at the now fully opened drawbridge. It was quiet at this late hour, except for the bridge operator, who was yelling in her direction at the top of his lungs. Vera jammed the Ford into gear, praying that she hadn't done enough damage to cause the car to stall, leaving her stranded and alone on the side of the road.

She checked her rearview mirror repeatedly as she drove through the quiet neighborhood streets to her house. That was no accident. They were trying to kill her—and almost succeeded. It couldn't have been Scarlet—or Vincent. So, who was it? Vera thought about the nanny's phone call she overheard at Priscilla's mansion.

She slowed after turning onto her street. Having calmed down a little, she was now aware of the squeaking and groaning the car was making. *What will Hugh say?* In the next instant, her breath caught in her throat when she spotted a dark car parked in her driveway. *They know where I live!* She peered inside the car as she prepared to keep driving. She could go to Dari's.

A honk sounded from the parked car, making Vera jump in her seat. Her knuckles gripped the steering wheel as she watched two figures step out the car. Illuminated by her headlights, they waved in her direction. Vera exhaled and pulled to the curb.

Dari opened her driver's door as soon as she turned off the car. "I've been trying to call you since yesterday! Where have you been?"

Her friend's smile faded as she assessed Vera beneath the streetlamp. "You're soaking wet! And you're bleeding!"

"Cripes! What happened to your car?" Opal appeared beside her and put a hand on her shoulder. "And your face! Vera, are you all right?"

Dari wrapped her arm around Vera's shoulders. "You're shaking! Come inside."

Vera broke down in tears as soon as they entered her house.

"Let's get you into some dry clothes." Dari led her toward the stairs.

Opal headed for the kitchen. "I'll make a cup of hot tea."

Vera was still trembling after Dari helped her get changed. Opal appeared holding a steaming mug and a damp washcloth. After placing the hot mug in her hands, she sat beside Vera on the edge of her bed and pressed the washcloth to her forehead.

Vera winced from the sting of the cool cloth. She pulled it away from her head and saw it was stained with blood.

"What happened?" Dari's dark eyes were wide with worry.

As Opal pressed the cloth back to Vera's forehead, she told them everything, from Priscilla asking for her help to being nearly driven off the bridge.

"You should go to the police," Opal said.

Vera remembered what Priscilla had said about the Ellises having police on their payroll. "I don't see what good that would do. I didn't even get a good look at the car."

Dari stood. "I think you should stop working for them. This is the Ellises's problem—not yours." She pointed to Opal. "Like she said, you should definitely leave this to the police."

Vera looked at Dari, whose arms were crossed, seeing she was smartly dressed in a fitted twill skirt and blazer with a matching hat pinned to her hair. She'd hardly ever seen her friend in anything but pants.

"Are you going somewhere?"

Dari's expression softened. "It's what I've been calling to tell you. I got a phone call yesterday from Nancy Harkness Love, herself. She said my name came highly recommended."

Priscilla. That was fast.

"When she heard my qualifications, she asked why I hadn't previously applied. I told her I'd written to our local congressman, but she said my application never made it to her desk."

Opal shot Vera a look. "Can you believe it?"

"She asked me to be a squadron leader, Vera! I'm to report to Delaware immediately for training. She got me a seat on a C-47 leaving Boeing Field tonight." Dari bent down and placed her hands on Vera's knees. "But now I'm worried about you. Maybe I should stay. I could telegram that I need a little longer to get my affairs in order."

Vera shook her head. "No. You have to go—you've worked too hard for this." Vera smiled at her friend as pain shot through her forehead. "I can handle this."

Dari and Opal exchanged a look of concern. "Okay, but you have two pretty smart women standing here saying you should go to the police."

Vera thought again of how quickly Priscilla had come through on her end of the deal. It made her feel ashamed to tell her she was giving up on finding her son, even after what she'd been through that night.

"I'll think about it," Vera promised. But she knew it wouldn't do any good—possibly put her in even more danger. She started to get up, but winced from the throbbing in her head.

"You need to lie down." Opal took the hot mug from Vera's hands and set it on the dresser.

"I want to see you off." Vera smiled at Dari, despite the pain. "I'm so proud of you."

"Oh, stop. You're making me blush." Dari swatted her playfully with her gloves then turned serious. "Opal's right. You need to rest. Will you be okay here, alone?"

"I can come back after taking Dari to the train," Opal offered.

"Thanks, Opal. But I'll be fine."

Dari pursed her lips. "You can stay at my place."

Vera shook her head. She wasn't about to be run out of her home. And her head was spinning. "I just need to rest."

Dari checked the time on her watch. "I better go, or I'll miss my plane."

Vera stood and Dari pulled her into a tight embrace.

"Be careful."

Vera nodded.

Dari reached into her pocket and withdrew a key. "Oh. I almost forgot. I was wondering if you could water my Frangipani while I'm away. It only needs it once a week." She stopped herself and turned to Opal. "Wait, Opal, considering Vera's condition, maybe you should—"

Vera took the key from Dari's hand. "Don't be silly. I can do it."

Dari had brought the root of the small, flowering tree with her from Hawaii when she moved to Seattle, and Vera knew it represented more than just a pretty plant to her friend.

"Are you sure you'll be okay alone?" Opal asked.

Vera gave her a reassuring nod. "I'm sure."

She followed them downstairs, where Opal stopped at Vera's secretary desk and jotted something down on a piece of scrap paper.

"Here's my number," she said, extending the paper to Vera. "If you want me to come back, just call."

Vera thanked her and gave Dari one last hug before they left, promising to call Opal if she needed anything. After locking the door behind them, Vera turned back for the stairs, stopping when she caught her reflection in the hallway mirror.

A swollen red bump had formed above her right eye, and there was a small gash along her hairline. She looked away from her reflection and forced her feet up the steps. Before getting into bed, she went to Hugh's side of the closet and found the revolver he kept on the top shelf.

Her hand trembled as she released the cylinder the way Hugh had shown her to make sure it was loaded. After setting it on her nightstand beside their wedding photo, she lifted the black-and-white photograph and ran her finger over Hugh's handsome smiling face.

What had she gotten herself into?

"I wish you were here," she whispered, as a tear landed on the framed photo.

She wondered what he was doing, feeling suddenly guilty for not having written him since he'd left. The house was painfully quiet without him. And now Dari was leaving, too, although she couldn't be happier for her friend. Vera turned and set the photo on his pillow before lying down beside it.

Vera turned off the bedside lamp, but after a second in the darkness of the room, she switched it back on, closed her eyes, and immediately drifted off to sleep.

30

Vera gave a few hard raps on the brass door knocker on the front door of Priscilla's mansion. She'd slept fitfully the night before, waking before dawn to a nightmare of crashing her car into the black water beneath the Ballard Bridge. She heard the drone of a large airplane and looked up to see a B-17 bomber, just like the one Hugh had flown to Hawaii, that was descending overhead toward Boeing Field.

Footsteps sounded in the foyer and the door swung open. Priscilla wore a fur-trimmed robe. She looked expectantly at Vera.

"Oh," her face fell. "I thought you might be the FBI. They've taken Scarlet Fox in for questioning."

Vera was surprised at the way Priscilla mentioned her name. Had she known about her husband's affair?

Priscilla drew in a gasp, as if just noticing the red welt above Vera's eye. "What happened to you?"

"Can I come in?"

Priscilla opened the door wider. "Yes, of course."

Vera stepped inside. The house was quiet aside from Vincent's rhythmic snores reverberating from the upper level.

"Vincent has been sleeping in the spare room for years," Priscilla said, "but his damn snoring still manages to keep me awake most nights."

Vera knew she was risking her job if Vincent learned she'd shown up unannounced, but she no longer cared. She wasn't exactly sure what she'd come for. But after last night, she needed answers.

"We can talk in the library."

Priscilla led her into a different room than she had the last time. Vera caught a glimpse of her hair in the hallway mirror, which had dried into frizzy curls after her jump into Lake Union last night. She noticed Priscilla's dark waves were perfectly smooth and bet her hair even looked good when it rained. If Hugh had taken a likening to the banker's beautiful wife, what chance did she stand?

Vera followed Priscilla through a set of double doors.

Priscilla gestured to a velvet davenport in front of built-in floor-to-ceiling bookshelves. "Please, have a seat."

Vera waited until Priscilla had closed the doors and then she turned, too upset to sit down. "I was nearly run off the Ballard Bridge last night. And it wasn't an accident." She paced back and forth in front of the long sofa, realizing for the first time how angry she was. "I followed Vincent and Scarlet Fox to her houseboat last night. After the police came to arrest her, I left. And a car followed me all the way to the Ballard Bridge. And tried to run me into the Fremont Cut along the way." She crossed her arms, assessing Priscilla's reaction.

Priscilla's eyes travelled to the window. "I see."

"You *see?*" Vera's chest heaved with rage. "I was nearly

killed last night doing the thing you asked me to do, and that's all you can say?"

Priscilla's eyes darted to the closed double doors. "Keep your voice down." She took a seat on the davenport as Vera gaped at her. "I'm sorry. I should've warned you there would be risks."

"What are you talking about? Do you know who did this to me?"

Priscilla exhaled and crossed her legs. "They've been spying on me for years. Hattie has this strange fixation with Rex. I'm not exactly sure what their arrangement is, but she does whatever he tells her. She must've told them I enlisted you to help me find Max."

Vera thought back to the phone call the nanny had made to Rex Ellis during her last visit. But was she supposed to believe the multi-millionaire bank executive tried to run her off the road? "Told who? What are you saying?"

Priscilla reached for a cigarette case and took her time lighting a cigarette as Vera waited expectantly for an answer. "Rex. And likely Ruth. She may seem like a refined old woman, but she runs this family like a wolf controls its pack. Ever since I gained notoriety for attending a march for equal wages for women a few years ago, the family watches everything I do. They hate when I get positive attention in the papers. It makes it harder for the public to overlook Vincent's affairs if they ever become known. And the Ellises will do anything to protect their precious reputation for fear that if people don't trust them, they'll take their money somewhere else." She let out a snort. "Which is laughable since they're as corrupt as it gets. If they see someone as a threat, they remove them. When you give people so much power and money, it changes them. Corrupts their entire way of thinking. Vera, the Ellises don't value human life the same way you and I do—unless that life is their own."

Vera recalled what Hugh had said about the Ellises right before he left.

"Are you saying your *mother-in-law* tried to kill me last night?" Vera didn't buy it.

Priscilla seemed to read Vera's face. "Shortly after Vincent and I were married, there was a reporter who started coming around, threatening to write a story about Vincent's father bribing a bunch of city officials when he first started the bank. It was true, of course. Vincent had a meeting with Rex and his mother about it, and the guy stopped bothering us. We never heard from him again." Priscilla puckered her lips and blew out a puff of smoke.

Vera shrugged. "Maybe he moved. Or they paid him to keep quiet."

"Oh, he moved all right. Three months later, his body was found in a trunk on the shore of Vashon Island. He'd been brutally murdered, and the trunk had been weighted down and tied shut. Some people on the beach came across it on a low tide."

Vera couldn't recall ever hearing about it, which seemed strange since it would have been big news.

"It was the same week that Jean Harlow died, so it didn't get much news coverage," Priscilla added.

Vera's mind leapt to her dad, how he would know about this if it really happened.

"So, to answer your question, Ruth would've hired someone to follow you and run you off the road. Probably just to teach me a lesson not to go behind their backs. I know Ruth wants to find Max. She just doesn't want me getting involved. Even though I'm his *mother*." She clenched her fists, and Vera's heart went out to her.

Again, she thought of Hugh. *How could he turn a blind eye*

on these kinds of monsters?

Priscilla stood as Vera's jaw dropped open. "I'm sorry. I should've been honest about the risks when I asked you to help me." Tears brimmed above Priscilla's lower lashes. "I'm just so desperate to find my son."

Vera backed away from Priscilla, taking in what she said. "I could've died."

A tear slid down Priscilla's cheek. "I'm sorry, Vera. I had no intention for you to get hurt. Only to find Max."

Vera pressed her lips together and moved toward the davenport. She assessed Priscilla after sitting down. Her dark eyes were pronounced by even darker circles beneath them. Despite the danger she'd put her in, Vera couldn't help but feel sorry for her.

"Earlier this year, Rex was left at the altar by his fiancé. Actually, she didn't even show up to the wedding."

This, Vera remembered. The local papers had a heyday with the story.

"She skipped town and Rex never heard from her again, aside from a note she left saying she planned to travel abroad. To Switzerland, I think. He was devastated. The public couldn't understand why she would throw away the opportunity to marry into the Ellis family." Priscilla lifted her gaze and stared out the front window. "She was the smart one." She lowered her eyes until they met Vera's. "Anyway, now that the FBI have this Scarlet in custody—and found the connection with her and Howard Mills—I'm hoping we will have answers soon."

"I hope you do." And Vera meant it. She stood. "I don't want to be involved anymore. I'm not sure what I could even do anyway."

"I understand." Priscilla followed her to the library doors and pressed her palm against the wood as Vera reached for the door handle. "There's just one more thing I need you to do."

Vera turned. She wanted to help her, but not enough to risk her life. "What?"

Priscilla's chest fell with relief. "I need you to find out what Vincent's investigator knows. He was the man on the plane with us yesterday. They're keeping something from me. And I need to know what it is. What I do know is that they've been meeting with the PI in Rex's office at the bank. And I bet he's kept records of what the PI has dug up."

"But how would I—"

"You're working for him now. You'll think of something."

"Priscilla—"

"I can't do it. They'd have me followed. But *you* could say it's something about an upcoming trip." Her voice broke. "Please."

Vera nodded.

"Rex is a very organized man. Anything that's not related to the bank will stand out. You find something, grab it."

"I'll try."

Priscilla pulled her hand away from the door. "Thank you."

Priscilla turned to Vera when they reached the foyer. "Have you heard from your friend Dari?"

"Yes!" Vera's mood changed at the mention of Dari's name. "She got a call from Nancy Harkness Love asking her to be a squadron leader in the WAFS. She left for Delaware last night. I assume it was you who sent her Dari's qualifications. Thank you."

Priscilla unlatched the door and opened it wide. "Don't mention it. I always come through on my promises."

Vera didn't respond, knowing what Priscilla meant.

Instead, she crossed Priscilla's cobblestone driveway in the early-morning sun and climbed into her banged-up Ford, squinting from the pain in her head.

31

How the hell could this have happened?" Vincent slammed his palm onto the reception desk at Seattle's FBI headquarters, making the woman behind the partition jump. "You should've been watching her!"

"I'll get Agent Steincamp," she said, before fleeing the room.

Vincent's face flushed with anger as he and Priscilla watched her scurry down a hallway. Vincent had climbed into his Speedster less than five minutes after Gregory woke him with a telephone call from a Seattle Police officer who gave Vincent inside tips on occasion for the proper compensation. Priscilla had barely gotten in beside him before he tore out of the driveway and sped downtown.

She'd known from his yelling into the phone that it wasn't good news. But it wasn't until he parked the car that Vincent finally admitted that Scarlet was dead.

The receptionist returned and stepped out from behind the partition. "You two can follow me." She led Vincent and Priscilla to a windowless room at the end of the hallway. "Agent Steincamp will be right with you."

The couple sat in two of the four chairs surrounding a small wooden table and stared at the walls. When the older FBI agent heading up Max's investigation appeared in the doorway, Vincent jumped to his feet.

"You better not have let her die before learning where she hid my son!"

The agent put his hands in the air. "Mr. Ellis, I need you to calm down."

"And I need you to do your damn job!" Vincent shouted. "So don't tell me to be calm!"

Agent Steincamp took a seat across from them as Vincent remained standing. "How nice. You've got a mole in the Seattle Police, Mr. Ellis. We haven't even released her death to the public."

Priscilla interrupted their banter. "What did she say about who has our son?"

The agent shook his head. "Both Howard and Gilbert were killed the same night, that much the coroner has confirmed. Likely within a few hours of each other. Miss Fox had an alibi that has checked out—she was at a gambling hall in Chinatown until four in the morning." He stared up at Vincent. "And, as you know, she was with you until just before your son was discovered missing." He shot a wary glance at Priscilla before continuing to address her husband. "However, she did admit to faking an affair with you as part of a blackmail scheme with the Mills cousins."

Vincent slammed his fist on the table. "That's horseshit!"

The agent raised his hands in the air. "But she claimed to have been kept in the dark about your son's abduction, having no involvement in it. We've searched her houseboat, and Gilbert's home, and the boy isn't there. No sign that he ever was. We were going to release her this afternoon."

Vincent paced back and forth in the small room.

"How did she die?" Priscilla asked.

The agent folded his hands atop the table. "She hanged herself with a bedsheet from the top bunk in her cell. She appeared to have been dead for a few hours when the guard found her this morning."

Priscilla felt the blood drain from her head as the room seemed to close in around her. She shut her eyes, trying to force away the image of Scarlet Fox's limp corpse being found in the same fashion as her father. "What about Max? She must've known something!"

But Priscilla knew the answer from the frown on Steincamp's face.

"I'm afraid not."

Priscilla pressed her hands against the cold table to steady herself, her heart feeling like it might give out. The hope of getting Max back—alive—only for it to be extinguished was more than she could take. Vincent continued to pace behind her as she fought the urge to throw up.

She didn't believe for a second that Scarlet took her own life. Somehow, Ruth had managed to keep her and Vincent's affair out of the papers, even after the FBI found out. But Ruth wouldn't risk Scarlet blowing the whistle on it, especially once she learned the actress couldn't lead them to Max. Priscilla imagined Ruth had also worried about what family secrets and security details Vincent had likely let slip during his drunken pillow talks with his hard-up lover. She knew her mother-in-law well enough to be certain Ruth would never allow those risks to remain unchecked.

A knock sounded before the door to the room swung open. Priscilla recognized the tall fair-haired agent as he leaned forward and whispered into Steincamp's ear. Vincent had grown still, and she wondered if he was thinking the same thing she was about Scarlet's death.

Agent Steincamp's eyes grew wide as the younger agent pulled away from his ear. He looked between Priscilla and Vincent before he spoke.

"Earlier today, a small child was found walking the streets of Spokane, claiming to be lost after he'd been dropped off at a nearby gas station by a man he didn't know."

Priscilla gripped Vincent's arm behind her as she took in the agent's words.

"He fits your son's description. The Spokane police haven't gotten much out of him—aside from the boy saying his name is Max."

Priscilla inhaled an audible gasp.

"They've requested you come to identify the child."

"Yes!" Vincent said. "Oh, thank God. Of course, we will!"

Still at a loss for words, a whimper escaped Priscilla's throat.

The agent nodded. "I'll telephone Spokane and tell them you'll be there before nightfall."

"It'll be much sooner than that," Vincent said. "We'll take our plane."

32

Vera's Ford puttered to a stop in front of her home. She lifted the paper sack of groceries from the passenger seat before climbing out of the car. She'd felt several eyes on her at her local grocer as shoppers noticed the darkening bruise over her swollen eye. One older, grandfatherly man even slipped her a note with his telephone number, saying she could call him if she was ever in trouble, probably assuming she was a battered wife. Vera thanked him for his concern but assured the man her injuries were from a minor car accident. He hadn't looked convinced, telling her to keep the number anyway.

She grimaced as she climbed out of the car. Her head had begun to throb on her drive home, but she now had a splitting headache. She planned to lie down once she put away the groceries. She slowed as she moved past her mailbox, using her free hand to open the letterbox. Her heart quickened when she spotted the Honolulu postmark, even though Hugh had only been gone for five days.

She set her bags onto the sidewalk and tore open the

envelope. She smiled at Hugh's neat handwriting as she unfolded it. A patch of clouds covered the sun, and a light mist fell as she began to read.

Dear Kitten,

I can't believe it was only this morning I left you at Boeing Field. It feels much longer, and I miss you so much already. I smile thinking of you behind the controls of the Lockheed Electra, just like Amelia Earhart—only more of a looker. You're one hell of a pilot, Vera Chandler, and the Ellis family is lucky to have you. I hope they are treating you well, and that they might be able to part with you when I return.

Vera stopped reading, remembering what Priscilla told her about the Ellises getting rid of people who got in their way. Had Ruth Ellis really put a hit on Vera's life to teach Priscilla a lesson?

The island is beautiful, and it gives me a clearer picture of Dari's stories of growing up on Oahu. While I think of how much you'd love the palm trees and warm beaches, the evidence from the destruction of Pearl Harbor reminds me of why I am here. I can only imagine what it must have been like for those that were here the day of the attack. Seeing the keel of the USS Oklahoma *protruding from water with the hundreds of souls still resting inside is a constant reminder of why we must fight—and what we must defeat.*

Vera swallowed, knowing that Dari's husband, James, was one of those souls.

You remember the duty I had last summer? Well, I have

that exact same duty now, so you may not hear from me for a while.

Vera tried to remember what duty he was referring to. She knew he couldn't say the ship name because it would've been censored. She recalled Hugh saying last summer that he was qualifying for carrier landings on the *USS Hornet*.

Vera stood still, in shock of Hugh being shipped out so soon. Although, she knew more pilots were needed on the warships in the Pacific and that was why they'd deployed him with such short notice. But now it was happening. Nearly every week in the papers, an Allied ship was sunk by enemy fire. She could hardly bear that Hugh could be among them.

But know that you are always in my thoughts.

All my love,
Hugh

Despite her worries, she also felt relief at reading his words. He loved her, she was sure. She felt a stab of guilt for thinking he could have been mixed up with Priscilla.

P.S. I hope by the time this letter arrives, you've been able to taste my tomatoes. I'd love to know how they are turning out.

His tomatoes. Vera swore as she hurried inside the house, holding Hugh's letter in one hand and her groceries in the other. As soon as she'd set the bag of food onto her kitchen counter, she opened the back porch door.

She righted one of the patio chairs that lay on its side as she crossed their small yard. The wooden tomato cage

Hugh had built to support the vines had been blown to a forty-five-degree angle. Vera recalled the storm on Orcas, and how it was forecasted to head this way. She drew in a short breath at the sight of the browning tomatoes lying in the wet dirt of Hugh's garden bed. The few that were still on the vine were split open, with several gashes in their skin that were starting to rot around the edges.

She put a hand over her mouth as she leaned closer. *Oh, Hugh....*

The shrill ring of her telephone from inside the house pulled her from her thoughts. Keeping Hugh's letter in her hand, she hurried inside to answer it. Every ring made her head ache more as she pulled the receiver to her ear.

"Hello?"

"Vera, it's Vincent." He sounded out of breath. "I need you to fly us to Spokane right away. We're headed to the airport now—so hurry!"

Vera lifted a hand to the painful pulsation in her temple. *This man can't be serious. Another fling?* "Mr. Ellis, this is not the time—"

"Come now! We think we've found Max."

Before Vera could say another word, Vincent hung up.

33

Priscilla pushed past Vincent and Ruth when they stepped inside the Spokane Police Headquarters. She'd never been more grateful for their private plane. Having to take several hours to drive over the Cascade Mountains would've been excruciating. Their hour and a half flight had been long enough.

"We're here to get our son—Max Ellis," she said to the uniformed officer sitting behind the front desk.

"Oh, yes." He stood slowly from his chair as Priscilla willed him to move faster. "Right this way."

He led the three of them to a stairwell. Priscilla followed at his heels as Vincent helped Ruth up the steps. When they reached the top, a young couple holding hands turned in their direction, along with another uniformed officer.

"These are the parents of Max Ellis," the policeman said to the other officer.

The second officer reached out and shook Vincent's hand as Priscilla scanned the upstairs hallway for a sign of her son.

"I'm Officer Blakeman. After we got off the phone with the Seattle FBI, we learned that another boy had disappeared from his Idaho campsite this last weekend." He gestured toward the young couple at his side. "Coincidentally, that boy's name is also Max. So, we've called that child's parents here too."

Priscilla assessed them, recognizing the ravaged look in their eyes. Their clothes were well-worn, and the woman's eyes looked red from crying. *No. It has to be our Max.* Her heart went out to them; it would be agonizing to have to return home without their child. Priscilla looked away and noticed Ruth staring at the couple through narrowed eyes.

Officer Blakeman cleared his throat as the other policeman retreated downstairs. "Now that you're all here, we'll take you to the child."

Priscilla held her breath as they followed him down the hall, until he stopped to knock on a closed door. A woman opened it, and Priscilla peered into the room to see a small, freckled brown-haired boy appear behind her.

"Mama!" He ran toward the other young woman as she crouched down to receive him.

"Max!"

Tears of joy streamed down the other couple's face as they enveloped their son in a hug. Vincent hung his head as Priscilla watched the scene of the reunited family unfold in front of her in disbelief.

Officer Blakeman turned to Vincent. "I'm so sorry to bring you all this way."

The room spun as he continued to speak to her husband. "Priscilla?"

She felt the floor move beneath her feet and turned to see Ruth frowning at her. She smacked her cane against the floor to get Priscilla's attention. As if she was having a silly daydream, instead of the shock of losing her son all over again.

Priscilla pulled at the collar of her dress. *This cannot be happening.* "I can't breathe."

They'd had their chance to get Max back last week at Kinnear Park. And they would likely never get another.

"Madam?" Officer Blakeman shot her a look of concern as Priscilla's legs gave out, and he reached out to catch her before she collapsed to the floor.

34

Raindrops showering against the Electra's windshield was the only sound in the cockpit as Vera waited for the Ellises to return. They had been gone nearly an hour, and dusk had settled over the gray Spokane sky.

She could only imagine the relief they must be feeling by finding their son. It seemed remarkable that, at this point, they'd found him at all. Spokane was a long way from Seattle, and she wondered what horrors the little boy might've experienced in these last eight days.

Scarlet must have been innocent of the boy's kidnapping after all. It was also a relief that, now that they had Max back, she would no longer have to get involved in the family's affairs.

Vincent, Priscilla, and Ruth had already boarded when Vera had arrived at the Everett Airport. She'd been surprised to see the family's matriarch and noticed Ruth hadn't appeared surprised to see her—*alive*. Although, Vera concluded, Ruth's hired hitman would likely have reported back to her that Vera had escaped.

After she landed in Spokane, Vera watched the elderly woman get off the plane, wondering if the poised bank heiress was really capable of murder. Or was Priscilla delusional about the level of the Ellis family's corruption? *One way or another, someone did try to kill me. And nearly succeeded.*

Vera pulled Hugh's letter from her jacket pocket and reread his words. She wished she could ask him about the Ellises. Hugh was perceptive. He wouldn't have missed what kind of people the Ellises were.

She closed her eyes and smelled the letter, hoping to drink in Hugh's familiar aftershave. But the paper held no smell.

"Please stay safe," she whispered. "I need you to come home to me when this is all over."

Headlights shone against the cockpit's side window. Vera turned, watching expectantly as Vincent climbed out of the taxi's front seat and opened the rear door. Vera leaned closer to the window. Ruth got out cane-first as Vincent held an umbrella over her head. Priscilla stepped out of the car behind them. Without Max.

Vera's heart ached as she registered the devasted expression on Priscilla's pale face. She followed behind her husband and mother-in-law, the rain soaking her dark curls against her mink coat. Priscilla looked to be in a trance as she followed them onto the back of the plane, disappearing from Vera's view.

"Let's go!" Vincent barked, after boarding the plane.

Vera turned in her seat. Priscilla let out a gut-wrenching sob as she sank into a seat in the back. Vera longed to comfort her, shocked by how Vincent and his mother acted as though she wasn't there.

"It wasn't Max," Vincent added, as Vera looked from

165

Priscilla to Ruth, who turned to her daughter-in-law with a hard-set expression.

"You could've saved your emotions for our private flight home, rather than humiliate us with your huge spectacle at the police station."

Vera's jaw dropped at Ruth's heartless words. "I'm so sorry," she said, directing her words toward Priscilla.

After no response, she turned toward the controls and flipped on the Electra's master switch. A few minutes later, with both engines started, she taxied to the runway for takeoff.

On the flight back to Seattle, Vera thought about what Priscilla had said about Vincent's hired PI knowing something they weren't telling her. Seeing the devastation in Priscilla's eyes tonight, Vera knew she had to help her by finding out what it was. Dari's words from the other night echoed in her ear. *Be careful.*

And Dari didn't even know the half of it. From all Vera had learned about the Ellis family, they were just as dangerous as the people who had kidnapped Max. If not more.

But if she wanted to help Priscilla find her son, the Ellises finding out she was continuing to help Priscilla behind their backs was a risk she would have to take.

35

Two days later, Vera pulled into the gravel parking lot at the Everett Airport and saw that Rex's Lincoln Continental was already there. She checked the time on her dash, afraid she was late. But it was still fifteen minutes to nine. She grabbed her flight bag and stepped out of her car into the cool October morning. As she moved past Rex's car, she saw he was still sitting inside, and there was a man in his passenger seat.

Vera looked away before her employer caught her staring and headed toward the tarmac. She'd been unable to sleep the night she flew Max's devastated parents back from Spokane. A heavy despair had hung in the air of the Electra's cabin the entire flight home. She was worried about Priscilla, and what might become of her if they never found Max. After tossing and turning, Vera had gotten out of bed and written to Hugh, tossing the first five drafts into her wastebasket before finally deciding to leave out any mention of the Ellises in her letter—nor the fate of his cherished tomatoes. Then she'd written to Dari.

She'd put her letters to Hugh and Dari in the mailbox yesterday morning. She wondered, if Hugh had already been shipped out, how long it might take for her letter to reach him.

She was surprised to find the Electra's rear door already open when she reached the plane. An attractive middle-aged woman seated in the front row turned her head when Vera climbed aboard. Vera had assumed she was flying Rex to Boise for business. But now she wondered if this was another lovers' rendezvous.

The woman smiled as Vera moved down the aisle. "You must be the new pilot. I'm Silvia, Rex's secretary."

"Nice to meet you." Vera returned her warm smile, relieved this wasn't another secretive, off-the-books venture. "I'm Vera."

"My niece is a pilot," Silvia said as Vera climbed into the cockpit. "She's hoping to apply for the Women's Flying Training Detachment."

"Wow. So am I." Vera settled into her seat and turned on the plane's master switch. "Eventually."

"And give up this job?" Silvia leaned forward. "I mean, the Ellises aren't the nicest people on the planet, but they sure do pay well."

Vera nodded, unsure of what to say. She couldn't argue, but she wondered how much Silvia knew about the inner workings of the Ellis family. She started her pre-flight checklist when she saw Rex and his passenger get out of the car. She recognized him as the man who had joined the family on Vera's first flight, Vincent's private investigator.

Rex tucked a folder under his arm and said something to the man before the PI got into a dark sedan parked nearby. Vera moved her attention to the controls as Rex started toward the plane.

"Good morning, Silvia," she heard Rex say a few moments later. "Mark my calendar for one p.m. on Friday. I'm going to meet with my investigator at the office as soon as I'm back from lunch."

Rex's musky aftershave filled the plane as he took a seat behind his secretary.

Vera turned around. "Are we still heading to Boise, Mr. Ellis?"

"Yes. Thank you, Vera." He smiled cordially, his demeanor starkly different from the first time she'd met him.

Vera faced the controls and pulled on her headset. She eyed the parking lot, thinking of his private investigator. From the burly looks of him, he seemed more like a man who did Rex's dirty work.

She tried to picture the car that had nearly run her off the road. *Was it the man she'd just seen with Rex?* Rex's warm smile from a moment ago stuck in her mind, sending a shiver down her back.

Vera took a bite of the ham sandwich she'd packed as she reread a paragraph in *Rebecca* for the third time. After refueling and using the Boise airport bathroom, she'd returned to the cockpit where she'd been waiting for nearly two hours for Rex and Silvia to return. She'd read the Daphne du Maurier novel three times, and it never failed to keep her attention. But today, she couldn't bring herself to focus on the story.

She looked up from her book at the snowcapped mountains beyond the city and remembered coming to

Idaho with her parents as a little girl. Thinking of them, she felt a stroke of sadness, wishing she could call them. Especially with Hugh and Dari so far away. But she knew that even if her parents spoke to her, they'd be unhappy to learn she was still flying planes. Hearing someone climb aboard the plane, Vera turned to see Silvia.

"Last night I dreamt I went to Manderley again," Silvia said, sinking into her seat in the front row. "I loved that picture. Never read the book, though."

Vera lifted the faded novel in her hand and smiled at Silvia's quote of the first line. "I like the book better, although it was a good film."

Vera looked behind Silvia, expecting Rex to board the plane any second.

"It gave me shivers when Mrs. Danvers told the second Mrs. DeWinter to jump from the top of the mansion." Silvia shook her head. "So evil."

It was one of Vera's favorite scenes too, but she didn't think the picture had quite done it justice. Films were never able to evoke the level of emotions in her that books did.

"And I just love Joan Fontaine," Silvia continued. "I used to read quite a lot, but now I spend all my extra money on war bonds. Anyway, I see you're married."

Vera followed Silvia's gaze to her wedding band, taken aback at her abrupt change of subject. "Yes." She stared at her ring, imagining Hugh risking his life fighting in the Pacific Theater while she sat aboard this private airliner reading her novel and chatting with Rex Ellis's secretary.

"I hope Rex can find a wife someday. It would be so good for him."

Vera shot a glance again at the rear door, afraid her employer would catch them discussing his private life. "Is Mr. Ellis here? Should I request clearance for takeoff?"

"Oh, no." Silvia waved her palm through the air. "After lunch, he went for drinks with a few of the branch executives. You know…" she rolled her eyes. "Boys only."

Vera thought about Rex's ex-fiancé jilting him at the altar.

"He was engaged once, right?"

Silvia's eyes lit up. "Oh, yes. To Evie Calloway. She was lovely. That was so tragic how she left him at the altar. He's never been the same, if you ask me. And those horrible accusations from the girl's parents were so cruel." She lowered her voice, even though they were still the only ones on the plane. "I mean, the Ellises are no saints, but they'd never kill anyone."

Vera's book dropped to the floor. "I'm sorry?"

"Oh. Well, the Ellises somehow managed to keep it out of the news, thank goodness. But the girl's parents were convinced the Ellis family killed her. They just couldn't believe their daughter would leave without saying goodbye." Silvia shrugged. "But people get cold feet all the time. Although, between you and me, Rex's mother almost seemed happy about the girl leaving him like that. He moved in with Ruth not long after."

Vera's mind reeled. Priscilla hadn't mentioned any murder accusations from his ex-fiancé's parents. "Was there an investigation?"

Silvia nodded. "Not a public one though. From what I gathered, it didn't take long for the police to conclude that the Calloways' accusations were completely unfounded. Rumor has it that Evie joined a utopian society in Switzerland. Evie's father is a senator, you know, but Ruth has publicly supported his rival in next month's election." She shook her head for emphasis. "He doesn't stand a chance of getting reelected. If you ask me, he burned the wrong bridge accusing the Ellises like that."

With all she'd learned since she'd taken this job, Vera doubted the family's accusations were unfounded.

"Do they still live around Seattle?"

"They have a beautiful Victorian home on Green Lake, just down the hill from my own." The secretary smoothed the top of her skirt after crossing her leg. "Called the Calloway House. I've always been a sucker for Victorian architecture." Silvia lifted that morning's *Tribune* from the seat next to her. "I better stop gabbing, so you can eat your lunch. I doubt Rex will be too much longer. He's got a meeting back at the office at four."

Silvia lowered her gaze to the top page of *The Tribune.* "Humph. Looks like one less problem for the Ellis family."

Vera strained to see what Silvia was referring to as the secretary continued to scan the article. After a minute, Silvia opened the paper and lifted it in front of her face. Vera's jaw dropped as she read that morning's front-page headline:

FILM SIREN SCARLET FOX HANGS HERSELF
AFTER BEING JAILED IN CONNECTION WITH
ELLIS KIDNAPPING

36

Vera touched down at the Everett Airport, her mind still reeling over Scarlet's death as she laid on the brakes. Silvia had offered her the paper after she finished reading, and Vera had managed to read most of the front-page article before Rex returned. The police were calling her death a suicide. The article went on to say that while the police had originally suspected Scarlet in Gilbert Mill's murder, she had an alibi for the time of Mills's death, and for Max's kidnapping.

She thought of Rex sitting in the back of the plane. *How far would the family go to keep Vincent and Scarlet's affair out of the headlines?*

If the Ellis family had police on their payroll, maybe they had jail guards, too.

Vera parked the plane and slid off her headphones. She grabbed Amelia's faded photograph from the dash and tucked it inside her blouse pocket.

"It was lovely to meet you, Vera."

She turned at the sound of Silvia's voice. "Likewise."

Rex stood at the rear door, briefcase in hand. "I'll have Silvia telephone you with the next time I need the plane. Probably later this week."

Silvia followed him off the plane, and Vera watched them move toward the parking lot in the afternoon sun as she turned off the master switch. After she climbed out of the cockpit, her eyes traveled to a pale folder sitting atop Rex's seat. When she moved closer, she recognized it as the folder he'd tucked under his arm that morning after meeting with his investigator.

Noticing that the side was labeled *Max Ellis,* she lifted the folder. Her heart skipped a beat as she glanced out through the windshield. She could no longer see Rex or Silvia. She looked back at the file and started to open it, recalling Priscilla's plea to find out what the family was hiding from her.

Her eyes fell to the top page of the folder, a typed summary marked *CONFIDENTIAL.* Vera jumped from Rex's voice as she read the first line.

"Oh, thank you. You found it."

Vera snapped the folder closed as Rex watched her from the rear door.

He outstretched his arm. "I knew I forgot something."

Vera swallowed and extended the file toward him, hoping he didn't notice her trembling hand.

"Of course," Vera said.

His gaze lingered on hers before he turned from the door.

"Oh, and Vera?"

He reappeared in the rear opening, his ice-blue eyes locking on hers.

"Yes?"

His expression turned serious, and she braced herself to be berated for prying into his file.

"I need the flight ledgers from the last six months. Hugh kept them for me. Could you bring them next time we fly?"

Vera nodded, feeling the tension in her chest dissipate. "Of course."

Vera watched through the side windows as Rex walked toward the parking lot. After he reached the front of the plane, she collapsed into one of the seats.

There was no doubt he saw her snooping in Max's file. Goosebumps formed on her arms. She should stop. Quit this job and apply for the Women's Flying Training Detachment. She'd explain everything to Hugh once he came home. He'd have to understand. She longed to speak to him now about everything that was going on.

She knew she should leave Max's abduction to the police. But Rex was already onto her.

She gripped the metal armrests, thinking of what happened to those who got in the way of the Ellises. Rex already knew she was helping Priscilla. The memory of nearly being driven off the Ballard Bridge played in her mind. If Rex and his mother wanted her dead, there would be no outrunning them.

If she didn't want to end up like Scarlet or Evie, her only chance was to find Max. If she could bring him home, the Ellises might be grateful enough—at least publicly—to spare her life. All she could do was aim to learn the truth about Max's whereabouts before they silenced her—for good.

37

Dari looked up at the sound of a fist rapping against the bathroom door shared between the six women in her tiny dorm.

"Time's up, Lily! This isn't a beauty pageant. I gotta go!" Barbara shouted.

Dari smiled as the ex-lingerie model pounded a second time on the door, knowing there was no rushing Lily in the morning. Ruby, a recent graduate of UCLA, stifled a yawn in line behind Barbara. They had to report to ground school in less than five minutes, and both women were already dressed in their baggy flight suits that had originally belonged to the men who had trained before them. After less than a week of training, Dari had figured out the secret to being ready for the flight line after their six-a.m. alarm went off.

While her five roommates waited in line for a turn in the loo, Dari would throw her ill-fitted flight suit on over her pajamas and tuck her toothbrush into her pocket before heading to the mess hall. Being one of the first to arrive, she'd use the dining hall's restroom before getting her breakfast, while her roommates were still battling for their shared bathroom time.

Normally, she stayed in the mess hall until it was time to walk to the ground school building. But after shoveling down her oatmeal, she had rushed back to her room to write to Vera. Yesterday, she'd become the first in her squadron to pass a cockpit check in the XP-51 prototype. Being a single-seat aircraft, her flight check consisted of ground school training on its controls, specifications, and emergency procedures. Today, her first time up in the fighter, would be a solo one.

With a top speed of 445 miles per hour and a service ceiling of 42,000 feet, the single-engine high-speed fighter was only slightly faster than the last air racer she'd flown. But the prototype's sleek design and Packer-built Merlin engine made it more powerful, and likely smoother, than anything she'd flown before. She could see why the army had already placed an order for four hundred of them. Being at the controls of the XP-51 would be an exhilaration like no other, and she couldn't wait to tell her best friend all about it.

A bell went off overhead, signaling that it was time to walk across to the adjacent building where ground school was held.

After only a brief orientation five days ago, the WAFS recruits had begun a rigorous combination of ground school and flight training. All the trainees came with commercial and 200-hp ratings, along with an average of over 1,000 flight hours. Since Nancy Love had selected only highly qualified female pilots, and they were needed immediately, the program was packing several months of training into one.

Although their sixteen-hour days were exhausting, no one complained—except when Lily hogged the bathroom. There was a palpable energy among them, as they excelled through their courses and flight checks, grateful for the opportunity to use their skill of flying to serve the war effort.

"*Lily!*" Barbara yelled as the bathroom door swung open.

Lily emerged, and a waft of hibiscus perfume filled the air. Her lips were coated in a ruby-red lipstick, and she was completely unfussed as the two women rushed into the bathroom behind her.

"Finally!" Ruby said, closing the door behind them.

Dari stood, hurriedly licking the envelope after tucking Vera's letter inside. She shook her head, following Lily out of their sleeping quarters.

Dari placed a hand on Lily's shoulder as they marched down the narrow hall. "You look impeccable—don't get me wrong. But you do know that's not the way to make friends, right? *And*, you don't have to impress these planes with your looks."

Lily winked before looping her arm around Dari's. "You're one to talk. I've seen the way you look at that XP-51. I've never seen you look at a *man* like that. You were practically drooling over it yesterday."

Dari laughed. "I guess there's no use hiding it. I'm in love. Just wait until you fly it. Trust me, you'll understand."

"XP-51, requesting permission to land at runway 26." Dari looked beyond the slender nose of the fighter at the triangular runways at the New Castle Army Air Force Base.

178

A light fog had settled over the airfield since she took off, but she could still make out their position.

"XP-51, you are cleared to land at runway 26."

She flew through a patch of clouds as she began her descent over the murky waters of the Delaware River. "Roger, XP-51 cleared to land on runway 26."

Dari eased the control stick forward, amazed at the plane's smooth response to her command.

She smiled, thinking of Lily's words to her earlier that morning. Her friend was right, she hadn't looked at a man the way she looked at this plane—not since the last time she saw her husband. A lump caught in her throat at the thought of James. And what his final moments must have been like on board the USS Arizona.

The sight of the battleship exploding in the harbor below her parents' home would be forever burned in her memory. She pushed the painful memory aside as she broke through the clouds and continued her final approach.

"I'm going to miss you, baby," she whispered to the aircraft without pressing down on her mic button.

Tomorrow would be her last training flight in the XP-51 prototype before it would be flown back to Long Beach. During her flight, she'd taken the speed up to four hundred miles per hour and was amazed at how well the plane handled. She couldn't wait to get behind the controls of this lightweight fighter again.

The fields below disappeared as she flew into the low hanging fog. She continued on course, knowing it would clear before she touched down. She eased back on the throttle as she soared through the dense haze. A moment later, she emerged from the fog, glad to see she had stayed on course and the runway was in clear view.

Suddenly, a powerful jolt accompanied the sound of an

explosion on the left side of her airplane. She looked toward the flash, but all she could see was the underbelly of a large plane, which darkened the sky above her. Despite her steady hand on the control stick, the fighter dove to the left. Dari fought to level the plane.

Flames and black smoke erupted from her shattered wing. Less than ten feet above her, a B-24 Bomber banked to the side, moving out of her path. As her plane spun out of control, she spotted a chunk of aluminum from her wing hanging from the bomber's landing gear.

"Mayday! Mayday! This is XP-51. I repeat, mayday!" she yelled into her radio.

"State your emergency. Can we be of any assistance?"

"I'm going down!"

As she spun toward the fields below, Dari pressed the right rudder to the floor with her foot, hoping to recover from the spin in time to bring the plane down right-side up. Her spinning slowed as the fighter started to bank in the opposite direction. But without her left wing, the airplane was incapable of recovering from the spin.

"XP-51, state your position."

The nose dipped toward the earth as she whirled toward it with increasing speed. She could bail out and pull her parachute, but it would be useless. She was seconds from impact, leaving no time for her chute to open.

She took one last look at the flames erupting out her side window and let go of the microphone. "I'm sorry, baby," she whispered.

In a final, futile effort, she pulled back on the control stick before she pressed her other hand against the plane's army green side paneling. She closed her eyes, filling her mind with James, knowing he'd be waiting for her on the other side.

38

Vera pulled her Ford up to the curb across from the park that lined Green Lake. It had taken her less than fifteen minutes of driving around the lake to find Evie Calloway's parents' home. On her way home last night, rattled from Rex catching her snooping at Max's file, she'd picked up an application for the Women's Flying Training Detachment, a twenty-three-week training program in Houston, Texas. She had put it in the mail that morning.

No amount of money was worth working for the Ellises. But before she could take a chance on escaping the evil family, she needed to know exactly what she was up against. She got out and moved past the metal sign that hung in the front yard marked *Calloway House*. After climbing the stone staircase that zigzagged up the steep hill to the home's front porch, she knocked on the front door.

She turned to take in the view of the lake while she waited. The leaves on the trees surrounding the deep blue water had turned to shades of copper and gold. After debating what she would say to Evie's parents on her drive over, she'd decided on the truth. But now that she was here, it felt like a ridiculous plan. How could she expect them to open up about their missing daughter to a stranger? One who worked for the Ellis family, no less. Vera spun around, hearing footsteps come toward the door.

It opened just enough for a woman's face to be seen.

"Can I help you, Miss?"

The woman looked to be in her late fifties, probably close to Vera's own mother's age.

"Sorry. I—" She racked her brain for what she had planned to say. "I—um—I work for the Ellis family."

The woman's face darkened. "What on earth are you nosing around here for?"

"I don't know them very well, but I'm trying to help find their son, Max. I was wondering if I could ask you a few questions about your experience with the Ellises? I'm an old friend of Priscilla's, and with the kidnapping on top of her father's suicide, I'm worried about her."

"Oh, Priscilla, poor dear." The woman started to close the door. "But it seems like that family finally got what was coming to them. You can only dish out so much evil before it lands back on your doorstep. Maybe you can find my daughter while you're at it. I have nothing to say."

Vera held the door open with her palm. "Please. It's for the child's sake. I won't stay long."

"Wished someone gave a damn when my daughter went missing. No one ever believed me that something happened to her. Not the police. Not even the papers. They made her sound like some flighty, nutcase runaway bride."

"So, you don't think your daughter could've gotten cold feet and run away? I understand she left a note saying she wanted to travel abroad."

She turned to Vera with furrowed brows. "That's what

Ruth Ellis wanted everyone to believe. But no, Evie would never do that. If my daughter did pen that letter, it's because she was forced to. It's been seven months since we last saw her, and she was head over heels in love with Rex Ellis. She couldn't wait to start a family with him." Evie's mother crossed her arms. "Ruth tried to buy us off before the wedding. Offered us a hefty sum to make Evie call it off."

"Why would she do that?"

"Ruth only supported Evie and Rex's engagement when she thought their alignment would mean Evie's father would support policies that benefited the bank. When Ruth learned we backed the government's plan to peg interest rates at low levels for the remainder of the war and supported increased taxation for large corporations—including Pacific Bank—to help fund the war effort, her attitude completely changed." Evie's mother took a step toward the threshold. "But what really worried Ruth was Rex's bond with my husband. They'd grown close after he and Evie's engagement, and Rex expressed interest in a life of politics. Ruth couldn't bear the idea of leaving her precious bank to be run by her younger, delinquent son." She stared out at the lake before returning her gaze to Vera's. "But we refused to take her money. Rex and Evie were in love. And we wanted them to be happy." Evie's mother crossed her arms, making no effort to close the door, but still not inviting Vera inside. "You say you work for them? The Ellises?"

Vera nodded. "Yes, ma'am. I'm their private pilot."

"Hang on," she said, turning from the door.

Vera heard the squeak of a drawer open and close from somewhere inside as she waited for Evie's mother to return.

"Here." She reappeared in the doorway, holding a newspaper clipping out to Vera. "If you get the chance, ask

Ruth where my daughter's body is."

Vera looked at the photo above the engagement announcement. Evie's sleek blonde waves reminded Vera of Veronica Lake as she beamed beside Rex, who smiled down at her.

Evie's mother put her hand on the door. "But I'd be careful if I were you." Her eyes travelled up and down Vera before settling on the lake behind her. "Evie was just about your age when she…." Her chin quivered.

"You think Ruth had Evie *killed*?"

Evie's mother locked her eyes with Vera's. "I don't think so. I know so. At the wedding, Ruth leaned into me after Evie didn't show. And you know what she said?"

Vera shook her head, waiting for Evie's mother to go on.

Her eyes narrowed. "She whispered in my ear, *Guess you should've taken my money.*"

39

Priscilla woke to sunlight streaming through her tangerine silk bedroom curtains. She sat up in bed, surprised she'd finally fallen asleep. Since returning home from Spokane—without Max—she'd hardly slept. She'd tossed and turned for hours last night and remembered looking at the clock a little after six a.m.

She pulled on her robe and went downstairs. She heard two male voices on the other side of the library's closed doors. She recognized her brother-in-law's voice as she moved past the room.

"That's all he's told me for now. I'll be meeting with him again on Friday at my office at one. You should come."

"Should we invite Priscilla?" Vincent asked.

She stopped, staring at the double doors.

"No. Not until we know more."

Her heart quickened. She was dying to open the doors and demand what they were talking about. It had to be something the family's PI had found out.

She put her hand on the doorknob, but let it fall away as

footsteps came toward the door from the other side. She turned down the hall so she didn't appear to be eavesdropping. There was no way she could strong-arm them into telling her what they were talking about if they didn't want to.

"Priscilla."

She pivoted at the sound of Rex's voice after the library doors opened.

His eyes fell to her pajamas beneath her robe. "Good afternoon."

Hattie appeared out of nowhere behind him, but Priscilla knew better than to be surprised. She always managed to make her presence known when Rex was around.

"Good afternoon," Priscilla said.

Rex followed Vincent to the front door, and Priscilla watched Hattie's expression change when she caught Rex's eye. The nanny bit her lip before the edges of her mouth upturned into a playful smile.

He's using you, Priscilla wanted to say. Hattie moved to the edge of the foyer and watched Rex go out the front door.

Priscilla folded her arms when Vincent turned back toward the library. "What were you talking about?"

"Business." His expression betrayed nothing as he tried to move past her.

Priscilla took a step to the side, blocking his path. "It didn't sound like *business.* It was about the investigator wasn't it? He's learned something. I heard you say my name."

Vincent flexed his jaw and assessed her eyes with his. He looked as tired as she felt, and she guessed he hadn't slept at all last night.

"Why are you acting so nervous?"

Priscilla uncrossed her arms and balled her hands into

fists at her sides. "My son's been abducted! Why wouldn't I be nervous? Aren't *you*?"

Vincent ran his hand through his pomaded hair. "I'm sorry. Of course, you are. And yeah, I'm wrecked."

Priscilla felt at a loss for words. In all the years she'd known Vincent, she couldn't ever remember him apologizing.

"Rex is meeting with the investigator again on Friday. He's requested that I attend." The look in her husband's eyes told her she was certainly not welcome to join him.

"There's something I need to tell you," Priscilla said. "About Max."

He leaned toward her, taking her hands in his. "What is it?"

Priscilla squeezed her eyelids shut as she debated about what she was about to say. When she opened them, Vincent was staring at her intently.

"I know why Howard took him. It wasn't out of revenge for getting fired from the bank." She swallowed. "It was for money."

Vincent's face fell. He ripped his hands away from hers in a single, rough motion. "Damn you, Priscilla! I thought you were about to say something *useful*." He scoffed. "Of course, it was for money. Howard left us a *ransom* note!" He turned around and put his hands on his head, as if wanting to tear his own hair out.

Priscilla watched the heave of his chest with each angry breath, knowing there was nothing she could say that would calm him down. She'd been stupid to think she could tell him.

His jaw was set and his eyes narrowed when he turned back around. He pointed at her face. "When my mother finally has you committed, don't ask why."

She reached for his arm.

"Vincent, I—"

"I'm going out." He pulled out of her reach.

After the door slammed behind him, Hattie shot her a look of victory before she moved past Priscilla and went upstairs.

Priscilla gripped the pointed wood newel at the base of the staircase and stared at the front door.

After she heard Hattie's bedroom door close on the third floor, she moved toward the telephone. There had to be more than what Vincent was saying. She needed to know what Rex's investigator had found out. Before she ruined herself unnecessarily.

Hurriedly, she flipped through the little black notebook next to the telephone. She stopped when she found the page she was looking for. *Pilot* was scrawled in black ink at the top of the page. Beneath it, *Hugh Chandler SU 5335.*

40

Vera walked straight to her mailbox after pulling up to the curb in front of her house, despite seeing the flag was down. She opened its metal door. It was empty. She bit her lip, knowing she shouldn't have expected another letter from Hugh after what he had said in his last one, but she couldn't keep herself from hoping.

With a sigh, she remembered his tomatoes. It was time to face them. She went straight through the house and out the back door, cursing at the sight of the shriveled and rotting tomatoes still lying in Hugh's garden bed.

She'd just finished washing her hands in the kitchen sink after disposing of every last tomato into the compost when her phone rang. It was probably Rex's secretary calling with that week's flight schedule. She moved toward the phone, thinking of what Evie's mother had said about Ruth Ellis getting away with murder.

She lifted the phone's earpiece. "Hello?"

"Oh, Vera. Thank God! I've been trying to call you all morning."

"Lily?" *Why would she be calling?* The long-distance call would cost a fortune. Vera couldn't remember Lily ever calling her even when she was in Seattle.

"There's been an accident."

Vera's heart caught in her throat.

"It's Dari."

"Is she all right?"

Lily was quiet, and a shiver ran up Vera's spine.

"No, Vera. I'm afraid she's not. She was getting checked out in a new fighter prototype and was coming in for a landing when her plane collided with a B-24 bomber. The control tower cleared them both to land but didn't calculate the speed right of the new fighter Dari was flying. The visibility was poor—there was fog—and the B-24 came down on top of her."

Lily's voice broke into a sob on the other end of the line, and Vera's back slid down the wall until she sat on the floor.

"Is she...." Vera couldn't bring herself to say the word.

Lily sniffed. "She's gone, Vera."

Vera squeezed her eyes shut. "Do her parents know?"

"Nancy Love telephoned them this morning. We're all pitching in some money to have her body shipped to Hawaii."

"Isn't the army paying for it?" Vera envisioned the honorary burials the war veterans received. Surely this wouldn't be any different.

"No. We took the same oath of enlistment, but we don't have any military status."

Anger welled in Vera's chest along with her grief. Dari died serving her country, and she deserved to be honored for it.

"I'll send some money, too. Thank you for calling. I would've hated to read about it in the papers."

"Goodbye, Vera."

"Lily?"

"Yeah?"

"Stay safe."

"I will."

Vera broke down in sobs after she heard the click on the end of the line. It felt inconceivable that her beautiful best friend was gone forever. She'd been so worried about Hugh, she hadn't given any regard to the dangers Dari and Lily might face in their training.

"Oh, Dari," she cried.

She was the most incredible woman she'd ever met; she hadn't let any obstacle come in the way of her purpose.

Her poor parents. They'd already experienced loss due to the war, and now their only daughter was gone, too. Vera vowed to write to them as soon as she could compose herself.

The sky outside her front windows was darkening when she finally picked herself up off the floor. She thought of her own parents, how she longed to hear her mother's voice. *How would they react if it had been me?* Life was too short to hold grudges.

There was no promise of tomorrow, especially during these times. She needed her parents, even if they didn't see eye to eye. She took a deep breath, lifted the receiver, and dialed the long-distance operator.

A pert voice came over the line. "Long distance...."

Vera gave her the number she knew by heart and waited for her call to be routed through. A familiar voice answered after the third ring.

"Hello?"

Vera choked back a sob that came to her throat. "Mom, it's Vera."

41

Vera used Dari's spare key to open the door to her and Lily's one-bedroom apartment, carrying an empty cardboard box under her arm. The sweet fragrance of Dari's frangipani filled the air when she stepped inside. She felt a waft of emotions as she took slow steps across the small living space and spotted the flowering tree. Today was the first time Vera had left her house since the fateful telephone call from Lily three days ago.

She looked out at the balcony where she'd stayed up late sharing stories with Dari, Lily, and Opal on Lily's last night before leaving for Delaware. The few potted herbs that comprised their victory garden looked in much better shape than Vera's. She sighed, making a note to water them before she left.

She took a steadying breath as she stepped into the bedroom Dari had shared with Lily. It was easy to tell which bed was Dari's, and Vera nearly smiled at the stark contrast between the two sides of the room. Dari's bed was neatly made, while Lily's blankets were tossed in a messy heap, with the September issue of *Vogue* lying in the middle. Vera turned for the closet.

After calling her mother, Vera had decided to phone Dari's parents through the radio telephone service, knowing a letter wasn't enough to express her condolences over the loss of her best friend. Vera's father had been at work when she spoke to her mom, and she hadn't said anything to her about working for the Ellises. Her mother hadn't asked if she was still flying, knowing she likely was. But they'd spoken, and she'd consoled her about Dari's death.

The war was changing things. While her mother hadn't apologized for not supporting Vera's dreams, she was warm, and it was a step in the right direction. She invited Vera to come home for a visit, and Vera agreed she would when she got a chance. Her mom had seen in the papers that Hugh had been deployed and said they were praying for his safe return.

When Vera called Dari's parents, she'd offered to send money to help cover Dari's funeral expenses but learned that Priscilla Ellis had wired Nancy Love enough money to cover everything, plus some. The reminder that she'd gotten Dari her placement in the WAFS hit Vera like a punch in the gut. If it wasn't for her, Dari would still be alive. She choked back the thought and ran her hand across the few cotton blouses Dari had left behind.

After folding Dari's shirts into the box to mail to her parents, she sat on the edge of Dari's bed and reached for the framed photo of Dari and James, taken in front of the *USS Oklahoma*. Vera ran her thumb over the photo of the vibrant couple. Dari wore a sundress beside James in his white navy sailor uniform, and they both smiled brightly for the photograph. A tear slid down Vera's cheek. They were finally together again. She wiped it away before setting the photograph atop Dari's blouses.

She opened the nightstand's top drawer to find a hairbrush, a jar of cold cream, a few *FLYING* magazines, and two photographs: Dari and James's wedding photo and Dari standing beside the Aeronca Chief she gave lessons in. Vera added the drawer's contents to her box for Dari's parents but kept the second photo of Dari in her hand.

She lay back on Dari's bed and stared at the photo of her friend. It felt almost impossible to believe someone so full of life could be gone forever. As long as Vera had known her, Dari was unwavering in her purpose as a pilot and helping the war effort. Vera had always admired her strength, wanting to be more like her.

She set the photo on her lap and thought again of her role in Dari's death. If only she hadn't gotten mixed up with the Ellises. But she'd never seen Dari happier than when she told Vera about her phone call from Nancy Love. She could only imagine the things Dari would have gone on to do if she'd had more time. Even in her short years, she'd accomplished and overcome more than most people do in a lifetime.

Vera rolled onto her side, inhaling the faint scent of jasmine that lingered on Dari's pillow. She vowed to honor Dari's life by flying for the Women's Flying Training Department if she ever got the chance. Dari should go down in history as one of the great female pilots of their time. But if the U.S. government wouldn't even pay for her body to be shipped home, Vera worried that the WAFS wouldn't get the honor they deserved.

Vera's stomach churned at the thought of continuing to work for the Ellises. Thankfully, they hadn't asked her to fly in the days since Dari's death. She looked at Dari's confident smile staring back at her in the photograph. She always had the best advice.

"I don't know what to do," Vera said. She pulled the photograph close to her chest. "Oh, Dari." Her voice broke. After a few moments, she spoke again to the empty apartment. "I miss you so much. I'm so sorry. What am I possibly going to do without you?"

It had grown dark by the time Vera got home. She felt inside her mailbox before going into the house, holding Dari's frangipani pot under one arm. Feeling the lone envelope at the base of her letterbox, she felt a flush of relief. Hugh must have been able to write again sooner than he'd thought. A light rain began to fall, and Vera hurried inside to open the letter.

But after she got in the house and set the frangipani by the front window, she saw the cursive handwriting on the envelope wasn't Hugh's. It was Dari's.

For a moment, it seemed her friend was alive again, but Vera realized she must have mailed it right before she died. Flooded with emotions, she lifted the letter to her face, closing her eyes as she pressed the paper against her skin.

She found a letter opener on her kitchen counter and used it to slice open the envelope, not wanting to risk tearing Dari's final words to her. As she unfolded the letter, a square photograph slid out from the paper. Vera snatched the photo out of the air before it fell to the floor, admiring the confident grin on Dari's face. She stood in front of a military fighter plane wearing a leather flight helmet and loose-fitting military coveralls.

Vera's lip quivered as she began to read Dari's beautiful cursive that filled the page.

My dearest Vera,

I've settled into the army barracks at Wilmington (a long green barn that was formerly the Bachelor Officers' Quarters), where I'm staying with Lily and a dozen other women who've joined the WAFS. Our accommodations are bare, but we are rarely in our rooms other than to sleep. With only 30 days of orientation before we fly for the WAFS, we are cramming several months of flight training into one.

The other women are wonderful. Like Lily and me, most were employed as flight instructors before coming here — although we all come from very different backgrounds. One was a teacher with a master's degree in psychology who was forced to quit after getting married, so she is teaching flight school instead. Another is a wealthy Southern socialite with a Texas drawl, one comes from a very prominent east coast family, while another of the girls was raised by adoptive parents who struggled through the Depression in rural Nebraska.

We start the day by lining up for inspection by Colonel Baker and Nancy Love before we march in formation along with the men on base. While the days are long and the training can be grueling, watching Lily march in her high heels (we were not issued any footwear) beneath her baggy coveralls while she keeps an eye on the boys marching beside us is well worth the physical exertion! I only wish you were here to see it too.

And Vera, the planes! In my first week, I've already flown a Taylorcraft L-2M, a Piper L-4B Cub, and an AT-6. Lily and seven other girls will be the first to graduate as WAFS at the end of the month, and I and five others will be soon to follow. Nancy Love is still planning for me to become the WAFS Squadron Leader, so I'll be training in increasingly larger and

faster aircraft, including the P-47 Thunderbolt!
  But my best news of all is that I've met the love of my life.

Vera paused before flipping the page to read on. Her eyes brimmed with tears, as she felt simultaneously overcome with happiness and grief. For what Dari had gained—and what she'd so quickly lost. She sank to the kitchen floor, turned the paper over, and read on.

The XP-51B prototype.

A tear slid down Vera's cheek as a laugh bubbled out of her throat. "Oh, Dari." She should've known it would be a plane.

The USAAF placed a contract for 400 to be built last August, so Packard brought over the prototype for some initial flight tests. It has a surface ceiling of 42,000 feet, and a top speed of 445 mph! Since I have the most flight experience of all the women in training, I'm going to be the first woman to pilot it—weather permitting. I had a cockpit check in the fighter prototype yesterday, and even on the ground, I felt a sense of belonging like I'd never felt before. An exhilaration that can only be compared to true love.
  I pray you are staying safe. I worry about you working for those people. Promise me you'll do whatever you need to protect yourself. They shouldn't be allowed to get away with what happened to you. Stay at my apartment if you need and keep yourself out of danger.
But don't let them get the best of you.

Much love, my friend,
Dari

Vera pulled her knees into her chest and pressed the letter to her heart. "I'll never forget you, Dari."

She looked again at Dari's vibrant smile in front of the plane that took her life before she buried her face in her hands.

42

Vera awoke to the shrill sound of her phone ringing. She peeled her cheek from her forearm and gathered Dari's letter and photograph off the kitchen floor before getting to her feet. She squinted from the morning light that shone through the front window as she moved toward the persistent ringing.

She'd reread Dari's letter several times last night, unable to move herself off the linoleum floor. At some point in the night, she must have fallen asleep. She lifted the earpiece from the telephone.

"Hello?"

A cheery voice came over the line. "Good morning, dear. It's Silvia, Mr. Ellis's secretary."

An image of the chatty woman came to her mind. "Oh, hello."

"Sorry it's taken me all week to call with your flight schedule. Rex finally gave me the dates he'll need the plane next week before he left for lunch."

Vera brought a hand to her forehead. "What day is

today?"

"Why it's Friday, dear." There was a pause on the line. "Are you all right?"

Vera remembered Rex's meeting with his PI. She checked her wristwatch but saw that its second hand wasn't moving. Unable to recall the last time she'd wound it, she swore under her breath. She leaned forward as far as the telephone cord allowed and strained to see the time on her kitchen clock. It was quarter to noon. Rex would be at lunch for the next hour. And Max's file was likely in his office.

"Um. Yes, I'm fine. Rex requested that I bring him the flight ledgers from the last six months. I completely forgot until now. I was just heading downtown. Could I bring them to his office?" Rex had never expected her to bring them to the bank. While she hated to give cause to any sexist notions, she hoped he would attribute her mistake to female incompetency.

"Oh, well I'm afraid I'm just heading out for my lunch break. How about after one o'clock?"

"I'd like to make sure Rex has them when he gets back from lunch. They're already late as it is. Could I leave them on your desk?"

"I don't—"

"I also have a few crime novels I wanted to loan you. I think you'll love the new Patricia Wentworth. I could leave those for you, too."

Vera held her breath as she waited for Silvia to respond.

"That's fine. I'll let Arnold, our elevator operator, know to send you up."

"Wonderful. Thank you."

Vera hung up and rushed upstairs to get dressed...hoping that Rex Ellis kept his office unlocked during the lunch hour.

Vera held the flight ledgers and her detective novels against her chest as she stepped inside the elaborate doors of the Maxwell Ellis Building. Even though she'd been to Pacific Bank before, she was struck by the opulence of the gold-leafed ceiling that arched three stories high above the lobby. The lunch hour lines for the tellers had been long, filled mostly with women. From their attire, Vera guessed many were Boeing workers. But there'd been no one waiting for the elevator when she found Arnold standing guard, dressed in a tailored three-piece suit with a matching bow tie, ready to take her upstairs to the executive offices.

She'd been ready to explain the reason behind her visit, but the older man spoke first.

"You must be Vera."

"Yes."

He'd flashed her a kind smile as he held the elevator doors open and motioned for her to step inside. She thanked him as the doors closed. Arnold pushed a bronze lever forward.

He turned to her as they started to ascend. "Silvia said you're the Ellises' new pilot."

"That's correct." She kept her tone pleasant but braced herself for whatever sexist comments might come next.

"You know, if there's one good thing about this damn war, it's that women are getting to prove they can do things that most men from my generation never believed that they could."

Vera met his gaze.

"And I think it's wonderful," he added.

"I agree." Vera smiled at the man, feeling at a loss for words at his forward-thinking remarks, when he pulled the lever back and the elevator slowed to a stop.

"Here we are." He extended his arm through the door opening. "The fifteenth floor. You'll find Silvia's desk down the hall to the left."

"Thank you." Vera turned to Arnold after stepping off the elevator. "And that was the smoothest elevator ride I've ever had."

He nodded as the doors began to close. "I guess thirty years of practice makes perfect. Imagine the planes you'll be flying thirty years from now."

Vera shrugged. "Planes will probably be flying themselves by then."

Arnold winked before the door closed. Vera was glad to see there was no one in the hallway as she moved past a gold-plated sign for the executive offices. *RUTH ELLIS, Chief Executive Officer* was printed in bold letters at the top. Beneath it, she found Rex and Vincent's names, along with a handful of others.

She strode beneath the crown molding, slowing when she reached a glass door on her right. She stopped in her tracks, seeing the name *RUTH ELLIS* etched across the glass. She dared a glance inside the office, though it made her heart race to think of the old woman catching her in this part of the bank.

But the corner office was empty. If you could even call it that. It was the size of the main level of her house. In her limited view of the space, Vera spotted a kitchenette, two sofas, and a coffee table, along with expansive views of the Seattle waterfront beyond the buildings below. She guessed it was bigger than the apartment she and Hugh shared before buying their home, though it was her understanding that Ruth Ellis hardly ever stepped foot in the bank.

She continued down the hall until she came to a large desk across from a frosted glass door. *Rex Ellis, Vice President* was etched in gold letters near the top. Vera set her small stack of novels on the edge of Silvia's desk and looked both ways down the long hallway.

The floor was quiet, and there was no one in sight. Vera gave a final glance at the elevator, making sure the doors had closed before she crept toward Rex's office. She put her ear to the door as she gripped the door handle. Hearing no noise from inside, she turned the handle.

The large office was empty. Vera closed the door gently behind her as she took in the mahogany desk in front of a window that offered a spectacular view of the Seattle shipyard beyond the base of the hill. A large clock above the window showed the time as 12:40. She didn't have long before Rex returned.

With the flight ledgers in hand, Vera hurried toward the desk, eyeing the bookshelves on the far wall as she went. The shelves were lined with leather-bound books, a signed baseball and mitt, and framed photographs. The largest of them was of Rex and President Roosevelt shaking hands.

The top of Rex's desk was immaculate. The only things on it were a name plate, an accounting ledger, and two framed photos: one of Ruth and one of a man she guessed was Rex's late father. She looked around the office for the briefcase she'd seen Rex carry, but it wasn't there. After setting the flight ledgers atop Rex's desk, she glanced at the door before opening the top drawer.

The drawer was nearly as tidy as the top of the desk. Vera flipped through a notepad before replacing it beside a silver Montblanc pen. She pulled open the next drawer. If Max's file was in his office, it had to be somewhere in this desk.

Vera lifted the recent edition of *Forbes* that lay on top only to find a copy of *Newsweek* beneath it, but nothing else. She shut the drawer and opened the one below it.

Her pulse quickened, seeing Max's file that Rex had retrieved from the plane. She lifted the tan folder. When she opened it, something slid out and fell onto her shoe. Vera set the folder on Rex's desk and lifted an envelope off the floor. She opened the Manila envelope and saw it contained a handful of photographs. Her heart skipped again as she withdrew the first photo, wondering if she were about to see an image of Howard Mills with a bullet in his head at Kinnear Park.

Her jaw dropped as she stared at the image. Priscilla sat on a park bench beside Howard Mills. A sinking feeling filled Vera's stomach as she pulled out another photograph. Priscilla was handing Howard a thick envelope. In the next photograph, Howard looked over his shoulder, away from the camera as he tucked the envelope into the inside pocket of his suit jacket. Vera flipped the photograph over. A date was written in the upper right corner: *September 18.* Three weeks before Max was abducted.

Voices from the hallway interrupted the questions that tumbled in her mind. She recognized Silvia's voice right outside of Rex's office door. Vera shoved the photographs inside the envelope and stuffed it into her purse as the door to Rex's office swung open.

She grappled for what she'd say to Silvia. She glanced at Max's file, knowing it was too late to put it back in the drawer. Hopefully, Silvia wouldn't recognize it.

She lifted her eyes to the open doorway, and her heart sank. It wasn't Silvia who glared at her.

It was Rex.

43

"What the hell are you doing?"

"I—" Vera stammered and moved away from the desk, praying Rex wouldn't see Max's file until she was out of his office. "I was just bringing those flight ledgers you asked me for."

Rex's eyes darted to Max's file atop his desk before he narrowed his eyes at Vera. "By sneaking into my office? The hell you were. I told you to bring them on our next flight!"

Before she could think of a response, Rex crossed the room and encircled his large hand around her arm.

"What do you think you're doing?" he hissed through gritted teeth.

As his fingers dug into her flesh, Vera felt a rush of fear travel down her spine. Surely, he wouldn't harm her in his office, with Silvia right outside. Would he?

"This is just a big misunderstanding." She fought to keep her voice level.

"Silvia!" Rex shouted, inches from Vera's face.

Silvia appeared in the doorway, and her wide eyes met

Vera's.

"Call security and have them hold Mrs. Chandler until the police get here," Rex said, keeping his eyes trained on Vera's. "I'll call them personally."

Silvia looked uncomfortably between Vera and her employer.

"*Now!*"

Silvia retreated toward her desk at Rex's booming command.

"You're fired. *And* you're going to jail."

Vera thought of the photographs in her suede handbag as Rex squeezed her arm tighter. She hadn't had time to zip it closed and hoped he wouldn't see the thick envelope she'd tucked inside. But she didn't dare look down to check.

"I know what Priscilla put you up to. But helping her was a big mistake."

Vera knew better than to deny it. "I was only trying to help find Max."

"Priscilla's crazy. You can't help her. If you knew what's good for you, you should've stayed out of my family's affairs." Rex brought his face within an inch of Vera's. "It would be a shame for Hugh to come back from war and no longer have a wife."

Rex was still gripping her arm when the elevator chimed its arrival. Through the open doorway, Vera watched two uniformed guards who looked like retired beat cops march down the hallway. Silvia stood from her desk and pointed them in Vera's direction.

Rex threw Vera toward them when they reached his office. She clung to her handbag which hung from shoulder, afraid the photographs might fly out as the guards each grabbed one of her arms. Silvia bit her lip, avoiding Vera's gaze as the guards led her back to the elevator.

"Take it easy, will you?" Arnold said when one of the guards shoved her inside the elevator. "She's the Ellises' pilot."

"We're just following orders. Mind your own business," the guard snapped back.

"You're hurting me!" Vera exclaimed, when Arnold brought the elevator to a stop on the first floor.

"You heard her," Arnold said, an air of authority in his voice. "Take it easy."

"Shut your trap," the guard snapped.

"This is *my* elevator."

In an instant, Vera pulled her arms out of their grasp. She slid behind Arnold as he took a step toward them. She pushed the lever forward as she'd seen Arnold do. As the elevator door opened, Vera jumped through the narrow gap.

She ran toward the busy lobby and snaked through the crowd of women workers. Straight ahead, she spotted two uniformed police enter the building.

"Hey! Stop that woman!" one of the guards shouted from behind her.

Several heads turned in the guard's direction as the two cops drew their weapons. A scream erupted from one of the bank patrons upon seeing the guns. Vera spun around and crashed into a man who'd been filling out a form at the central desk.

"Watch it!" he cried, grabbing his hat as it bounced off his head.

The police charged through the crowd as customers ran in opposite directions, some ducking to the floor with their hands covering their hands. Vera darted through the series of lines as bank patrons dispersed in a panic.

"That's her!" Vera heard the guard shout.

The police waved their pistols, searching the crowd for the woman they'd come to arrest, which was met with more screaming. Vera followed a group of panicked women out of the revolving doors, nearly tripping over her own feet after being propelled onto the sidewalk of 2nd Avenue.

Pedestrians slowed and gawked at the scene as the bank customers dispersed. Vera clung to her purse and took brisk steps away from the bank. A woman walking toward her pulled her young daughter close and steered her away from Vera, while giving Vera a cold stare. Vera looked up at the top floor, imagining Rex staring down at her as she pushed through a small crowd waiting patiently to cross the street.

Anger filled her chest as she pushed past the crowd to the other side. Walking alone now, it took all her willpower not to turn around and check if the police had come after her. Her steps quickened as she approached her car, rolling the images of Priscilla and Howard over in her mind. All this time she'd felt sorry for Priscilla and thought she was helping her. It made sense why Priscilla wanted to know what Rex's PI had found out.

Priscilla wasn't worried about her son. She was worried that she'd get caught in her own scheme. Vera climbed inside her Ford, still parked beside the meter two blocks from the bank. She slammed the driver's door shut and peeled out into the midday traffic.

She'd stuck her neck out for Priscilla. *And for what?* This whole time, she had tricked Vera into believing she was helpless and distraught over Max's abduction.

But she wasn't helpless at all. Priscilla Ellis had paid Howard Mills to kidnap her own son.

44

Priscilla lay her head back against her porcelain clawfoot tub. Holding the 1929 vintage Cabernet by the neck, she finished what was left in the bottle as Benny Carter's "Nightfall" played from her bathroom radio. She shivered as the acidic liquid ran down the back of her throat. She'd always hated the taste of wine. It had been six days since that dreadful night in Spokane, and two weeks since Max was taken from their home.

Dear God, what have I done?

She closed her eyes and sank lower into the now cool water as the midday sun shone through the corner window of her upstairs bathroom. At Vincent's demands, the FBI had come to their home yesterday with their latest update in Max's investigation. They now theorized there had been three people involved in Max's abduction: Howard and Gilbert Mills, and the person who killed them. But they had no leads on who that was.

They'd officially ruled Scarlet's death a suicide and determined she wasn't a party to Max's kidnapping. Given how long Max had been gone, and that the Ellises had not received another ransom note, the agents admitted that the probability of him being alive was slim. Before they left, it was clear they were all but closing his case.

The jazz song faded, and a male announcer came over the radio. "And now a brief break from these delightful melodies to bring you our daily war update. In the Pacific, it remains in question whether the Allies will be able to maintain control of Guadalcanal after the Japanese victory last month in the Battle of Savo Island, considered one of the worst naval defeats in U.S. history. The fight for control wages on, with the most recent loss of the carrier *USS Wasp*, torpedoed by a Japanese submarine on September fifteenth. The sea-lane between Guadalcanal and Florida Island has earned the nickname Ironbottom Sound by the Allies, owing to several warships and planes lying on the ocean floor. Japanese drives against the Allied ground forces on nearby islands continue to counter the American offensive in the Solomons...."

The announcer continued with news of the war in Europe, and Priscilla thought of Hugh, wondering if he was on his way to fight in Guadalcanal. Or perhaps he was already there. If only her biggest problem was the news of the country at war. The empty bottle suddenly felt heavy in her hand, and she released it into the water. The glass clinked against the porcelain tub.

She thought back to the weeks prior to Max's abduction. When the news of the war and the Ellises' threat of institutionalizing her seemed so horrific. A laugh escaped her lips as tears blurred her vision. How trivial that had been compared to this.

The bathroom door opened without a knock and Hattie appeared in the doorway. The radio announcement faded into a peppy Glenn Miller tune. Hattie's dirty blonde hair was pulled into a tight bun at the nape of her neck, making her appear older than her forty years. A few weeks ago, Priscilla would have snapped at the intrusion. But without a word, she watched Hattie close the door behind her and walk toward the tub.

Hattie lifted an opened bottle of wine and held it toward her.

"I've already had one," Priscilla said.

"I know."

Priscilla sighed before taking the bottle from her nanny's hands. Priscilla lifted it to her lips as Hattie knelt beside her on the marble floor.

"That's it," Hattie soothed, as she stroked Priscilla's hair. "It will make it easier."

Despite her normal revulsion toward the nanny, Hattie's touch felt strangely comforting.

"I'll hold you down if you want."

Priscilla shrank back from Hattie's touch and a short, desperate moan came from her lips.

"It would be an easy way to go," Hattie added, her voice soft. "Think of how much better you'd feel—all you'd be free from. You might even find Max on the other side."

Priscilla tore her eyes away from Hattie's and stared into the waist-deep water. Hattie's gentle touch returned to her hair. She leaned over and spoke into Priscilla's ear.

"It would save you from the horrors that await at the asylum. And the embarrassment. Imagine Max coming home one day—if he's still *alive*—and learning how his mother went crazy."

Priscilla felt Hattie's warm breath on her ear.

"It would haunt him. Think of your son. Think...."

Priscilla's chest heaved with sobs. Hattie took the wine

bottle from her hand before it spilled into the water.

"*Shh.*" Hattie patted her back. "There now. It will all be over soon."

Priscilla allowed her back to sink lower into the water.

"That's it," Hattie cooed.

There was a sharp rap on the bathroom door as the tepid water rose over Priscilla's nose. She lifted herself up, drawing in a breath.

"Excuse me, Mrs. Ellis. But you have a telephone call. It's Mrs. Chandler, your pilot. She says it's quite urgent."

Hattie's eyes shot daggers toward the sound of Gregory's voice coming from the hall. "Not now!"

There was a pause. "Should I tell her you'll ring her back?"

Priscilla stood from the tub. It had to be news of Max.

"I'm coming! Thank you, Gregory. Tell her to hold the line." She extended a dripping arm toward the towel rack. "Hattie, please fetch me my towel."

Hattie's thin lips pursed into a hard line. The softness from a moment ago was erased from her face.

"Yes, ma'am." She lowered her gaze to the tub water before turning to retrieve the towel.

45

Vera pressed her hat against her head as she waited for Priscilla on the upper deck of the *Leschi*, the steam ferry that ran from Madison Park to Kirkland. There were only a handful of other passengers on the afternoon crossing. Afraid the police might be waiting at her home, she'd driven around the city after fleeing the bank, in a rage over the photos she'd discovered. She nearly went to Priscilla's mansion, but thought better of it, unsure if Vincent knew about his wife's secret meeting with Howard Mills. And, Rex had likely called Vincent and told him what had happened at the bank.

She finally parked at a downtown hotel. After pacing the lobby for nearly an hour, Vera telephoned Priscilla and told her to meet her at the Lake Washington ferry. She didn't say why, only that it was urgent.

Vera glanced at her watch. The ferry was due to depart in five minutes. Beneath her, a ferry worker secured a chain behind the last car to drive on. Vera felt a fury build in her chest, thinking Priscilla wasn't going to show. That she'd been had for the second time.

There was only one thing those photographs could mean. Priscilla arranged for Howard to kidnap her son. *But why?* Vera was about to turn from the railing when she spotted Priscilla's Cadillac speed into a parking lot beside the ferry terminal.

Vera felt a spark of rage as she watched Priscilla get out of her car and head to the terminal ticket counter. All this time, as Hugh was preparing to fight in the Pacific, and Dari had given her life for the war effort, Vera thought she'd been helping a desperate mother find her abducted son. But she'd only been used by a woman too wealthy for her good.

She was glad Rex had fired her. Though she dreaded having to tell Hugh that he'd no longer have a job when he came home. After today, she never wanted to see any of the Ellis family again. All she could do was hope she'd be accepted into the WFTD. Priscilla could likely get Vera in with so much as a phone call, but Vera didn't need that kind of help ever again.

Priscilla trotted toward the ferry in her mink coat, boarding the boat seconds before the propellers rumbled to a start, vibrating the entire vessel. As Priscilla started up the stairs toward the passenger deck, Vera was surprised to see that her hair was damp, even though it hadn't rained all day. When Priscilla reached the upper deck, her red eyes locked with Vera's.

Aside from the mascara smudged beneath her eyes, Priscilla wore no makeup and was as disheveled as Vera had ever seen her. But this time she felt no pity.

"What is it?" She came to a stop beside Vera as they pulled away from the ferry terminal. "Please tell me you found *something*."

Vera assessed the woman who had deceived her,

wondering why Priscilla would bother asking for her help when she had orchestrated the crime.

Was she crazy? Vera thought of Priscilla's wealthy father, who'd gone insane before hanging himself at the Moore Mansion. The ferry horn blared, and Priscilla turned toward her.

"Tell me." Priscilla's eyes searched Vera's.

She inched closer to Vera, and Vera smelled wine on her breath.

"Is it bad news?"

Vera turned away and stared at the white wake behind the ferry as it increased in speed. She felt Priscilla's hand on her arm.

"Vera, please. Tell me now. I have to know."

She eyed Priscilla in confusion. She was either a very good actress or clinically insane, and right now, she was inclined to think the latter.

Vera pulled the envelope filled with photographs that she had found in Rex's office and thrust it at Priscilla's chest. "You tell me."

Priscilla's eyes widened as she opened the envelope. Vera watched her face turn pale when she withdrew the first photograph.

"Where did you find these?"

"In Rex's office at the bank." Vera watched Priscilla closely. "I broke in, as you asked me to."

Priscilla's hand trembled as she lifted another photograph from the envelope.

"So, where's Max? You must know."

"I *don't* know." Priscilla's voice was barely audible.

Vera furrowed her brows. *"You don't know?* But you plotted his kidnapping." She pointed her finger at the photographs in Priscilla's hand. "Don't you dare tell me that's not what this is!"

A young mother chased her squealing toddler as he ran in their direction.

Vera lowered her voice. "I'm not falling for any more of your lies."

Priscilla looked up with tears in her eyes. "Yes. I—I arranged for his kidnapping. But you must believe me—I have no idea where he is. Or whether he's even alive."

Vera shook her head. "This is ridiculous!"

A couple of heads turned toward them from the other side of the deck.

Vera leaned toward Priscilla. "I'm not helping you anymore. You've been playing me like a deck of cards this whole time. I risked my life to help you. I lost my job. You need to turn yourself in. Tell the police what you've done!"

"Wait. Please, you have to help me." Priscilla gripped Vera by both shoulders.

There was a crazed look in her eyes. Vera took a step back.

"You have no idea what the family will do to me now that they know what I've done. Before Max's abduction, they were planning to have me committed to Rainier Psychiatric Hospital—where I would never see Max again. The Ellises have always seen my eccentric father as an embarrassment. Then, when the press took a liking to my political activism, Vincent's mother decided I was outshining the Ellis family and putting them in a bad light. So, Ruth concocted a plan to have me institutionalized. Even got Vincent to go along with it. You don't understand—they'll go to any length to protect their fortune."

An American flag flapped in the wind above Priscilla's head at the front of the deck.

"Staging Max's kidnapping was the only move I had. But Max was supposed to be safely returned to us that night at the park. Howard was supposed to call the *Tribune* with an anonymous tip about the kidnapping after we left the house, so the reporters would be waiting when we arrived home, with Max in my arms. I'd hoped it would employ enough public sympathy to stop Ruth from having me committed and make Vincent see how much Max needed his mother." Her voice broke, and she cleared her throat. "It was only one lie. I never imagined it would turn into this. You must believe me. I have no idea who killed Howard or where Max is." She gripped Vera's shoulders tighter. "I'm begging you. Help me find my son."

Vera stepped out of Priscilla's hold. Whatever Priscilla's motivations had been, Vera had been used. And it had nearly cost her own life. She thought of Dari. If it weren't for Priscilla's 'favor,' she'd still be alive.

Vera gripped the railing with both hands and stared out at the lake as the boat neared the Kirkland terminal. While Priscilla had betrayed her, the woman was clearly in desperate straits.

"If you won't do it for me, please do it for Max," Priscilla added.

Vera's mind filled with the image of the sweet young boy on his *Missing* posters around the city. And now, she had no job, no husband at home, and not even Dari to talk to. Dari, who never backed down for fighting for what was right.

"You know, Priscilla, when you're flying a plane, even a single mistake can be fatal—all it takes is one. You must get it right the first time, or you might never have another chance."

"I'm sorry. I promise I'll be straight with you from here on out." She choked back a sob. "Please help me find my son."

Vera's eyes settled over the water.

"So, will you?"

The ferry docked, and cars began to drive off the lower deck past a group of commuters, probably from the Lake Washington Shipyard, waiting to board.

Vera faced Priscilla.   "On one condition. There can't be any more lies."

46

It was dark when Vera parked her Ford against the curb in front of her house. She'd circled the block before she parked, relieved and a little surprised the police weren't waiting for her. The entire drive home from the ferry terminal, her thoughts were consumed with Priscilla's role in Max's abduction. No wonder she'd been so desperate for Vera to learn what Rex's PI had discovered. Why she was so jumpy around her husband. She must have been terrified her criminal act would be discovered.

Vera wondered why Rex hadn't confronted Priscilla about it. He'd had those photos at least since Monday, when he met his PI before boarding the plane, probably before. How could he wait when Max's life hung in the balance?

Vera thought of Evie and the reporter who'd washed ashore after being thrown into the Sound inside a trunk. And Priscilla's excuse that the Ellises would send her away to the asylum. What would Ruth do to Priscilla when she found out what she'd done?

Vera felt inside her empty mailbox on her way into the

house. Despite what Hugh had said in his last letter, she couldn't help but hope to find a letter from him. She shook off the disappointment and went to unlock her front door. She stopped cold, seeing it was ajar. A chill crept up her back when she gripped the door handle, which hung loose from the door.

Vera glanced around her dark street before she cautiously pushed open the door and flicked on the light. The house was quiet, and she stepped inside, taking in the state of her home. The cushions and pillows from her living room couch were strewn across the floor. Her bookshelf was bare, her crime novels scattered on the hardwood beneath it. Every drawer of her secretary desk had been emptied of its contents, and a mess of papers was piled atop the desk. A mirror and framed photographs were smashed, leaving shards of glass all over the floor.

She stood still, noticing a light on at the top of the stairwell. She listened for a sign that the intruder was still in her home, but the house was quiet. She hadn't seen any strange cars parked on her street.

She thought of the envelope that was still inside her purse. Priscilla had given the photographs back to her on the ferry, since she couldn't dare take them home. Rex must've sent someone here to find them. *What if they came back?* Priscilla would go to prison if the photos got to the police, which was probably what Rex wanted.

Vera set her purse on the secretary desk and withdrew the envelope. After a quick look around, she took the photographs into the kitchen and set them inside the ice box.

When she returned to the living room, she stepped over the broken glass to the phone, relieved it didn't appear to have been tampered with. She lifted the receiver before

220

replacing it on the hook. She bit her lip, knowing that she should call the police. It was possible that Rex was only trying to scare her, or find out what else she knew, after catching her in his office at the bank. But if Priscilla was right about the Ellises having Seattle police on their payroll, then calling them might put her in more danger.

She turned away from the phone and turned on the nearby light before starting upstairs for Hugh's gun. She slowed when she reached her bedroom doorway. Her bedside lamp must have been the light she'd seen from downstairs. The drawers of the dresser were open, and her underwear and stockings had been emptied into a messy heap on the floor. The bed had been stripped down to the mattress. But none of that bothered her as much as her bare nightstand, where she'd been keeping Hugh's revolver since she'd been nearly run off the road.

She stepped over the pile of bedding at the end of the bed and opened her nightstand drawer. Aside from the latest edition of *LIFE*, it was empty. She slammed the drawer closed and looked around the room. Whoever did this had taken the gun with them.

Vera stiffened, hearing the soft tick of two hangers knocking together from inside her closet. She stared at the closed closet door as her heart thumped against her ribs. The closet was between her and the bedroom doorway, but she ran past it anyway as the door flew open.

She heard heavy footsteps behind her when she reached the hall. She turned for the stairs, but something caught around her neck, propelling her backward as it tightened around her throat. Her hands flew to her neck, but she struggled to get her fingers between the silky fabric and her skin.

Out the corner of her eye, she spotted the sleeves of a

man's tweed suit jacket as he tightened the grip around her throat. She coughed from the constriction to her airway. She dug her nails into her skin as pressure built inside her head, but her attacker pulled the fabric even more taut around her neck.

Vera jabbed her elbow into her assailant. Hearing him grunt, she did it again with as much force as she could muster. She kicked her heel into his shin, and his grip behind her neck loosened enough for her to grab one of his hands. She brought it to her mouth and sank her teeth into his palm.

"Ahh!"

She tasted blood before her attacker pulled his hand out of her mouth. As soon as his hand was free, she threw herself forward. She gasped for air when she landed in a heap at the top of the stairwell, pulling at the fabric wrapped around her neck. She tossed it over the banister, realizing it was one of Hugh's neckties.

The man charged toward her as she got to her knees, and Vera recognized the burly man as Rex's PI. His thick hands reached for her throat. She clawed at his face while she struggled to her feet. He snarled as his fingers completely encircled her neck. Vera pushed her thumb into his eye socket as she fought the urge to pass out from her lack of oxygen.

The man shook her hand away from his face as Vera's strength was drained from her body. She blinked as her vision grew blurry, knowing she only had a few more seconds of fight left in her. A smile reached the edges of the PI's mouth, and Vera felt a surge of energy from the rage he triggered inside her. She gritted her teeth and slammed her forehead into his nose.

The PI's head snapped backward, and his hands dropped

from Vera's neck. She jumped away from him and fell through the air, landing on the stairs halfway down. She moaned as her body bumped and rolled down each step until she slammed into the wall at the bottom.

She scrambled to her feet as the man started down the stairs. Blood oozed from his nose, and his earlier smirk was replaced with a hateful sneer. A wheeze sounded from her aching throat as she sucked in a deep breath. The room around her spun, and she pressed her hand against the wall. There was no way she could reach her front door, let alone her car, before he caught her.

She lifted the earpiece of her telephone above her head as the PI charged toward her down the steps.

"Operator! Operator!"

The man ripped the receiver from her hand and slammed it back on the hook. He raised his other hand in the air, holding Hugh's revolver in his grip. Vera lifted her arms in front of her face as she looked into the barrel that was aimed at her head.

"Please—"

A fist banged against her front door. She heard whistling coming from her porch as the PI's eyes darted toward the sound. Another knock.

"Who's that?" the PI hissed.

"Mrs. Chandler?"

She recognized the high-pitched voice of her newspaper delivery boy.

"I'm here for your weekly collection fee!"

The PI swung the revolver toward the movement outside her front window.

"Please!" Vera held out her hand. "He's just a child."

"Mrs. Chandler?"

Vera thought to call out and tell the boy to run for help.

But out of the corner of her eye, Vera saw the muscular man raise the gun above his head. Before she could react, the PI slammed the butt of Hugh's revolver against her skull and her world faded to black.

47

Vera woke to a razor-sharp throbbing in her head. Her eyes adjusted to her surroundings as she recalled her struggle with the brawny PI. She felt cold, and her house was dark aside from the faint light from her upstairs bedroom. She winced as she pushed herself to her feet and felt for the telephone that hung on the wall. She'd have to take her chances that the police would be on her side.

She tore the earpiece from the hook and pressed it to her ear. "Operator, I need the police."

She was met with silence. "Operator?"

Vera depressed the hook on the wall and let it go. "Operator!"

But there was nothing, not even static. As she went to replace the earpiece, she spotted the frayed wires sticking out from the severed telephone cord. She brought her hand to the back of her head. Feeling the tender bump from the PI's blow, she winced.

She remembered the newspaper boy and hurried across the room and opened her front door. She exhaled. There was no sign of the kid or his bicycle.

Her mouth was dry, and she went into the kitchen, which felt colder than the rest of the house. She turned on the light and saw that her back door was ajar.

Several cupboards were open, and her silverware had been dumped all over the counter. She opened the ice box, relieved to find the photographs still inside. After closing her back door and filling a glass with water, she spotted the envelope from Dari among the cutlery. She slid the silverware aside, looking for Dari's letter. But it wasn't on the counter. Vera's eyes scoured the rest of the kitchen, scanning the counters and floor for the letter.

She checked the wastebasket and recognized Dari's handwriting lying atop the trash. Vera pulled out the letter, which had been ripped in half and stained from coffee grounds.

She clenched her jaw at Dari's final words to her, which were now practically indecipherable. She pressed the letter onto the counter and smoothed the tattered paper as best she could.

Rex hadn't just wanted to scare her by sending his PI to her house. She had no doubt the brute would have killed her if it wasn't for the newspaper boy's interruption. She thought of Hattie, who likely snooped on the phone call to Priscilla before they met on the ferry.

Vera took one last look at Dari's tattered letter before she grabbed the photos from the ice box. She found her purse still on the secretary desk with its contents spilled out around it. She gathered the items and tossed them back inside, along with the cold envelope, and stormed outside toward her car. If Rex thought he could get her to back down, he was wrong.

Her street remained quiet and dark aside from a few

streetlamps that lined the road. She imagined her neighbors soundly asleep in their beds, oblivious to Vera's break-in and subsequent attack.

When she reached for the door handle, her fingers grazed the side window. She bent over to grip the handle, realizing her Ford was several inches lower to the ground than it normally sat. She pulled open the driver's door, which scraped across the sidewalk.

Vera took a step back, assessing her tires in the dim light of a nearby streetlamp. From what she could tell, they appeared completely flat. She crouched down and pushed her hand against the tire, which was devoid of air. She ran her hand along the rubber until her fingers reached a long slit.

She moved to the other side of her car, only to find a similar puncture. She swung her head toward their detached garage at the back of the house, then quickly jogged to the side door. She pulled the string connected to the light bulb hanging from the ceiling. In the small space, it took only a moment to find what she was looking for.

She strode toward the tall wooden gun cabinet that had belonged to Hugh's uncle. He had passed away before they were married, but had left the cabinet to Hugh, along with a hunting rifle and his Colt pistol he'd smuggled home from the Great War. Vera bent down, opened the cabinet drawer, and withdrew the pistol. *Model of 1911* was engraved across the side of the barrel.

She released the magazine as she'd seen her father do countless times at the kitchen table throughout his career in law enforcement. It wasn't loaded, but there was a small box of ammunition next to the gun. She reached inside and fed eight bullets into the magazine before replacing it. After pulling back on the slide to chamber a round, she pushed the hammer to the half-cock position and flicked on the safety. She tucked the firearm into her purse, turned off the garage light, and started down the street. The Ballard Police station couldn't be more than two miles away.

Vera walked as fast as her heeled pumps would allow, fueled with adrenaline from her earlier attack. She turned off her street and headed for the waterfront, her anger growing with each step. She started down the last mile to the police station, deciding to tell them everything she knew. She could easily identify the man who'd been inside her home.

She slowed her pace along the dark street. *But then what?* Would they honestly believe that Rex Ellis, the heir of Pacific Bank, was behind this?

And even if they did believe her, could they do anything about it?

She heard a car engine slow to an idle beside her, and she felt inside her purse for the pistol as she shot a glance at the car. She brought a hand to her chest as she exhaled, seeing the lit-up *TAXI* sign on its roof. The driver leaned over and rolled down the passenger window.

"You need a lift, miss?"

Vera glanced around the dark street, wondering what the chances were that Rex's PI was following her.

She opened the cab's rear door. "Yes. To the Ballard Police station."

"You got it." The gray-haired driver eyed her from his rearview mirror. "You in some kind of trouble?"

Vera looked out the window as they drove slowly through Ballard's town center. What would happen to Priscilla after she went to the police? Would they ever find Max?

In the backseat, she wondered how long Rex had known

about Priscilla's arrangement with Howard Mills. The driver slowed as they neared the police department. Vera thought about her secretary desk, emptied of all its contents. What was Rex so worried that she had discovered in his office?

The taxi came to a stop in front of the Ballard Police Department's lit-up sign. "Here we are, miss."

"Actually, never mind. Take me to upper Queen Anne."

Her driver turned around. "You sure, miss? The police are right inside."

"I'm sure. Drop me on the corner of Prospect and Kinnear."

48

At the top of Queen Anne hill, Vera spotted the lights of Ruth Ellis's mansion that overlooked Vincent and Priscilla's a few streets below.

"This is good. You can drop me here."

The driver whistled as he slowed the cab to a stop. Vera checked her wristwatch. It was nearly midnight.

"Can't say I've ever driven anyone up to this part of the city before." He turned in his seat. "Are you sure you're all right? Maybe we should head back to that police station and let them sort out whatever you're mixed up in."

"I'm fine." Vera handed him two dollar bills and climbed out of the taxi, thinking that a big tip would stop his questions from coming.

He rolled down the side window as she walked past the car. "You know someone up here?"

Vera stopped and let out an exacerbated sigh. "I told you. I'm fine. Just going to see a friend. Thank you for the ride, but now leave me alone."

"Just tryin' to help, miss. I know trouble when I see it."

Vera waved her purse at him, and the cab pulled away. She waited until it turned down the hill before she climbed up the steep concrete stairs that looked to lead to the Ellises' private drive. At the top, she stepped onto a cobblestone street and walked the rest of the hill to the enormous home. She slowed when she neared the front gate.

Beyond it, a towering brick mansion made Priscilla's look like a modest home. The front porch lights were on, along with several decorative lampposts lining the lawn's perimeter, but Vera was far enough away to stay in the shadows. *If the Japanese wanted to bomb the Ellis compound, it certainly wouldn't be hard to find.* She took a deep breath and hoisted herself over the wrought-iron gate. A dog barked, and she paused, her legs straddling the gate.

She held her breath as she scanned the grounds of the Ellis estate, envisioning an attack dog racing toward her through the immaculate lawn. The bark sounded again, and Vera exhaled. The animal's cry was too distant to be coming from the Ellises' place.

She swung her other leg over the fence, hearing her skirt tear before her feet landed on the driveway. She ran her hand down her side, feeling the slit in her skirt's fabric, wishing she had worn trousers. She crept past the pristinely trimmed hedges and imported palm trees that lined the lawn, careful to stay far enough from the house so as not to be seen.

As she came to a statue that towered above a large fountain, she noticed a light shone from inside one of the second-story windows. *Had it just come on?* It was past midnight now, and she hadn't anticipated either of the Ellises to be awake. She moved around the side of the house, which was dark aside from a single lamppost at the edge of the lawn. Although maybe the light was just left on. The

Ellises were not exactly fretting the electric bill.

Vera stopped at the first window she came to, pressed her hands against the glass, and pushed upward. It didn't budge. She moved to the next window but was met with the same result. When she came to a set of French doors, she tried both handles, which were locked. She swore under her breath. She'd been so furious after being attacked that she failed to think through how she would get inside the house.

She took a step back and looked up at the huge home. If she broke a window, it would no doubt alert them. She continued across the back of the mansion, trying every window she came to. She rounded the corner, surprised to see a light coming from one of the first-floor windows.

Vera quietly scrambled toward the window frame. There was no mistaking that someone was still up. When she got close, she spotted Rex, a drink in his hand, standing only a few feet from the window. Instinctively, she crouched down. She placed a hand over her hammering heart, assuring herself it was far too dark out for Rex to have seen her. She leaned her back to the home's exterior, and something hard protruded against her spine.

She pivoted on her heels and ran her hand over the wall. The rough bricks changed to something smooth and cold. It had to be metal. Her fingers closed around a handle, which must have been what she felt against her back.

A coal chute. The home was at least twenty years old, maybe older. Of course, it had a coal chute. Although many homes now burned fuel oil instead of coal, it was possible the Ellises still used coal—or at least hadn't sealed up their chute.

She gripped the handle and pulled. With a groan, the small heavy door lifted. Vera glanced up at the window, waiting for a sign that Rex had heard the noise. When he took a sip of his drink, she tucked her legs inside the chute, which felt just wide enough for her to squeeze through. She scooted toward the edge of the chute and pushed herself down the slope into the darkness before she had a chance to think twice.

She landed with a thud at the bottom of a coal bin. She sat up slowly and pushed herself to her feet atop a thick layer of coal. Wincing from the raw scrapes on her hands, she dusted herself off after climbing out of the brick bin. She put her hands out in front as she struggled to adjust her eyes to the dark space, wishing she had something she could use as a flashlight. Though Rex didn't seem as if he heard her open the coal chute, she couldn't be sure about her catapult into the basement.

She waved her hands through the air in front of her in search of a dangling light bulb string. Instead, she felt a cold concrete wall and followed alongside it until she spotted a light coming from beneath a door at the top of a nearby staircase. She climbed up the steps on the balls of her feet so her heels wouldn't clack against the wood. When she reached the top, she pressed her ear to the door. After a moment of silence, she opened the door and stepped out onto the main floor of the Ellis mansion.

She recognized Rex's deep voice coming from one side of the house, and she tiptoed down a corridor along a set of tall, arched windows until she reached a staircase. From this spot, she noticed light coming from the room down the hall where she had seen Rex from outside.

"So, he left her *alive*?"

Vera stopped in her tracks at the base of the stairs, recognizing the Ellis matriarch.

"I told you, Mother, he was spotted by a newspaper boy. What was he going to do? Kill her right in front of a witness?

She'll be arrested tomorrow. And she doesn't have a thing on us."

"She has the photographs, Rex! That's bad enough. I don't want that getting out."

Vera gripped the banister.

"Think of how it would reflect on the family," the old woman continued. "It would look much better that Priscilla goes crazy due to Max's kidnapping. The public will sympathize."

A light came on in the corridor behind her as footsteps came toward her. Vera spun around. She had only seconds before the person came into her view. With no time to think, she hurried up the stairs. She didn't turn around until she reached the top of the staircase and watched a middle-aged woman in a maid's uniform stride toward the room where Rex and Ruth were talking.

"Excuse me, madam. Are you ready for me to help you upstairs?"

"A few more minutes, Nessie."

Vera retreated into the upstairs hallway as the housemaid returned down the corridor from where she had come. Light spilled from a door ajar farther down the hall. Vera moved toward it and peered in, making sure it was unoccupied before she stepped inside the room.

Against the far wall of the large room was a four-poster bed with pale satin bedcoverings that had already been turned down. There was a mirrored dressing table to her right, across from a fireplace flanked with two over-stuffed chairs. But it was the desk in the corner that Vera moved toward.

She glanced behind her before reaching over the monogrammed stationery and letter opener, lifting the small stack of mail from the desk. She flipped through the envelopes, pausing when she saw a return address from Rainier Psychiatric Hospital. She withdrew the paper from inside and saw that it was a bill. For a patient named Edith Hamilton.

Vera racked her brain but was sure she'd never heard the name before. She cast another look behind her and continued reading. *Admission date: March 30, 1942. Diagnosis: Delusional Disorder.* She scanned the list of ongoing treatments, which included electroshock and several medications she'd never heard of.

Vera slid the envelope into her purse beside the gun, knowing Ruth and her maid would be up any minute. She'd have to ask Priscilla who Edith Hamilton was. And why Ruth was paying for her treatment.

There were still murmurs coming from the room off the stairs as Vera descended the steps. When she got to the bottom, she crept toward the sound of Ruth's gravelly voice, pressing her back against the wall outside the room.

"I don't like it," she said. "Priscilla will be immediately arrested. Imagine how that would look."

Vera heard Ruth's cane hit the hardwood floor.

"We won't keep this secret much longer," Ruth continued. "Not with that Chandler girl holding those photographs."

"Mother, I will get the damn photos back, one way or another. I will personally—"

"But I can't trust that you will, son."

"What are you saying?"

"You know what I'm saying."

The room went quiet. Vera worked to keep as silent.

"Have Hattie do it," Ruth added.

"How?"

"Tell her to slip a few of those sedatives our doctor

prescribed for Priscilla into her drink. She better make it several to be safe. Priscilla's too distraught to question it. Once she's out of the picture, along with the Chandler girl, this mess will all be over."

Vera pressed her palms against the wall behind her. She had to warn Priscilla. She could get another cab to Lily's and Dari's apartment, then she'd call Priscilla first thing.

The crack of Ruth's cane in the doorway beside her tore Vera from her thoughts.

"Nessie! I'm ready."

Vera turned toward the doorway beside her. One more step, and Ruth would be staring her in the face.

49

Vera stepped as far to the left as her skirt allowed, feeling the wall with her hands behind her. She took another step and this time felt a door behind her. She reached for the handle as the tip of Ruth's cane came into view and beat against the marble tile in front of the doorway.

Nessie's footsteps started down the corridor in their direction. Vera kept her eyes on Ruth's cane as it lifted off the floor. Just before it hit the marble, Vera twisted the handle. She slid into the room behind her, praying the sound of the door opening had been covered by the clack of Ruth's cane.

She left the door open a crack as Nessie's footsteps grew louder, and Ruth shuffled away from the adjacent room. Vera turned in the dark space, wondering what it contained. She stepped farther inside the room, hearing Ruth and Nessie start up the stairs. Her legs collided with something waist high, and she fell forward. Her torso landed on something round, which spun beneath her hands when she tried to push herself up.

She felt around and, using a chair to her right, managed to stand up straight. She didn't move for a moment, waiting to hear if she'd been discovered. But she could only make out the faint voices of Ruth and her housemaid from upstairs.

As her eyes adjusted to the light, she spotted a desk in front of the window with a lamp sitting on it. Vera crossed the room and pulled the lamp cord. She scanned her surroundings. *Rex's study.*

Her eyes rested on what she had fallen over a moment ago. Why anyone needed a globe that big was beyond her. Vera focused her attention on Rex's desk, and why she had come. She rifled through the drawers as quietly as she could. They weren't quite as bare as the ones in his office at the bank, but she couldn't find anything that seemed connected to Max.

There was only one drawer to go. She pulled it open and found a single bank statement from Pacific Bank, the balance containing an astonishing number of digits. She closed the drawer and looked around.

She moved toward a wastebasket beside the desk. She lifted a receipt from Vito's and a couple of scrunched up memos from the small pile of trash. At the bottom was an empty matchbook and packet of Luckies, along with a few more crumpled pieces of paper. Vera crouched down and unfolded the small balls of paper, seeing they were receipts. One was for a pack of cigarettes, and the second from a gas station in Centralia, just north of where Vera had grown up.

She was about to toss the receipt back into the basket, disgusted for going through Rex Ellis's garbage, when she saw it was dated October 9. The night Max went missing.

"Rex!"

Ruth's voice resounded from the top of the stairs. Vera

238

stuffed the receipt into her purse when she heard Rex step out of the next room.

"What is it, Mother?"

Vera froze. He was right outside the door to his study. She stared at the door, hoping he didn't notice the light coming through the crack.

"Call Hattie and have her do it tonight. I'll sleep better knowing it's taken care of."

Rex sighed. "All right."

Vera turned to the window. She had to try to warn Priscilla somehow. And she was only a few blocks away. As soon as she heard Rex move away from the door, Vera leaned over to turn off the lamp.

But she'd forgotten about the pistol in her purse, which clanged loudly against the wooden desk. Rex's footsteps stopped. Vera had just unlocked the window when the door to Rex's study flew open. The room flooded with light.

Rex sneered. "*You!* How the hell did you get into my house?"

Vera pushed the window open, and a cold breeze blew into the room.

He charged toward her, his pointer finger outstretched toward her face. "Stay where you are!"

She dug the pistol out of her purse and pointed it at Rex. Rex slowed, but he didn't stop.

"Nessie!" he called over his shoulder. "Call the police! I've caught an intruder!"

Vera used her thumb to pull down the hammer and flicked off the safety. She waved him back with the gun. "Don't come any closer."

"An *intruder!*" Ruth exclaimed. "Rex?"

Rex continued toward her but put his hands in the air. He turned his head over his shoulder. "It's all right, Mother. I

239

have it handled." Turning to Vera, a smile crept over his lips. "You won't shoot me. You'd be hanged for it."

Keeping the gun aimed at his chest, Vera sat back onto the windowsill and lifted a leg over the side. Rex reached the desk and extended his hand.

"Give me the gun, Vera."

"What have you done with Max?"

He lunged over his desk for the gun. Vera fired a warning shot into the mahogany. The smell of gunpowder filled the air, and Vera's ears rang from the shot.

Rex reflexively brought his hands to his face at the sound of the blast as tiny wood chips burst into the air, giving Vera just enough time to escape out the window. And run.

50

Vera flew down the steep concrete steps to the street below.

"Vera!" she heard Rex shout from the window of his study.

A dog barked from a neighboring home, followed by another. When she reached the pavement, she raced down the hill as fast as her heels would go. After a block, the outside lights of Priscilla's white mansion came into her view. She raced down the next street and saw a light come on inside the third story of Priscilla's house.

She was less than a block away when she heard a siren coming up the hill. She ran faster as the wail of the police car grew closer. She'd reached the neighboring property to Priscilla's when the patrol car turned onto Priscilla's street, the strobe of its flashing light causing Vera to squint.

Vera ducked behind a hedge, her heart hammering against her ribs, as the cop car sped up the hill toward Rex's mansion. Vera peered over the hedge and waited for the car to turn up Rex's drive before she sprinted toward Priscilla's house. She hopped the gate just as she'd done at Rex's mansion.

She'd nearly crossed the lawn when headlights lit up the dark neighborhood street. She turned to see a dark car speeding down the hill, before rounding the corner of the house. A light was on beyond the double doors of the second-floor balcony, in what Vera presumed was Priscilla's room.

The hum of the car's engine grew closer as Vera stared up at the white pillars that supported the balcony above. She scanned the area beneath the porch lights for something she could throw against Priscilla's balcony doors. The pillars were flanked with potted shrubs, and the planters came up to Vera's hips. Hearing Rex's car pull up to the front gate, she stepped into one of the pots, her heels sinking into the damp soil. She grabbed hold of the iron porch light, willing it to support her weight, as she lifted her leg toward the balcony.

Her sole slid off the balcony's edge and her feet dangled in the air before she swung her leg up again, this time flexing her foot to catch around the ornate railing. She lifted her other leg and crossed her ankles around the railing before moving one hand from the porchlight to the balustrade and then the other. With a grunt, she heaved her body over the side, landing in a heap atop the hard tiles of the balcony. Ignoring the pain radiating through her knee, she pulled herself to her feet and put her ear to one of the French doors.

Sheer white curtains covered the glass, but Vera could make out movement inside. She raised her hand to the glass and tapped. Her heart drummed wildly in her chest as a figure came toward the door. She could only hope Vincent wasn't in the room, as well.

The doorbell chimed from below. Vera tapped on the door again. She watched as Priscilla looked to the direction of the doorbell and then back to the balcony. With caution, she approached the French doors, and the door opened a crack.

"Priscilla!" she whispered.

"Vera?" She opened the door wider, exposing her sheer black negligee and satin nightgown. "What on earth are you doing?"

"*Shh!*" Vera brought a hand up, hearing someone approach the bedroom door.

A sharp knock sounded against Priscilla's door. "Priscilla? I brought you something to help you sleep."

Hattie. Priscilla turned toward the nanny's voice.

Vera stepped inside the doorframe and took hold of Priscilla's shoulder. "I just came from Rex's house."

Priscilla looked confused. "Rex's ho—"

"I don't have time to explain," she whispered.

"Good grief, what happened to you?"

Vera looked at her torn skirt, filthy from the coal chute, along with her soot-covered hands. From Priscilla's wide eyes, Vera guessed her face hadn't fared much better.

The knock came again, only louder. "Priscilla!"

Priscilla stepped back. "Let me just see what she wants."

Another knock.

Vera grabbed her wrist. "Don't take anything Hattie gives you!" She lowered her voice, realizing she'd spoken too loud. "You're in danger and you need to get out of this house."

The knocking ceased, and Vera heard the creak of the front door opening from below.

"What are you doing here?" Vincent slurred from the downstairs porch. His voice echoed through the foyer. "It's after twelve. You're not one to stay out late, are you, Rex ol' boy?"

"Where is she?" Rex demanded.

"What? Priscilla, she's up—"

"The pilot!"

"What are you talking about?"

The front door slammed, and Vera gripped Priscilla by the shoulders. "I'll explain later, but right now you need to come with me."

"Where's Priscilla?" Rex's angry voice sounded up the stairs.

"Let's go." Vera stepped onto the balcony and Priscilla followed, closing the door behind them.

Priscilla shook her head as she watched Vera swing her leg over the banister. "I don't know about this...."

"You have to trust me." Vera let her feet hang before she dropped to the ground. "Hurry!"

Priscilla glanced back toward her room before climbing over the railing. Vera heard voices from inside.

"Now jump!" she whispered.

Priscilla let go and landed on the cobblestone with her bare feet as the door to her balcony opened. Vera grabbed Priscilla's arm and pulled her beneath the balcony.

"I swear I just heard her," Hattie said from above. "It sounded like she was talking to someone."

Priscilla gawked at Vera as they stood frozen still, their backs pressed against the siding.

"They can't have gone far," Rex said. They were all now standing on the balcony above.

A red flashing light from the driveway illuminated the front lawn.

"Are you going to tell me what's happening?" Vincent shouted. "Why are you looking for our *pilot* in the middle of the night?"

"It's nothing, Vincent, don't worry."

"What the hell's going on, Rex? Where has my wife gone to?"

"Hattie, why don't you take Vincent inside, now? The police are here. We'll let them find her. They can't have gone far."

The women stared at each other as the voices retreated inside the house. Priscilla pointed toward the rear of the mansion.

"This way," she mouthed.

Vera nodded and took off after Priscilla, who ran toward a narrow alleyway behind the home. Water sloshed her legs as Vera sprinted through a puddle. They had nearly reached the end of the lane when headlights lit up the dark street from behind them.

51

The beam of the headlights grew brighter, but Vera didn't dare turn around. She grabbed Priscilla by the hand and pulled her through a backyard beside the alleyway. They dodged a clothesline and rounded the side of a house.

"Stop where you are!"

A flashlight shone in their direction as a barking dog ran through the yard.

"Whoa, whoa. Easy now," the copper placated, his flashlight waving from side to side, as the barking grew louder and more incessant.

Lights came on from inside the home, but Vera and Priscilla had already reached the street. They continued down the hill, and Priscilla turned right when they came to a major cross street.

"There's an apartment building down this way," she panted.

Vera followed, ignoring the burn in her lungs, until they reached The Greenbelt Apartments. Priscilla opened the door, which was thankfully unlocked. Vera watched a squad car cruise down the hill in their direction before she followed her into the lobby.

The entrance to the apartment building was unlit, aside from the streetlights outside, which cast a soft glow around the small space. Vera made out an empty desk against the wall and a telephone booth beside the stairwell.

Priscilla turned to her after the door closed behind them. "Are you going to tell me why you dragged me out of my house in the middle of the night?"

"After I broke into Ruth and Rex's house—"

"You *what?*"

"I overheard Ruth telling Rex to have Hattie mix sleeping pills into your drink—enough that you'd overdose. And it would look like an accident." Vera shrugged. "Or suicide."

"They were going to kill me?" Priscilla sank against the wall.

Vera nodded. "I'm afraid so."

"So, what do we do now? We can't hide in here forever. If they want me dead, there's nothing I can do to stop them." Priscilla stared at the empty desk on the far wall. "I was hoping you had news of Max."

"They want me dead, that's for sure."

"No, Vera."

"Listen to me, Priscilla. Before I had to shoot my way out of that house—"

"*What?* Did you hit someone?"

"Just Rex's mahogany desk."

Priscilla laughed, and for moment, Vera joined her.

"After we met on the ferry, I went home to find my entire house ransacked."

"Oh, Vera. You don't think that—"

"I don't have to *think*, Priscilla. Rex's PI was in my house! He was hiding in my bedroom closet and nearly strangled

247

the life out of me."

Priscilla covered her mouth with her hand.

"He had a gun in my face, ready to shoot me dead. Then my newspaper boy came to collect, knocked on the door, and scared the goon away. He socked me cold before he escaped." Vera pointed to the door. "He's still out there, somewhere."

Priscilla's eyes followed the direction of Vera's hand. She shuddered. "I should have never, ever gotten you into this. This madness…."

"Here's what's mad. *You* sent me into that bank to find evidence. Now, Rex and Ruth want those photographs of you and Howard Mills. They can't have them leaked to the press."

"Oh, right, what would the public think?"

"Exactly what Ruth said—you know your mother-in-law very well."

"Too well. She would rather have me dead than an embarrassment to the family."

"If Rex's PI took those photos of you and Howard, then Rex would've known about your scheme to stage Max's kidnapping for weeks before it happened."

Priscilla remained quiet, thinking it over.

"And Hattie knew Max was kidnapped, and that you were going to Kinnear Park at midnight to retrieve him, right?"

Priscilla drew in a short breath. "Yes."

"So, maybe Rex decided to intercept your plan. I can't imagine he'd allow you to make that kind of power play against the family after he learned of it."

Priscilla raised a hand to her face. "If Rex knew…that would mean that Max is *alive*. Right?"

"Let me show you something I found before Rex caught

me going through his study. Could be nothing, but...." Vera dug around inside her purse in the dim light. "It's in here somewhere. Here, hold this." She held the pistol out toward Priscilla.

"Oh, I don't—"

"It's fine, just hold it."

Priscilla reluctantly took the gun from Vera's hand.

Vera reached back into her handbag. "It's a gas station receipt from Centralia, from the night Max was taken. I fished it out from the bottom of Rex's wastebasket."

Priscilla took a step toward Vera. "Vincent has a cousin who lives in Chehalis. We visited them once when I was pregnant with Max. That's close to Centralia, right?"

"I grew up in Chehalis. Those two towns are only a few miles apart."

"The cousin has a farmhouse there. What if it's where they're keeping Max?"

"*Shh!*" Vera tilted her head, afraid Priscilla might have woken the tenants sleeping above them. "Okay." She paced back and forth. "We'll go there. But we can't take my car. Rex's PI slashed my tires."

"Does Rex know you found the receipt?"

"No, I put it in my purse before I escaped." Vera lifted her purse toward the lights from the street and rummaged through the bottom. Her fingers closed around a folded piece of paper. "Here it is."

She lifted it up triumphantly, only to discover it was Opal's phone number written on a scrap piece of paper.

"It's not here." She looked up at Priscilla. "I thought I took it with me. But it must've fallen out when I reached for Hugh's gun."

Priscilla groaned. "Then Rex could be on his way there right now! What if he calls his cousin and tells him to move

Max somewhere else?"

Vera strode toward the telephone booth. "I'll call my friend to come pick us up. You keep watch while I make the call. And for goodness sakes, *keep quiet!*"

She turned on the light in the telephone booth just long enough to read Opal's number and dial it.

"Come on, pick up…" Vera murmured after the third ring.

"Hello…?"

She sank with relief hearing Opal's groggy voice. "Opal, thank God! It's Vera. I'm in trouble and I need your help. Can you come pick me up?"

"Of course. I'll be right there. Are you okay?"

"I'm fine, but I'm not at home. Come to a brick apartment complex called The Greenbelt. It's just off Mercer Street, heading up Queen Anne hill. But make sure there's no police cars out front. I'm with Priscilla Ellis, and we think we know where her son is."

Opal drew in a sharp breath. *"You do? Where?* Okay, never mind—hang tight. I'll be there in twenty."

The door to the apartment building swung open when Vera stepped out of the booth. Priscilla retreated toward the booth, but it was too late. The stranger had already spotted her. He wore dark coveralls, with a metal lunch pail tucked under his arm.

"Oh, pardon me," he said, as Priscilla stepped out of his path, tucking Hugh's gun behind her back.

His eyes traveled to her negligee before it settled on Vera when she came up behind her. "You gals all right?"

Vera glanced at Priscilla. She could only imagine what her hair looked like, not to mention everything else. Priscilla gasped, and Vera followed her stare to the front window, where Rex's PI was striding toward the door.

She grabbed Priscilla's hand and brushed past the man. They'd no sooner ducked behind the front desk when she heard the PI's gruff voice.

"You seen a couple of dames come through here?"

Vera watched the stranger with pleading eyes as Priscilla squeezed her hand so tight it hurt.

The man shook his head. "Sorry. Not in here."

"If you do, call the police. They're lookin' for 'em."

"Sure thing."

The women waited a moment after hearing the door close, before lifting their heads above the desk.

"Don't worry. He's gone," the man said in a lowered voice, shifting his lunch pail to his other arm.

"Thank you," Vera whispered.

"You're welcome. Hope you gals got a good reason to be hidin' from the cops."

Vera stepped out from behind the desk and nodded to Priscilla. "We do."

52

Vera and Priscilla waited until Opal's white Chevrolet pulled up to the curb before they exited the building. Vera looked up and down the street before opening the passenger door and sliding in next to Opal, making room for Priscilla on the other side. A jazz melody played through the car's speakers. Opal reached for the dial and turned the radio off.

Her eyes fell to Vera's ripped skirt, then back to her face. "I thought you said you were okay. You don't look it."

"I'm fine," Vera said, as Pricilla shut the side door. She noticed Opal had thrown on a skirt and matching blazer. "Priscilla, this is Opal. Opal, Priscilla."

"Nice to meetcha." Opal gave Priscilla a big smile. "And, um, nice negligee."

Priscilla glanced at her sheer sleeves. "It's not what I normally wear when I'm run out of my house in the night and hunted by the police. But there's a first time for everything."

Opal turned to Vera. "I like her."

"Let's get out of here," Vera said. "And thank you—I didn't know who else to call." Thinking of Dari, Vera swallowed the lump in her throat.

"That's what friends are for." Opal threw the car in gear. "Where to?"

"Chehalis."

Opal shot them a sideways glance as she turned down the hill. "Is that where Max is?"

A pair of headlights sped up the street in the opposite lane, and Vera and Priscilla ducked as a squad car drove past them.

"We think so," Priscilla said, lifting her head off Vera's lap.

As Opal drove toward Highway 99, Vera filled her in on that evening's events, and their theory that Rex had been keeping Max with his cousin and his wife at their Chehalis farmhouse.

She turned to Priscilla. "Do you know an Edith Hamilton?"

Priscilla looked at her blankly. "No. Why?"

"I found a bill for her treatment at Rainier Psychiatric when I was inside Ruth's bedroom."

"Rainier?"

Vera watched a shadow come over Priscilla's face as they passed beneath a light.

"The bill said she was being treated for a delusional disorder."

Priscilla shook her head in confusion. "That's bizarre. I don't know anyone by that name. Could be a family member on Ruth's side."

"All right, but I'm just saying, Ruth paying for someone's psychiatric treatment—"

Priscilla placed her hand on Vera's arm. "I know, I

know."

Opal turned onto the highway and gunned the engine. "You guys know where we're headed, right?"

Vera leaned forward and opened the glove box to take out the map. "Do you remember where the farmhouse is?"

"Um...." Priscilla closed her eyes. "It's white. With a wrap-around porch. Green roof."

Vera thought of a few homes it could be. "What do they farm?"

Priscilla stared straight ahead.

"Priscilla?"

"Hops. They grow hops. And it's about half a mile from a schoolhouse."

"I know it. That's not far from my parents' place. Couple miles, if that."

Opal checked the gauge on her dash as they drove past the downtown Seattle waterfront. "I'll have to stop for gas. I don't think we have enough to get there."

"But Rex could be on his way there! We have to hurry!" The panic in Priscilla's voice grew with each sentence. "He—he could move Max somewhere else before we get there. And be waiting for us."

Vera put out her hand, hoping to calm her. "Let's hope he's still back there looking for us."

A whimper escaped Priscilla's lips. "I can't lose him. I can't."

Vera placed her hand on Priscilla's knee as Opal sped through a red light at an empty intersection. "I know."

Not long after they crossed over the Duwamish River, Vera pressed her hands against the dash as Opal made a sharp turn off the highway.

Priscilla leaned forward. "What are you doing? We don't have time to stop! Rex will beat us there!"

Opal reached for the radio dial and an upbeat jazz song flooded through the car. She leaned back, and with one hand on the wheel, floored the car, heading east. Vera realized where she was going.

Opal turned to them both. "Not if we fly."

53

"*Fly?*" Priscilla leaned into Vera as Opal took a sharp right turn toward the Kent Airport.

"Well, I haven't quite gotten my license yet. But Vera can." Opal turned to her. "Right?"

Vera bit her lip, mulling it over. "I can, but it will be hard to find our way in the dark." She looked through the windshield at the night sky. The full moon would help. "We could follow Highway 99. But the farmhouse where Max might be held is south of town. It's a long way to walk from the Chehalis-Centralia airport."

Opal pulled into the gravel parking area beside the airport. "Didn't you tell me you wanted to be a pilot ever since you watched a barnstormer land in a neighboring field as a kid?"

She was surprised Opal had remembered. The night they chatted on Dari's balcony over a bottle of wine seemed like a lifetime ago. "There'd be no way to land there in the dark. We wouldn't make it."

"What about your parents?" Opal asked.

"What about them?"

"They could light up the field. You can call them from the pilot's lounge. They could shine headlights on it, or something, couldn't they?"

Vera looked out at the darkness. It might work. *If* they were willing. "But how will we get in? The hangar is locked at this time of night."

Opal withdrew a set of keys out of her purse. "Dari left these with me and asked me to return them. My next lesson is tomorrow, so I've been hanging onto them until then." She jutted her thumb toward the hangar. "We won't all fit in the Chief, but we could take the Curtiss Robin."

The soft jazz music stopped, and a radio announcer crackled through the speakers. "We interrupt this broadcast to bring you breaking news from the Pacific campaign."

Opal went to turn off the engine, but Vera grabbed her arm, her eyes glued to the radio. "Wait."

"The Battle of the Santa Cruz Islands continued today, resulting in the sinking of the carrier *USS Hornet*."

Vera felt like she'd had the wind knocked out of her.

"Both the Allies and the Japanese are claiming it a victory. While no Japanese ships were sunk, only damaged, their most significant losses were in their aircrew. American death tolls are estimated around two hundred and fifty men, including twenty-six airmen."

Hugh.

"Meanwhile, the Battle for Henderson Field rages on in the Guadalcanal—"

Opal cut the engine, leaving them in a silent darkness. She opened her door and climbed out. "Let's go."

She felt Priscilla tug on her sleeve after Opal shut the driver's door. "Vera?"

She stared straight ahead, the darkened dash blurring in

her vision. She couldn't move. Couldn't breathe.

"That couldn't be Hugh," Priscilla said. "It's too far from Hawaii. And he's only been gone a couple of weeks."

"He wrote me. Right after he got to Hawaii. Saying he was being shipped out. On the *Hornet*." Her voice felt separate from her body, like it was coming from someone else.

"You can't know it's Hugh. Think of how many airmen were in that battle. You need to believe that he's alive. Don't give up hope." Priscilla pulled at her arm. "Come on."

The driver's door flew open, and Opal leaned into the door frame. "You girls coming?"

"Hugh was on the *USS Hornet*," Priscilla said.

"Oh, Vera. I'm so sorry. But they didn't give any names, did they?"

Priscilla shook her head.

Opal leaned into the car and rested her hand on Vera's shoulder. "Then, for now, we trust and pray that Hugh is okay. There's nothing else we can do."

Priscilla gripped her arm tighter. "Vera, Max needs us. He needs me, and he needs *you*. You're the only one who can get us there before Rex does. *Please*."

Vera had no recollection of climbing out of the car, but before she knew it, Priscilla and Opal were supporting her on either side, leading her toward the main hangar.

54

Vera had been too shaken to speak to her mother when they got to the pilot's lounge, so Opal did most of the talking. She left out most of the details, aside from Vera working for the Ellises and possibly knowing where their missing child was. And that it was an emergency. To Vera's surprise, her mom agreed to light up the field for their landing.

Thankfully, Vera's father was out of town on a fishing trip. Had he been home, he would have insisted they call the police. But Vera was sure they wouldn't believe them. They had no proof that Max Ellis was being held at the farmhouse, which was quite an accusation. There'd be no way to convince them to search the property in the middle of the night before Rex showed up.

By the time they pulled the red, three-seater plane out of the hangar, Vera was coming out of her shock. If they were going to get there safely to find Max, she had to keep her thoughts clear. Which meant clinging to the belief that Hugh had survived.

Vera opened the plane's side window as Priscilla climbed in the backseat.

"Contact!" Opal yelled as she took hold of the propeller with both hands.

Vera turned both of the magneto switches to *ON* and leaned out the plane's window. "Contact!"

Opal spun the propeller, and the engine sputtered to a start as Opal squeezed in beside Priscilla. Vera flipped the switch for the wind-driven generator. A red light from the ceiling illuminated the instrument panel.

Vera raced through the takeoff checklist as she taxied toward the runway. After rounding the corner, she eased the throttle forward and took off without stopping.

"We'll follow the highway south, but I'll need your help navigating." She turned to the southwest to pick up the lights of the cars on Highway 99.

"No problem." Opal looked out her side window. "Good thing they haven't called a blackout tonight."

For the next twenty-five minutes, the three of them talked through their plan for after they landed.

Opal pointed over Vera's shoulder. "That's Centralia up ahead. We're almost there."

Vera started their descent, recognizing the landmarks below as they passed over the town's lights. They were at only eight hundred feet when they flew over the main street of Chehalis. The ground beneath them faded to dark as they descended over the surrounding farm fields away from the town center.

Vera banked to the left, spotting the headlights of a parked vehicle amidst the darkness ahead. They cast a golden glow over the recently harvested hay field. She exhaled as she pushed in the yoke, bringing the plane down. A single light shined from the other end of the field, which

Vera knew was her mother marking the end of their makeshift runway.

Vera buzzed the farm truck, the plane's wheels only a foot above the roof, and touched down on the short-cut hay. The plane bounced into the air twice before coming down onto the field. Vera stood on the brakes and turned the plane around as her mother's form came into view, waving a lantern in the air up ahead. When the plane jerked to a stop, she could make out her mother's face from the lantern's light.

She wore a navy-blue bathrobe over her pajamas, and her eyes were deep with concern. Her mother's auburn hair was the same shade as Vera's, only now lightly speckled with gray, and fell in natural waves around her face. A tightness formed in Vera's chest, realizing how much she had missed her.

"Whew!" Opal said. "Nicely done."

"Let's go. We have to hurry!" Priscilla said, reaching across Opal's lap for the door.

Priscilla and Opal jumped out of the plane. Vera grabbed the pistol from her handbag and tucked it into the back of her waistband before she ran to her mother. She threw her arms around her neck and her mother returned the tight embrace.

Vera fought back the emotions bubbling inside her. "Thank you."

"What's all over your face?" her mother asked after taking a step back. "And your clothes?"

"Come on!" Priscilla called. "We need you to show us the way!"

Her mother shot a wary glance at Priscilla's sheer negligee and heeled slippers before turning back to her daughter. "Who flew the plane?"

261

"Why, Vera did, ma'am," Opal toward her mother with an outstretched hand. "I'm Opal, we spoke on the telephone." She pointed to Priscilla. "And that's Priscilla Ellis."

Her mother's jaw dropped as she returned Opal's handshake. For a moment, she seemed at a loss for words until her attention returned to Vera. "*You* flew at night? Good grief. Why don't you call the police?"

Feeling the hard barrel of Hugh's gun against her back, Vera was glad her mother hadn't felt it when they embraced. "We can't. At least not yet. First, we need to see if Max Ellis is there." Vera didn't offer any further explanation. There was no time.

Her mother frowned. "You be careful. I don't like this. Here…." She extended the lantern toward Vera. "Take this."

"Thank you."

"This way!" Vera called to Opal and Priscilla, as she started through the field.

"Vera!" her mother called.

She turned.

"Why don't you take our car?"

She shook her head. "If we cut through the fields, it's not that far." Plus, she didn't want Vincent's cousin to see them coming.

"I'll give you a couple of hours to do what you need to do. But, after that, I'm calling the police."

Vera nodded before she continued to jog through the field, using the lantern to light her way through the uneven hayfield, with Priscilla and Opal following right behind.

55

They were all out of breath when a dim light from the farmhouse appeared in the distance. They'd been running for about ten minutes when they came to a dirt road.

"I think that's it," Vera breathed.

She turned off the gas on her lantern. The three of them turned off the road and ran through the harvested rows of hops toward the house.

"Stop here," Vera panted when they got closer.

The outside lights were off, but there was light coming from inside one of the main floor windows. Vera assessed the house as she caught her breath, debating on their best plan of approach. A shadow moved across the window. It would have been easier if everyone inside the home was asleep.

"What time is it?" she asked.

Priscilla and Opal both lifted their wristwatches toward the full moon.

"It's nearly five," Opal said.

It wouldn't be light until closer to seven. But the darkness was on their side. For now.

"Do you think Rex called them? What if he told them we were coming?" Priscilla's voice was ripe with panic.

"Keep your voice down." Vera had already considered this. She withdrew the pistol from her waistband. "We need to see if there's a back door or an open window that we can sneak through. If we find Max, we'll have to try and get him out without them hearing." She looked down at the weapon in her hands, praying she wouldn't have to use it.

"I'll go have a look around the back," she added.

Priscilla hurried after her. "I'm coming with you!"

"Fine," Vera whispered. "But you must keep quiet!"

"I'll stay here and keep watch," Opal said. "I'll whistle if I see Rex or anyone coming toward the house."

As they neared the farmhouse, Vera could make out the inside of a kitchen through the front window. She reached for Priscilla's arm to lead her around the side of the house, but realized she was no longer at Vera's side. She scanned the front of the house and spotted Priscilla's silhouette creeping toward the front window for a better look.

"Priscilla!"

But Priscilla ignored her and continued toward the house. She was only a few feet from the covered porch when the lights flicked on. The front door flew open as Priscilla stood still in the spotlight of the porch lights. Vera gasped, then covered her mouth with her hand.

Damn it, Priscilla. You think you can get away with anything.

A man wearing a plaid shirt, jeans, and a mean scowl stepped onto the porch with a shotgun aimed at Priscilla's chest.

"Get off my property!" he barked.

"Where's Max?"

"Rex said you'd be coming."

"What have you done with my son?"

"That's no longer your concern."

Vera wanted to yell at Priscilla to stop as she charged toward the man. Instead, Vera cocked the pistol and pointed it toward the man's chest. The farmer pumped his shotgun, raising the barrel toward Priscilla as she started up the porch steps.

"Get back or I'll shoot!" he shouted.

But Priscilla didn't stop. "Where is he?" she demanded.

Vera ran forward to pull Priscilla back but came to a halt when she saw the man's finger slide over the trigger. "No!"

The man's head whipped in her direction, which brought Priscilla to her senses. Priscilla dove off the porch onto a stack of firewood as the man refocused his attention on her. Vera watched in horror as he followed her movement with the barrel. A blast rang out as the weapon's barrel kicked the man back a step.

Priscilla rolled off the pile of wood and landed in the dirt beside a chopping block. Vera couldn't tell if she had been hit, but she knew it was time to fire back.

"Ahh!" The farmer brought a hand to his chest before he pumped the shotgun a second time and swung the gun at Vera. She squeezed the trigger just as another blast erupted from the shotgun. The man jerked back against the wall and collapsed onto the porch.

Vera felt a sting in her arm where the buckshot had grazed her as she ran toward the house. She kept the pistol trained on the farmer, who lay unmoving on his porch, his shotgun at his side.

"Priscilla!"

She didn't respond. Vera knelt beside her. From the glow of the porch lights, Vera saw blood seeping through the side of her satin robe that had been peppered with buckshot.

Vera gently shook her side that hadn't been hit. "Priscilla!"

She moaned, and her eyelids fluttered open. Vera sank to her knees as Opal appeared beside her.

"Good golly, I thought she was dead!" Opal exclaimed.

"Can you get up?" Vera asked.

"I think so." Priscilla winced as the two women helped her to her feet.

"You better get his gun," Opal said.

Vera climbed the steps and crept toward the shotgun beside the man's still form. When she reached down, the farmer's lifeless eyes seemed to lock with hers. Her breath caught in her throat. She stepped back, seeing the crimson puddle that seeped onto the porch from the bullet hole in his chest.

I did this. I killed him. The porch began to spin as the blood drained from her head. Her stomach churned as the pistol slipped from her hand.

"Grab the gun!"

She barely registered Opal's voice, or the front door swinging open. Vera stumbled backward, losing her balance.

"Vera!"

Vera reached for the support beam beside her and realized why Opal was screaming. A woman with a long braid and a flannel robe pointed a revolver at Vera's chest from the front door. She fell against the support beam as a shot rang out.

Fire radiated from Vera's arm as her knees buckled. She dropped to the porch, her arm searing with pain. The woman's eyes fell to the man lying dead on the porch at her feet. She screamed, then turned and pointed her gun a

266

second time at Vera.

56

The woman's jaw clenched and her eyes narrowed as she came a step closer, lifting the revolver toward Vera's head.

Vera put her hand in front of her face. "Please! It—"

A gunshot erupted beside her, drowning out Vera's words. The woman was thrown backward into the house from the close-range impact of the buckshot. Vera's ears rang from the blast as she turned, seeing Priscilla on her knees beside her, gripping the shotgun with shaking outstretched hands.

The woman's gun lay beside her bare feet that protruded through the doorway. Opal reached their side and said something Vera couldn't understand over the ringing in her ears. She lowered Priscilla's arm holding the gun.

Opal bent over and assessed Vera's upper arm, which bled through the bullet hole in her blazer. "You okay?"

Vera nodded, casting a glance at her wound. "It's burning like hell."

After Opal helped both women to their feet, they heard

flames flickering from inside the doorway. Priscilla limped to the door.

She froze after stepping inside, seeing the large flames climbing up the curtains beside the woman's still form. Blood oozed through her robe where the shot had blasted away half of her chest. Next to her, there was a table on its side and a kerosene lamp smashed on the floor.

"Max!" Priscilla yelled.

Vera felt the heat from the flames on her face. Priscilla thrust the shotgun at Opal and ran past the growing blaze toward a stairwell. Vera stared at the woman on the floor. After lifting her pistol from the floor, Vera turned to Opal.

"She might still be alive."

"I'll drag her out." She grabbed the woman's feet. "Go help Priscilla." She cast a glance at the flames crackling up the wall. "I'll look for a telephone to report the fire. But then we need to get out of here!"

Vera ran past the scorching hot flames and coughed from the smoke when she reached the stairwell. Dark smoke hovered over the staircase, and Vera's eyes burned as she strained to see through the haze. She coughed again when she reached the top.

"Priscilla!"

"I'm here! Help me!"

Vera ran down a hall toward her voice. She found Priscilla frantically banging herself against a closed door at the end of the hallway.

"It's Max!" she cried, pointing at the door.

"Mommy! Mommy!"

With wide eyes, Vera turned toward the child's voice on the other side of the door. She grabbed the door handle, but it wouldn't turn.

"It's locked!" Priscilla banged her fist against the wood.

"Can you open it, Maxy?"

"No, Mommy. You need the key."

"What key, baby?"

"Aunt Beatrice has it."

Priscilla looked at Vera with horror in her eyes. The smell of smoke grew stronger. Vera turned to see the glow from the fire at the end of the hall. There was no time to find it.

Vera leaned against the door. "Max? I need you to stand back, okay? Step as far away from the door as you can."

"Mommy?"

"Yes, Max. Do as she says! Move to the other side of the room. Go lie down in the corner, and then Mommy's can come in to get you!"

"Are you far away, Max, in the corner?"

"Yes. Yes!"

His voice was far enough away. Vera stepped back and pointed the pistol toward the space between the handle and the doorframe. She fired. Wood splintered from the bullet's impact.

Vera tried the handle and pushed. The door budged, but only slightly. She lifted the gun a second time.

"Stay back, Maxy!" Priscilla called.

Vera squeezed the trigger, and the door rattled from the blast. Priscilla coughed as the smoke grew thicker.

Vera kicked the sole of her heel just below the handle. The door shook. She drew her knee back and kicked again. This time the door broke open. Early morning light filtered into the small room through the window.

Priscilla flew into the room as Max ran from the far corner toward his mother.

"Mommy!" A wide smile covered his face as he flung his arms around her neck when she lifted him off the ground.

"Oh, Max! My baby." A weighty sob erupted from

Priscilla's throat.

"Let's go," Vera said, leading them out of the room.

With Max still in his mother's arms, they started down the hall, which was now hazy with smoke. Vera felt the temperature rise as they neared the stairwell. She stopped after rounding the corner and held her arm out behind her to stop Priscilla.

Priscilla shrieked, seeing the flames and black smoke that shot up the stairwell.

Vera turned. "We have to go back!"

They ran down the hall, and Vera closed the door behind them after they reached Max's room. She rushed to the window and yanked it open with her good arm.

"We'll have to jump."

Max turned toward the open window with a look of terror. "No!" He shook his head firmly.

"We must, Max," Priscilla soothed. "It's okay. It's the only way out."

"No!" He flailed wildly in his mother's arms, and Priscilla set him down, grimacing at the pellet wounds in her side.

Vera knelt in front of the little boy and took a breath. "I can go first if you want, Max," Vera said. "Then, I can catch you." With Priscilla's wounds, Vera didn't think she'd have the strength to catch him. She only hoped she could coax him out the window by herself.

Max buried his face in the back of his mother's legs.

"Will you jump if I catch you, Max?"

"You can trust her." Priscilla brought him closer to the window and also knelt down beside him. "This woman has been helping me find you." She placed her hands on his cheeks and kissed his forehead. "I'll be right behind you. Don't worry. Mommy will never leave you again."

Vera was halfway out the window when a loud *crack*

erupted from below followed by the *boom* of a beam collapsing beneath them. She turned to Priscilla who held a wide-eyed Max in her arms.

"Go!" Priscilla shouted, as she pointed toward the window.

Vera tucked Hugh's pistol into her waistband again before she swung her other leg out the window and pushed herself off. She landed with a thud on the grass below. Pain tore through her ankle before she fell to her hands and knees. Through gritted teeth, she looked up at the window as Priscilla lifted a protesting Max through the opening.

"Mommy, no!" he wailed, kicking his feet against the siding.

Vera grunted and pushed herself up, despite the sharp pain in her ankle. She lifted her arms in the air. "Ready!"

Priscilla let go, and Max screamed as he fell through the air. Vera closed her arms around his waist before falling backward onto the lawn. A moment later, Priscilla landed and rolled beside her and took her crying son into her arms.

Vera sat up, seeing a black cloud of smoke billowing out the window of Max's room. Orange flames and black soot covered the windows of the main level, which had cracked from the intense heat. The women got to their feet and hobbled to the front lawn.

The bodies of the farmer and his wife lay still on the front porch. The early morning dawn lit the field surrounding the house, but there was no sign of Opal.

"Opal!"

Vera limped around the side of the house while Priscilla stayed in the front with Max.

"Opal!"

A side window shattered from the heat, and Vera covered her face with her hands as glass exploded onto the lawn.

Flames blew from the broken window, and Vera called Opal's name again. But there was no response.

She moved to the back of the house, staying a good ten feet from the burning structure, but there was nothing but an open field. *Where was she?*

"Vera!" Priscilla called.

Vera hurried to the front yard, where Priscilla was standing beside Max, pointing to a front window. Her jaw dropped when she saw movement, and realized what Priscilla was pointing at.

It was Opal. And she was trapped inside the burning house.

57

Vera ran toward the farmhouse, no longer able to see Opal through the haze beyond the window. Priscilla stayed back, keeping Max a safe distance from the burning structure. Vera's eyes darted toward the front door, now completely engulfed in flames. There was no way her friend could get out that way.

"Opal!" Vera cried when she neared the window.

Wood crackled from inside as she strained to see into the smoke-filled room. She banged her fist against the glass.

"Ahh!" She drew back her hand, burned from the heat of the window, and peered inside. "Opal! Where are you?"

If the window was that hot to the touch, she could only imagine the temperature inside. Ignoring the pain in her ankle, Vera sprinted toward the front porch, which was now ablaze. She bent over beside the stacked firewood and used both hands to pull an axe from the chopping block.

She ran to the window and thrust the axe head into the glass. Shards flew onto the ground as it broke through the pane. She felt a wave of heat from inside, causing her to step back.

"Vera! It's too late. Don't go inside!"

She turned to see Priscilla with her arms around Max, shaking her head. With the axe in hand, Vera ran around the corner of the house. Cautiously, she put her palm to the window that was still intact. It was warm, but not so much that it burned.

After turning her face away, she swung the axe through the glass. She swiped the axe head through the broken shards until there was enough room for her to climb through. Tossing the axe onto the grass, she pulled her legs over the window ledge, drawing in a sharp breath as a shard sliced through her palm.

When she got inside, the room was thick with smoke. She covered her nose with the sleeve of her blazer and blinked through the sting in her eyes.

"Opal?" She coughed. "Opal!"

She put out her hand before she stepped forward, keeping as low as she could, unable to see more than a foot in front of her. Although she couldn't see the flames, she could hear the roaring coming from the blaze that ripped through the house. She looked around, unable to tell what sort of room she was in. But she couldn't be too far from the front window where she'd seen Opal.

She took a few steps forward and ran into what felt like a rocking chair. She turned to the right, waving her arm through the darkening smoke. She hadn't gone far, but her visibility was all but gone. She coughed and turned, trying to remember which direction the window was in.

She closed her eyes, which burned from the smoke, and coughed into her sleeve. Priscilla was right. It was too late to get Opal out. Vera knew that if she didn't get out of the house now, she never would. She moved forward, trying to retrace her steps, when a loud *boom* resounded from upstairs, shaking the floor beneath her feet. She shuffled faster, feeling for the chair she'd bumped into.

She could taste the salt from the sweat on her lips. The temperature had risen significantly since she'd come inside. She thought of taking off her blazer when she tripped over something. It felt like a dog.

She caught herself before she fell and knelt to the floor. She ran her hands over what she'd kicked. Instead of fur, she felt a smooth fabric. And buttons. *Opal.*

Vera moved her hands across Opal's blazer and gripped her thin, limp arms. "Opal!" she shouted, her voice choked by the smoke.

Vera shook her.

She moaned. *"Hmm?"*

"We have to go!"

"Vera, is that you?" She was wheezing.

Vera noticed that Opal was clutching a telephone to her chest. She took it from her grip.

"I'm trying to call the fire department!" Opal protested.

"It's too late! Come on!" Using every ounce of energy she had left, Vera pulled Opal unsteadily to her feet and draped one of her arms over her own shoulder.

Vera squinted as they stumbled forward, straining to find the window. But she was blind to anything other than the hot black haze that surrounded them. They took a few more steps before she saw light.

Opal gagged.

"A little farther," Vera urged.

Vera pulled her forward until the air cleared enough that she spotted the opening in the window. She helped Opal out first, who collapsed on the grass, while Vera jumped out after her. A thunderous crack erupted from inside the house, and they both turned their heads toward the sound.

"We're too close!" Vera dragged Opal to her feet. "Come on."

When they rounded the front of the house, Priscilla was turned around, staring at something in the distance. Vera followed her gaze, seeing the dust cloud at the edge of the field trailing a dark car as it turned toward the farmhouse.

Vera filled with relief, finally letting go of Opal's hand. Her mother must have called the police. Or someone had seen the smoke and called the authorities. She watched the car speed toward the burning house, but as it rounded the corner just beyond the driveway to the farmhouse, the relief she'd felt vanished. It wasn't the police. This was a luxury sedan.

Priscilla turned around with wild, terrified eyes. She wrapped her arms around Max and pulled him toward her. "It's Rex!"

58

Vera grabbed Opal's hand and ran toward a tractor at the edge of the field. Priscilla looked back at Rex's car, which was halfway down the long gravel driveway before she scooped Max into her arms. They reached the tractor seconds after Vera and Opal. They crouched behind its wheels as the car pulled up to the front of the house.

With her back against the tire, Vera slid the pistol out from the waistband of her skirt. She released the magazine. There were two bullets left, plus one in the chamber. She replaced the magazine as a car door slammed.

Priscilla covered Max's mouth with her hand and silently kissed the top of his head.

"Argh! *Nooo!*"

Vera peeked over the wheel and watched Rex place his hands on his hips as he stared down at the two bodies on the front porch.

"Damn it!" He whipped around, withdrew a pistol from his side holster, and scanned the field. "Priscilla!"

Vera ducked behind the tractor wheel. Max squirmed in

Priscilla's arms, trying to see who was yelling. Priscilla lowered her mouth to his ear. *"Shh."*

Max pulled her hand away from his mouth and peered beneath the tractor. "It's Uncle Rex!" he shouted.

Priscilla pulled him onto her lap and clamped her hand over his lips. Opal put a trembling hand over her own mouth and squeezed her eyes shut. Vera leaned beneath the tractor and spotted Rex's legs taking long strides toward them.

Vera slid her finger onto the trigger and stood from behind the tractor. She aimed the gun at Rex, who stopped a few feet away. He jumped back a step and leveled his pistol at the center of her chest.

"Put the gun down, Vera."

Her hand trembled as she prepared to pull the trigger. She'd have to make sure it counted. She might not survive, but the others would.

"You won't get away with it, Rex. If you shoot me, I'll shoot you. But if you live, there will be three witnesses to testify against you. It will be *you* who's hanged."

He smirked. "That's where you're wrong. I *always* get away with it." He raised his pistol toward her throat.

As she kept her eyes trained on Rex's gun, she wondered about Hugh. Whether he was already dead, and if she was about to see him again.

"You can't hide behind your mother any longer, Rex. You're going down for this."

Priscilla came to a stop beside her, and Vera wanted to tell her to get back behind the tractor. Instead, she readied herself to shoot first if Rex turned his gun on Priscilla. She didn't dare tear her eyes from his pistol as Priscilla continued to lay into him.

"You let your mother control you, run off the woman you

loved, Rex. But you're never going to take anything, or any*one,* away from me again."

In her peripheral vision, Vera spotted Max clinging to the back of Priscilla's legs.

"Aside from Vincent, you're the most pathetic excuse for a man I've ever known."

Rex's eyes narrowed. He swung his gun toward Priscilla.

Vera pressed her finger against the trigger, ready to fire.

He raised his pistol toward the center of Priscilla's face. "Goodbye Priscil—"

The wail of sirens coming down the road muffled Rex's voice. He kept his gun trained on Priscilla as a brigade of police cars and fire trucks turned down the driveway to the farmhouse. Out the corner of her eye, Opal climbed onto the tractor and waved her arms through the air.

But Vera didn't dare look away from Rex. With a shaking hand, she kept her pistol pointed at his chest until the police cars came to a stop in front of the house. Two officers jumped out with their guns drawn.

"Drop your weapons!"

Rex didn't move. "These women killed my cousin! I'm Rex Ellis, owner of Pacific Bank!"

"Mister, if you don't drop that gun right now, all you're gonna be is dead!" the lead officer shouted back.

Rex lowered his gun.

"Miss, you too. Right now!" the officer demanded.

Vera slowly let the gun drop to her side, all the while keeping her eyes trained on Rex. Only when he stooped and set the gun on the grass did Vera lay hers to the ground.

"Hands on your head!" The police hurried toward them and picked their guns up off the ground.

"Get your hands off me!" Rex shouted, as the officers put them both in handcuffs. "Did you not hear me? I'm Rex Ellis of Pacific Bank!"

Max ran out from behind his mother before she could stop him. "Uncle Rex!"

Priscilla grabbed his hand. "It's okay, baby. It's okay."

Rex struggled with the officers, kicking one in the shin. "Mr. Ellis!" The officer grabbed him roughly by the arm. "We have orders to take you down to the station. In addition to whatever the hell's going on *here*, you're wanted for questioning regarding the death of your brother."

"Vincent?" Priscilla shrieked, covering Max's ears with her hands.

"He tried to kill *me*!" Rex tried to shake his arm away from the arresting officer.

The arresting officer yanked him toward his squad car. "Save it for the station."

Vera turned to see Priscilla's jaw drop in shock as the officer led her and Max toward an ambulance. Firefighters ran with hoses toward the house, now beginning to collapse, as two men from the ambulance moved in to help Opal, Priscilla, and Max.

Vera heard a fireman yell out: *We have two bodies here!*

"Are you arresting me?" Vera asked, as an officer led her toward his car.

"For now, you're coming down to the station until we sort everything out."

The officer opened the rear door of his car.

"That's my daughter. Let her go."

Vera whirled around and came face-to-face with her father.

"She needs medical attention!"

The young officer conceded and removed the metal cuffs from her wrists. "Fine, but we can't release her until we get everyone's statements."

"I'll stay with her." Her father put his arm around her and pointed toward the car in front of them, where Rex sat shouting at the arresting officer from the backseat. "Do not release him under any circumstances until I get to the station. Is that clear?"

The officer nodded. "Yes, sir."

Vera knew that with her father in charge, Rex wouldn't be able to buy his way out of this one.

"I always knew those Ellises were trouble." Her father led her toward an ambulance parked toward the end of the drive. "I've never been so worried in my life."

"I thought you were fishing," Vera said.

"There was too much swell. When I telephoned your mother from the Tacoma docks early this morning to say I was coming home, she told me everything. I got here as soon as I could." He waved down one of the medics who was assessing Opal behind an ambulance.

"I'm fine, Dad. Really." Vera coughed.

"She's limping," her father said, as the medic approached them. "And there's a nasty cut on her hand."

Vera lifted her hand and noticed the blood dripping down her fingers for the first time. Seeing the dark red liquid, she felt unsteady on her feet.

"*And* I took some buckshot in the arm, here." Vera pointed to her shoulder.

Her father shook his head, but he was smiling.

"Easy there," the medic said, as she swayed beneath her father's arm.

The medic blurred in her vision as the ground moved beneath her feet.

"She doesn't do well with blood," Vera heard her father say, before her legs gave out and everything went dark.

282

59

"You don't have to stay," Vera told her parents, after following them inside her home on crutches.

"Nonsense." Her mother gasped, seeing the mess of cushions, books, and papers on the floor. "We want to. Plus, it looks like you could use some help."

Vera opened her mouth to remind her mother that she didn't exactly have time to clean up after being attacked in her own house, but she was too exhausted to rehash the events of that night. The Ellises were in custody now, as was Rex's private investigator, who had admitted to being hired by Rex to kill Howard and Gilbert Mills. Still, she was glad not to be alone.

Her parents had offered for her to stay longer at their farm in Chehalis, but Vera wanted to be home in case there was news of Hugh. She'd heard nothing more about the Battle of the Santa Cruz Islands, aside from the fact that both sides had retreated and were each claiming it a victory. She could only hope that Hugh was on board one of the other carriers and headed back for Hawaii. But it was killing her not knowing for sure.

Her father had picked the *Tribune* off her front steps, covered with articles about Max being found and the Ellis family's downfall. Vera read the headline beneath her father's hand.

ELLIS NANNY TELLS ALL

She'd already read every article about it in the Centralia-Chehalis paper that afternoon.

After Vera's father had come back early from fishing, her mother told him of Vera's suspicion that the kidnapped Ellis child was being hidden in Chehalis. Her father had called his old friend Jim, the Special Agent in charge of the Seattle FBI Field Office, and learned that earlier that night, Vincent Ellis had been found dead on the floor of the foyer in his home, after apparently falling from three stories above.

The FBI had Hattie in custody for questioning, who, after learning that Rex and Ruth had been arrested, spilled everything she knew about the Ellises in exchange for reduced charges—including witnessing Rex push Vincent over the ledge after the older brother confessed to kidnapping Max to push Priscilla out of the family.

"Do you think Ruth Ellis's lawyers will be able to get her charges dismissed?" Vera asked her father.

Ruth had been arrested at her Queen Anne mansion yesterday evening for conspiracy to commit kidnapping and murder.

He shook his head. "Jim said the judge denied her bail due to being a flight risk. She and Rex won't have a chance at freedom, not until one, they've gone to trial for their role in Max's kidnapping and two, the murders of Howard and Gilbert Mills; and three, for *your* attempted murder courtesy of the PI they hired."

"I'll make up the couch so you don't have to climb the stairs tonight."

"Thanks, Mom." Vera sat beside her father in one of her floral armchairs, while her mother went upstairs to find linens.

She lifted her ankle onto the coffee table, which she was supposed to keep elevated, and saw it had nearly doubled in size during their drive from Chehalis. She and Opal had spent last night at her parents' home after being treated at the local hospital for smoke inhalation. She'd received stitches on both her hand and where the shotgun pellets had grazed her upper arm. As the doctor sewed up the gash on the base of her palm, he'd commented on how lucky she was. A centimeter lower, he'd said, and the broken glass would have severed her radial artery. He'd been amazed that a torn ligament in her ankle was her worst injury after hearing all she'd been through.

Then afterward, she'd spent the remainder of the day giving her father and two FBI agents her full account of her two weeks working for the Ellises.

Vera stared at the ashes in her fireplace as her dad lit a pipe beside her, the woody smell of his pipe tobacco reminding her of her childhood.

Her thoughts drifted to Priscilla, who was now in police custody, as well. After being taken to the hospital and assessed for injuries, Max had gone to stay with Priscilla's sister in Tacoma while she faced charges for kidnapping. After hearing about the Ellises' plan to institutionalize her, Vera's father assured her that a jury would be sympathetic at trial.

Her father pulled his pipe away from his lips. "When you were little, all you wanted to be was a pilot and a detective. I thought you were quite ridiculous."

285

"Yes, I know."

"But you proved us wrong. It turns out you're damn good at both!"

Vera turned from the fireplace to see her father beaming at her. Despite everything, a short laugh escaped her lips.

"You single-handedly exposed the crimes of the most powerful and corrupt family in Seattle, and I don't know any man who can say the same."

Her mother returned from upstairs with a bundle of blankets in her arms. "What your father is trying to say is that we're proud of you. But we were also worried sick we were going to lose you. So, in the future, know that we will always support you—but promise us one thing...."

"What's that?"

"Be careful."

"I'll try."

Her mother shook her head. "Don't try. Do."

Her father went back to smoking his pipe, and Vera's smile faded as she wondered if Hugh was in fact on his way back to Hawaii, or taken prisoner by the Japanese, or on a raft, stranded in the middle of the Pacific, or in a sunken Grumman Wildcat, lying on the ocean floor.

"There." Her mother fluffed a pillow after making up the couch. "Come on, dear," she said to Vera's father, "let her get some rest." She turned to Vera at the base of the stairs. "Just holler if you need anything."

Vera thanked her and prepared for a long night of restless sleep, plagued with worry about Hugh.

Vera woke to the smell of coffee and bacon and sat up on

the couch. She squinted from the bright morning sun that gleamed through the front window. She'd slept fitfully, tossing and turning despite her exhaustion. Through the night, she'd woken several times from the pain in her ankle.

She stood from the couch and hobbled to reach her crutches she'd left leaning against the armchair last night.

"You want some eggs, Vera?" her mother called from the kitchen.

"Sure, thanks." Her mother making her breakfast sparked a memory of being a kid on their farm.

Movement in front of the house caught Vera's eye. She leaned forward and saw that a uniformed messenger boy on a bicycle had pulled up in front of the house. Her lungs stuck with dread as she moved toward the window, leaving her crutches behind. A sign hung from the bike labeled *WESTERN UNION.*

"Vera?"

"No, no, no...." She ran to the door and pulled it open, locking eyes with the young boy who strode toward her, holding a tan telegram in his hand.

"Mrs. Chandler?"

Vera nodded, unable to speak through the tightness in her throat. The boy handed her a telegram and turned back for his bike. Vera's eyes fell to the paper.

REGRET TO INFORM YOU YOUR HUSBAND CORPORAL HUGH CHANDLER WAS ON OCTOBER 26 REPORTED MISSING IN ACTION OVER PACIFIC PERIOD IF FURTHER DETAILS OR INFORMATION ARE RECEIVED YOU WILL BE PROMPTLY NOTIFIED PERIOD
– THE ADJUTANT GENERAL

"What does it say?" Her mother appeared beside her

wearing an apron over her dress and a dish towel slung over her shoulder.

Vera silently handed her the telegram and waited for her mother to read it. She looked up from the telegram and pulled Vera into a tight embrace before they sat down together on the concrete steps.

"We mustn't lose hope yet," her mother whispered.

Vera buried her face into her mother's neck and cried, as the messenger boy pedaled down the quiet street to deliver more bad news. She couldn't imagine how she could go much longer without knowing if Hugh was alive or dead, captured or free. It was a wonder that Priscilla had held up as well as she did these last few weeks.

She wiped her tears with the back of her hand as her mother led her into the kitchen. Although she tried to stay positive, endless possibilities swarmed her thoughts about her husband. And none of them were good.

60

"Y ou sure you'll be okay without us?"

"I'll be fine." Clouds loomed overhead as Vera hugged her mother on her front porch steps. Her father was busy loading their bags into the car.

October had given way to November, and there was a damp chill in the air.

"Really," Vera added. "Opal's going to stop by this afternoon."

"That's good." Her mother patted her arm. "You just need to keep busy. Maybe you could join your local garden society. I read about it in the *Tribune*."

Vera cringed, thinking of Hugh's tomatoes. "I'll think about it," she lied.

She couldn't wait to get back in a plane as soon as her ankle healed. She hadn't yet told her parents, but she planned to apply for a job as a flight instructor at the Kent Airport while she waited to hear back from the WFTD.

"Make sure to eat!" her mother yelled, standing by the open car door.

After many goodbyes, Vera went inside the house, rubbing her arms from the cold. It was next to impossible to eat. Six days had gone by since Hugh was reported missing, and there had been no further word. If the carriers involved in the Battle of the Santa Cruz Islands had headed straight back for Hawaii, they could be arriving any day. Although Vera wasn't sure what would be worse: not knowing if he was alive or getting the news that he wasn't. At least now she had some hope, even though it was torture.

She looked around her house for something to occupy her mind. Her mother was right. She did need to keep busy. But without being able to fly, she had no idea what to do. Opal wouldn't be coming over for several more hours. When she'd called that morning, she'd asked if Vera had heard the news about Priscilla.

Max's mother was set to go on trial next month. Unlike Rex and Ruth, who faced life sentences if convicted, Priscilla was being charged with conspiracy to commit second degree kidnapping. If found guilty, she would serve up to five years in prison.

The FBI had also announced an investigation into the Seattle Police Department and the mayor's office for accepting bribes from the Ellis family in exchange for turning the other way from the family's criminal activities.

Since returning home from Chehalis, Vera had declined three interviews from reporters with the *Tribune*, and one from the *Star*. Her eyes settled on the secretary desk. Her mother had tidied it up by stacking the array of papers inside the drawers. But Vera figured she could go through the bills, statements, and other documents that needed to be organized. It was a distraction, at least.

After compiling a small stack of bills that needed to be paid, she found Dari's letter, which she'd taped back together. After rereading it, she folded the letter and tucked it inside one of the desk's upper cubbies, where it wouldn't get crumpled or lost. She opened the next drawer down and found her discharge instructions from the Centralia hospital. Setting them aside, she thought of the statement from Rainier Psychiatric Hospital that she'd found in Ruth's bedroom.

She'd given it to the FBI agents who had interviewed her, and her father told her later that they'd checked with the psychiatric hospital about the girl's identity. The facility's administrators stated that Edith Hamilton was Ruth's twenty-five-year-old niece, and Ruth had admitted her six months before. When Vera asked about Edith's parents, her father said that according to the hospital, they lived on the East Coast and had yet to visit.

She'd been getting around without her crutches for the last couple of days and took slow, uneven steps into the next room. She found Evie and Rex's engagement photo in the bottom of her purse, flipping it over to see the phone number Evie's mother had written on the back. Her telephone rang and she hobbled out of the kitchen, hoping to reach it before her caller hung up. It was probably Opal, telling her she was going to be *a little bit late.*

Vera lifted the receiver after the fifth ring. "Hello?"

"Hi, kitten."

Vera sank against the wall. Her lower lip quivered. She'd know that deep voice anywhere. She wanted to shout, but her voice came out barely louder than a whisper.

"Hugh!" She closed her eyes. "Oh, thank God. You're alive! I got a telegram that you were—" her voice broke.

"Yeah, well, I'm sorry about that, kitten. I was shot down by a Japanese Zero near the Santa Cruz Islands just before dark. A destroyer picked me up from my raft the next night, and I was in pretty bad shape—shot twice in the leg, which shattered my shin bone."

"Oh, Hugh...."

"It's all right. I'm on the mend now. I just spent the trip back to Hawaii recovering in the ship's infirmary, but the captain was under orders to maintain radio silence so the Japanese couldn't triangulate our position. Right now, I'm being treated at Pearl Harbor's Naval Hospital."

Vera exhaled into the line. "I was so worried."

"I'm sorry. It sounds like I'll be sent home, though, for the rest of my recovery, so you don't have to worry anymore. Well, at least not for a while. We'll see."

"That's wonderful." She could feel a smile lifting her cheeks.

"That night on the raft, I wasn't sure if I'd ever be found— by the Allies anyway. But it was thoughts of you that kept me going. Well, you and my tomatoes."

She envisioned him grinning at his own joke on the other end of the line. "Oh, Hugh."

61

Vera waited in a tense silence alongside Evie's parents in a small office at Rainier Psychiatric Hospital one week later. All three of them watched the medical director, Dr. Perry, as he studied Evie's photograph that her mother had brought. The massive four-story brick structure had been built in the late 1800s. With over eight hundred beds, it was the largest inpatient psychiatric hospital west of the Mississippi. To Vera, its ivy-covered exterior and peaked roofline seemed to belong in a Gothic novel.

When they arrived, an administrator led them down a long drafty corridor, as a patient's agonizing screams could be heard from the floor above. It sent a shiver up Vera's spine.

"I can see a faint resemblance in the eyes." The psychiatrist set the photograph on his desk and looked at Evie's father. "But I'm certain that meeting Ms. Hamilton today will quell your suspicions that she is your daughter."

Vera had telephoned the mental hospital before telling Evie's parents about Edith Hamilton, but they refused to give Vera any information. Evie's father, however, used his political connections to get a private meeting with the medical director, and Evie's mother had asked Vera to accompany them.

From Evie's parents, Vera had learned that Dr. Perry was one of the most prominent psychiatrists in the country. While his face wasn't unkind, Vera felt a certain detachment when she looked in his eyes. When they had arrived in his office and Evie's parents shared their concerns, the doctor had listened with a palpable lack of emotion. As if he'd already decided they were wrong.

"When she was admitted, she was underweight, probably twenty pounds less than the woman in this photo." Dr. Perry took off his spectacles and flipped them down beside the photograph. "And her brown hair—not blonde like Evie's—was cropped short. She'd cut it herself in a fit of rage prior to her admission."

"Evie's hair was dyed," her mother said. "It's naturally brown."

The physician looked unimpressed. "Ms. Hamilton has gained weight in her time here, a side effect of the antipsychotics, sedatives, and antidepressants she is on."

"Antipsychotics!" Evie's mother shrieked.

Her husband reached for her hand.

The doctor pursed his lips. "Normally, I wouldn't question the validity of the circumstances under which a patient is admitted from a respectable member of our community, but in light of Mrs. Ellis's incarceration, I'm inclined to entertain your suspicions. That said, I'm afraid you'll find you're mistaken." He folded his hands atop the desk. "Ms. Hamilton presented with classic symptoms of a delusional disorder. Within these disorders, there are different types of delusions. The delusions Ms. Hamilton displays are erotomanic and persecutory in nature."

"Erotomania," he went on, "is believing that someone is in love with you. In most cases, it's someone important or famous. In her case, it was Rex Ellis."

"But Rex *was* in love with her!"

The doctor continued, ignoring the outburst from Evie's mother. "With persecutory delusions, one believes that someone is out to harm them. Edith believed that her aunt, Ruth Ellis, had abducted and starved her and was only institutionalizing her to lock her away, rather than to help her. However, with medication and electroshock treatment, Ms. Hamilton's delusions have been under control for several months."

Beside Vera, Evie's father wrapped his arm around his wife while she shook with sobs. "How could you not have made the connection with our daughter in the papers?" he said.

"It was Ruth's determination, and mine as well, that Ms. Hamilton had read the news story of Rex Ellis being left at the altar before she took on Evie's identity as her own. She became obsessed with it, until she believed wholeheartedly that Rex was in love with her, and that Ruth was trying to hurt her to keep them apart. I had no reason to doubt Mrs. Ellis's claims at that point. And I promised her the utmost confidentiality due to their family's reputation."

Evie's mother pulled her handkerchief away from her face. "Our daughter was only telling the truth!"

"You fool!" Evie's father shouted. "I'll have your license revoked if it turns out you've imprisoned Evie here!"

Dr. Perry's mouth lifted into a slight smile as he smoothed his tie, seemingly unruffled by Evie's father's threat. Vera straightened as footsteps clacked on the tile floor outside the office door.

The doctor rose from his chair. "I haven't told Ms. Hamilton why you're here, of course. It would be very detrimental to Ms. Hamilton's emotional state for you to share your theory that she is your daughter, Evie. I think it's best we don't give her your names. So, I ask that you let Ms. Hamilton be the judge. Give her the chance to recognize you. If she truly is your daughter."

The door opened and a nurse in a white uniform entered, followed by a woman in a long, ill-fitting gown who shuffled in behind her. The patient's hands were clasped in front of her, and her eyes glued to the floor, as Vera and Evie's parents stood. Her brown hair was a few inches long and framed her round face in a shaggy mess. Vera had to admit, she looked nothing like the vibrant blonde she'd seen in photographs.

"Edith," the doctor said. "You have some visitors."

The woman looked up with blank eyes, her mouth hanging open slightly.

"Evie!" Evie's mother cried.

The young woman's eyes widened, and they darted between Vera and Evie's parents.

"Please! Don't call her that," the doctor said. "You're frightening her."

Vera thought for a moment that the unfeeling doctor was right. The woman looked terrified. Until something changed in the woman's glassed-over eyes.

"Mother?" She looked over Vera's shoulder. "Father?"

"Evie!" her mother exclaimed as she closed the distance between them.

A faint smile appeared on Evie's face as her parents enveloped her in a hug.

"I knew you'd come," she said.

"That'll be all, Nurse Ramsey. Leave us!" Dr. Perry

barked to the nurse, who by now had brought her hands to her face.

She backed out of the room, her wide eyes trained on the family's reunion. The doctor retreated to his desk chair with a look of defeat. Vera looked on with shock as Evie and her parents cried in each other's arms, astonished at what Ruth Ellis's money and power had allowed her to get away with. After a last look at the family's tearful reunion, Vera followed the nurse out of the room and strode with quick steps down the chilly corridor toward the hospital's main entrance.

She smiled at the sight of the Calloways' town car parked beside her Ford, imagining them soon driving away from this place with their missing daughter in tow. After getting behind the wheel, she checked her reflection in the rearview mirror and made a futile attempt to smooth her curls with her hand. Hugh's ship would be arriving in less than an hour.

She sighed and adjusted the mirror before pulling away from the psychiatric hospital. That morning, she'd tried to style her hair like Ginger Rogers. She'd failed miserably, but it would have to do.

62

Vera held her hat against her head as she weaved between reunited servicemen and their families at the Puget Sound Naval Shipyard. She scanned the bustling crowd for Hugh. All around her, men were lifting their children into their arms and embracing their wives. It was like nothing Vera had ever experienced.

"Vera!"

She whipped around.

"Hugh!"

She pushed past a kissing couple and ran to him. She flung her arms around his neck, nearly knocking him off his crutches. He laughed and fought to maintain his balance on his leg without a cast as she clung to his bomber jacket.

"Easy there, kitten."

She placed her hands on either side of his face and lifted her lips to his, hating to think of how close she'd been to losing him. She barely noticed the whistle from a passerby before she reluctantly pulled away. She wrapped her arms around his waist one more time, savoring the feel of his broad chest against her cheek before she led him toward their car.

"I've never been more worried than when I got the telegram saying you were missing."

"I wasn't going to let anything keep me from coming back to you."

A dimple appeared on his cheek when he grinned at her beneath his garrison cap. Vera bit her lip, already imagining the things they would do when they got home.

When they reached the parking lot, Hugh's grin disappeared as he stopped in his tracks, staring at the dents and scratches along the side of their Ford.

His jaw fell open. "What happened to the car?"

Vera bit her lip. "Oh. Well, it's a long story…I was hoping you wouldn't notice so soon."

Hugh raised his eyebrows. "Not *notice?* It looks like you ran into a bus. Twice!"

Vera stifled a laugh at the look of horror on her husband's face.

"Were you hurt?" he asked.

"I'm fine." She patted his arm as his gaze returned to the car. "I promise I'll tell you everything. But for now, let's go home so I can show you how much I missed you."

Vera pulled the blanket up to her shoulders as she lay beside Hugh on the couch, her body entwined with his. She wrapped her arm behind his waist and pulled him closer, careful not to bump his injured leg with hers. There was a hole in the top of his cast so that dressing changes could be made where the bullets had entered his leg. His bullet wounds had not only crushed his tibia, but caused nerve damage to his leg. While he would only need his crutches and cast for a few months, he'd likely have a cane for the rest of his life.

They'd made love twice since they returned home, stopping in between for Vera to make them sandwiches and tell him about Dari. He'd been saddened by the news and held her while she explained how it happened.

Now they lay in the darkness, the only light coming from the embers in the fireplace. For the last half hour, Hugh had listened in shock as Vera recounted everything that had unfolded with the Ellises while he was away.

"*All* of this happened in the time I was gone? You could've been killed!" His tone softened as he pulled her closer. "I'm so glad you're all right. I'm never leaving you again!"

She laughed, thinking that, if anything, this proved she could take care of herself.

"You're quite the detective, Vera Chandler."

She propped herself up on her elbow and traced the side of Hugh's chest with her finger. "Did you *really* not know what kind of people the Ellises were?"

"I knew they were likely corrupt here and there, and hadn't gotten to where they were without bribing some politicians and city officials. I didn't think they were dangerous. You know I tried to tell you, before I left, they were a different cut of people. I had no idea they were killers, Vera."

Vera pulled her hand back. "How could you have been okay with working for them, and *me* working for them, *knowing* they were dirty?"

He thought for a moment. "I suppose I wanted to provide for you, and I let that overshadow my conscience."

"Hugh, I don't *need* you to provide for me. I need you to be honest."

"I know. And I promise from here on out, I'll tell you everything."

Vera laced her fingers with his. "Thank you." She sighed. "I wonder what will happen to Priscilla. You know, when she first came to me and spoke about you, I was worried there might've been something between you two."

"Vera Chandler! I'm insulted. You know I only have eyes for you." He ran his palm down the length of her back. "I felt sorry for her, seeing how Vincent treated her, but nothing more than that."

She lay her head on his warm chest.

"She has nothing on you."

"I hope the jury is sympathetic to her."

He ran his hand through her hair. "With everything you've brought into the light about the Ellis family, I'm sure they will."

Vera yawned as she opened the oven to check on the roast. It had been nearly dawn by the time she and Hugh fell asleep the night before. Hugh nodded off first, and Vera had moved from the couch to her armchair, not wanting to risk bumping into his leg in her sleep. He was still asleep when she awoke, and she'd gone to the store to get everything to make Hugh's favorite meal. She wanted it to be perfect.

When she got home, Hugh had been in the kitchen drinking coffee.

"I know you had a lot going on, but did you have a chance to can any of my tomatoes?" he'd asked, while she put away the groceries.

She'd cringed and told him about the hailstorm.

"That's okay. I'll try again next year," he said, kissing her forehead before refilling his coffee.

She supposed the ruined tomatoes paled in comparison to them both nearly dying. She shut the oven door, deciding to give the roast another few minutes.

"Vera!" She moved toward the sound of Hugh's voice in their entryway.

"You got a letter. Do you know a Jacqueline Cochran in Houston, Texas?"

Her heart raced as she stepped out of the kitchen and saw Hugh leaning on one of his crutches, holding a white envelope in his hand.

She wiped her hands on her apron and took it from him. "It's from the Women's Flying Training Detachment."

"Well, what are you waiting for?"

She stared at the envelope. "What if I didn't get accepted?"

He grinned. "Then you'll start a detective agency."

"I'm serious."

"So am I."

She thrust the letter toward him. "You open it."

He took the envelope and unsealed it with his thumb. She held her breath as he unfolded the paper. He stayed silent as his eyes scanned the letter.

"Well...?" she finally said.

There was a flicker in his brown eyes when he looked up from the page.

He held the paper out to her. "I guess you'll have to wait to start that detective agency."

Her heart skipped a beat as she tore the paper from his hands and scanned the words. She blinked back the tears that blurred her vision and felt Hugh's hand on her shoulder.

"Congratulations, kitten!"

"I got in!"

"Of course, you did. Dari would be proud of you. I sure am."

She nodded as he slipped his arm around her waist and pulled her toward him. The letter fell to her side as she lifted her mouth to his. Her hands traveled down his chest before she pulled her lips away and led him to their living room couch.

He sat down and she unbuttoned his shirt. She knelt beside him, and he pulled off her sweater before kissing her neck. Vera closed her eyes and put her hand on the back of his head, when Hugh pulled away.

"What's that smell?"

She opened her eyes and sniffed.

"My roast!"

EPILOGUE

EIGHT MONTHS LATER

Vera donned her sunglasses as she lined up for takeoff at the Long Beach Army Airfield, admiring the palm trees beside the airport buildings. After completing the twenty-three-week training in Houston, she'd been in the second class to graduate from Jacqueline Cochran's flight training school, and the first to be stationed in Seattle.

That morning, she and another graduate from the WFTD ferried a B-17 from Boeing to Long Beach, where she'd been given a Mustang P-51 to deliver to New Jersey. She never knew how long she'd be gone, since there was often another plane that needed immediate ferrying, but she always eventually made it back home.

Last week, Priscilla had been acquitted of all charges after Ruth, Rex, and Rex's private investigator were sentenced to life imprisonment for their crimes. Afterward, Priscilla had telephoned her to thank her again and tell her she was moving to Tacoma for a fresh start and to raise Max near her sister.

Vera calculated how long it would be to her first stop, already regretting the second cup of coffee she'd downed in the pilot lounge after delivering the bomber. But she had run into Opal, who'd graduated from the WFTD last month, and they got talking a mile a minute. Now, Vera's cross-country flight would take ten hours, with a stop in El Paso and another in Indiana to refuel. She should arrive in New Jersey just before nightfall.

Due to his injuries, Hugh had taken a job as a flight instructor at Sand Point Naval Base. With her unpredictable schedule, he'd taken to cooking most nights, even when Vera was home. It turned out that Hugh was a much better cook than she was, and they hadn't had a burned meal in months. She watched an A-20 Havoc lift off the runway and eased the throttle forward as she moved to the front of the line in the Mustang P-51.

Last month, she'd been sent to Palm Springs along with three other women from the ferrying division—including Lily, who now had a man in each of several cities around the country. They were there to train in the North American Mustang. Vera had become the fifth woman to check out in the single-seat fighter, including Dari. She pulled the faded photograph out of her uniform jacket pocket and slid it into the dash.

"Army 7753, you are cleared for takeoff," a male voice crackled through her headset.

Dari stared back at her, standing confident in front of the plane that she'd taken up for her final flight.

"Roger, Army 7753 cleared for takeoff."

Vera pushed the throttle forward to full power and accelerated down the runway, pushed against her seat by the incredible power of the 12-cylinder Merlin engine. She drew back on the stick and smoothly ascended above the airfield with a rate of climb unmatched by any other aircraft she'd flown.

She eased the control stick to the right. The Mustang banked effortlessly on her command, and she spotted the Los Angeles city skyline in the distance. She glanced at her friend's photograph at the top of the instrument panel.

"I can see why you were in love."

"Army 7753...."

Vera went on alert as air traffic control came back.

"Thank you for your service...."

She swallowed the lump that formed in her throat, wishing her friend could have heard those words. And seen the look on men's faces when she climbed out of the cockpit and they realized a woman had delivered the hottest fighter plane in the inventory.

"Wish you were here."

She looked away from Dari and out over the Pacific, knowing that, in a way, she was. And always would be.

AUTHOR'S NOTE

During the writing process of *Only One Lie*, I thoroughly enjoyed learning about the Women's Auxiliary Ferrying Squadron, Women's Flying Training Detachment, and the Women's Airforce Service Pilots who played a vital role in World War II. I am sad to say that before writing *Only One Lie*, I didn't know much about their role in the war. Their willingness to serve our country, despite the limitations that had been placed on women at the time, is incredible to me.

Thirty-eight of these brave female aviators lost their lives during their service, but they were given no honorary burials, not even a flag on their casket. Despite transporting every type of military aircraft across the country throughout the war and participating in crucial training missions, the WASPs were not awarded veteran status until 1977. I am blown away by these women's courageous service and fight for equality, and grateful that they pioneered a path to women's rights not only during their own time, but for generations to come.

ACKNOWLEDGMENTS

A big thank you to my brilliant editor, Bryan Tomasovich, for all your hard work, many Zoom calls, and help in bringing this story to life.

To my agent, Jill Marsal, a huge thanks for your excellent advice in helping to shape this story from the early stages.

Dad, thanks for sharing your flying expertise to bring accuracy to the plane scenes in this book, and your knowledge of World War II. Mom, thank you for introducing me to books like *Rebecca*, and giving me a love for the time period of *Only One Lie*.

Detective Rolf Norton, thanks once again for answering my police procedural questions and giving me a picture of what Seattle, and the police department, looked like in the 1940s. And for naming Detective Gamble when I'd run out of ideas.

Keith Mann, thank you for taking the time to show me the B-17 bomber at The Museum of Flight and sharing with me the roles the B-17s and Mustang P-51s played in WW II.

Penny Lane and Nancy Brown, thank you for reading the early version of this story and finding the things my eyes can't see.

To the team at OrangeSky Audio, thank you for producing a fabulous audiobook version.

Jenifer Ruff, Timothy Browne, Danielle Girard, and Anne Srbinovski, thanks for your input, feedback, and friendship.

Keira, thank you for the hours you spent watching over my little ones while I wrote this story, and for all you do behind the scenes of the business of writing.

To my readers, I'm so, so grateful for all your support.

And last, but not least: Brett, Elise, and Anders, thank you for everything.

BOOK CLUB QUESTIONS

1. Before reading this novel, what did you know about the WAFS, WFTD, and the WASPs? Did anything you read in *Only One Lie* surprise you about the role these female aviators played in WWII?

2. How did your view of Priscilla change after learning she plotted Max's kidnapping?

3. Was there a character you identified with more than others? If so, why?

4. What can we learn from these women aviators who signed up to become the first female war service pilots, despite receiving no military benefits?

5. The Ellises are a fictional greed-driven family who abuse their power through corruption and coercion. Can you think of any other powerful families throughout history who have done the same? Is there a similar power structure among elites that still exists today?

6. How did the camaraderie among the women in this story help them achieve more than they would have alone?

7. Vera and Priscilla come from two different societal classes. But what do they have in common?

8. How did men, like Hugh, adjust from the social norms they were born into to help facilitate women fulfilling new roles in society after WWII disrupted the status quo?

WANT MORE?

Get your FREE bonus content and new release updates at
AUDREYJCOLE.com/sign-up

ABOUT THE AUTHOR

Audrey J. Cole is a *USA TODAY* bestselling thriller author. She resides in the Pacific Northwest with her family. Before writing full time, she worked as a neonatal intensive care nurse for eleven years.

Connect with Audrey:

facebook.com/AudreyJCole

bookbub.com/authors/Audrey-J-Cole

instagram.com/AudreyJCole

tiktok.com/@audreyjcole

You can also visit her website:

www.AUDREYJCOLE.com

CPSIA information can be obtained
at www.ICGtesting.com
Printed in the USA
BVHW061930271222
655042BV00016B/923/J